LENGTH OF DAYS
SEARCH FOR FREEDOM

A Novel

LENGTH OF DAYS
SEARCH FOR FREEDOM

Doris Gaines Rapp

The third novel in the Length of Days trilogy

Daniel's House Publishing

Copyright 2016 Doris Gaines Rapp

Daniel's House Publishing
P.O. Box 623
Huntington, Indiana 46750

This book is a work of fiction. Names, characters, places, and incidents are either products of the author's imagination or are used fictitiously. Any resemblance to actual events, locales or persons, living or dead, is entirely coincidental.

All rights reserved, including the right to reproduce this book or portions thereof in any form whatsoever.

For information contact: Daniel's House Publishing

Biblical Passages:
THE HOLY BIBLE, NEW INTERNATIONAL VERSION®, NIV® Copyright © 1973, 1978, 1984, 2011 by Biblica, Inc. ™ Used by permission. All rights reserved worldwide.

Cover Art:
© Daveallenphoto | Dreamstime.com - North Carolina Blue Ridge Parkway Autumn Sunrise Mountains Photo
(eyes) Gypsy Woman photo © Paul Hakimata/Thinkstock
The oval inset: A photo the author took while horseback riding near Dripping Springs Ranch, New Mexico, was later painted by a friend and then a photo was taken of the painting and cropped.

Library of Congress Control Number: 2016903959
ISBN: 978-0-9915033-9-1 (paperback)
ISBN: 978-0-692-66397-4 (eBook)

Contact Daniel's House Publishing at
www.danielshousepublishing@gmail.com

Table of Contents

<u>Dedication</u>

Dedicated to all freedom-loving people everywhere. Search for it. Capture it. And, never let it go.

ACKNOWLEDGEMENT

Again, a huge thank you to Debi Lindhorst of The Type Galley in Warren, Indiana, for your professional work on the cover. You have a way of interpreting my ideas and creating a fantastic design for the part of my novel readers encounter first—the cover. You're the best.

Thank you to Vicki Borgman for reading *Length of Days– Search for Freedom* and making helpful suggestions. I read what I assume is there and you read words as they actually appear.

My photo on the back cover is by Bonnie Tobey Manning: website—www.printroom.com/pro/btmanning. Thanks Bonnie!

To my dear husband Bill. I have loved you since the first time I saw you. You have supported my writing, my work as a psychologist and everything I do. Thank you for being you.

Proverbs 3:1-2 (NIV©2011)

My son, do not forget my law, but let your heart keep my commands, for length of days and long life and peace they will add to you. (Book One)

Isaiah 62: 6 (NLT@2007)

O Jerusalem, I have posted watchmen on your walls; they will pray day and night, continually. Take no rest, all you who pray to the LORD. (Book Two)

Luke 4: 18-19 (NIV©2011)

The Spirit of the Lord is on me, because he has anointed me to proclaim good news to the poor. He has sent me to proclaim freedom for the prisoner and recovery of sight for the bind, to set the oppressed free, to proclaim the year of the Lord's favor. (Book Three)

Zone Borders

PROLOGUE
Return to Capitol City, Central Zone, U.S.A.

Diary of Lady Christiana Applewait
2113

My heart is breaking and fear has flooded the craggy fissure. Dear, sweet Grand-père is missing. Dr. Jason O'Reilly and I must find him quickly, not only for his safety but because he is the presidential candidate for the newly formed *1787-Constitutionalists Party*. He is our only hope for freedom and a return to the original Constitution. My precious Grand-mère is in constant prayer.

It has only been four months since Silas Drummond broke the silence about the atrocities buried beneath Howard Mountain. Judge Carl Brunner issued a two-year stay on all those forced into the never-ending-sleep, thus ending their Length of Days, including my grandparents. Jason and I sneaked across all four closed zone borders, establishing a network to secure enough signatures to place a citizens' referendum, to overturn the Length of Days Law, on the ballot at the next election.

I am in a panic over Grand-père's disappearance. Who will help us? We can't ask Chief Inspector Ward Stoner, the head of the corrupt Blue Guard; he has stalked our every move and cannot be trusted. It isn't safe to get help from mass communication journalists; if word of Grand-père's abduction gets out, those who took him will surely kill him.

We will search for him with the few clues we have. I am willing to go all the way to the beautiful Pacific Ocean, wander through the hot and barren desert, cross the lofty Blue Ridge Mountains and tunnel again below the streets of New York City seeking my grandfather. When we find him, and we must, we will find freedom as well.

Lady Christiana Applewait

CHAPTER 1

April 2113

The year had rolled over from 2112 to 2113 while Jason and I were out of the Central Zone but I had not forgotten the evil buried beneath Howard Mountain. When we arrived back at the heavy door on the Valley side of the mountain it thudded and scrapped open on rusty hinges. Once inside the hollow rock chambers, the darkness of the subterranean lair ahead of us was as black as the evil that clung to the cold, damp, stone walls. I knew what waited there, and my stomach churned violently. With my friend, Dr. Jason O'Reilly so near to me I could smell the scent of him, I inched up as close behind Silas Drummond as I could. Sandwiched between the two men, I shuffled along with my eyes tightly closed, not wanting to see the frightening reality around me. I had seen it all before.

"Are you okay?" Jason asked.

"I just don't want to see them again," I said in a whisper. Then I shuddered. Would I ever get over the memory of seeing each body grotesquely stuffed and displayed like lifeless figures in a wax museum? Once the images burned a hole in my mind, I knew they would cling to me like black bats hanging from the walls of every safe sanctuary I would ever have.

Even though Silas had opened the massive door to the cold, vile cavern beneath Howard Mountain, I felt like I couldn't move, or keep up with the little stooped man in front of me. Jason moved up beside me and clutched my hand. I was desperate for comfort and cringed with every step we walked.

"They're just ahead, My Lady," Silas cautioned in a whisper. "The glass cases—they're in the next room."

I thought of how Jason must feel and tried to set aside my own fear and loathing. "If you want to pause for a moment in front of your parents' display cabinets and pay your respects, I can cover my eyes," I said as chills ran down my arms. "I can't look at them. The very fact they're on display for Alister Bedlum's bizarre pleasure, is reprehensible."

"Christy, there is no respect anywhere down here. And, certainly not in the glass coffins of the bodies Bedlum stole away from their loved ones." Jason paused a moment. "I don't need to see the violated, taxidermy displays of those I loved in life on display in Bedlum's despicable museum."

"The furnaces are just in front of us," I gagged. "I can still smell the burnt flesh."

"Remember, Christy, it is over," Jason reminded me. "No one will enter the never-ending-sleep just because they have reached the end of their Length of Days—thanks to you and Silas."

I pulled a cloth square from my pocket that Rebecca Spires gave me and covered my nose. "For two years, Jason. The stay is for two years—not forever—not yet. We have to finish the task."

Silas had said nothing since we entered the cavern until that moment. "Then breathe deeply, My Lady. Inhale the stench of death so you will never forget the wretchedness of it. All of our lives depend on the work that you and Dr. O'Reilly will do while the stay on exterminations remains."

I knew he was right. But, I was so tired, drained of every ounce of energy I had just a few days ago. The thought of so few of us overthrowing a corrupt and heinous government seemed impossible.

But, I knew impossible was not a word I could use. "I know. Grand-mère and Grand-père's lives depend on us."

"We all do," Silas said again. "All of our lives are cut short so we never live out our full Length of Days."

"I know," I said again, but inside, I thought about the very short time I had even thought about these things. Drugged with chemicals the government put in our water supply, robbing all of us of our emotions, our energy and our libido, I hadn't even thought about the Length of Days Law, terminating a person's life when they reached a pre-determined age, until my own grandparents arrived at their termination birthdays. Since I was a Legacy Citizen, my detoxification pills allowed me to begin to feel, to think clearly, and to recognize, not only my loss, but the loss of everyone around me.

Bedlum's private museum of the bodies of people-of-power was in the next hall. I had seen them once. I knew I couldn't see them again. I kept my eyes tightly closed and allowed Jason to lead me through.

As we came to the other side of the mountain within the peaks, my pulse quickened. "Do you see anything, Silas?" I whispered hoarsely, my voice raspy from exhaustion. We had entered the crypt-like space through the secret opening in the mountain-wall, walked on the nearly forgotten old road through the mountain, passed Alister Bedlum's despicable museum with averted eyes and emerged into the grand entry hall on the other side. There we waited.

"There's no one in the entry foyer," Silas's voice was gruff and weak. I could hear the pounding of his heart in the spacing of his words. He cracked the door open a little more, craned his neck and looked beyond the entry to the windows that flanked the front door. "I see nothing," he whispered. "I'll leave it up to you two. If you want to make a run for my car, that's fine with me. If we hurry, I can get you back to town before the city stirs."

"Let's run for it, Christy," Jason instructed.

"I'm ready," I agreed.

Nothing more was said. The only sound was that of heavy breathing and the crackling gravel beneath our running feet. Since few people owned personal cars, Silas's vehicle would be easy to spot. We would have to hurry. In silence, we all piled into the front seat of the old, broad vehicle of yesteryear.

The first blush of morning had already touched the eastern sky when the doors slammed closed on Drummond's car and we turned toward the city. The sweetness of the spring morning air filled my senses like a strong tranquilizer and my body relaxed. The empty road back to town stretched out like a magic carpet along the Devil's hideaway.

"Do you suppose Chief Inspector Stoner is up and out?" I finally questioned through a sluggish haze.

"He could be," Jason agreed. "But he shouldn't be out on the streets just because we're back. There would be no way for him to know we've returned, or that we were gone for that matter. He had his suspicions, but no evidence."

"He, or his minions, tracked us from the western ocean to the subterranean pits near the eastern shore," I insisted. "I don't think we were spotted, but Stoner *knew* we were beyond the hidden valley. He just *knew*."

Suddenly weariness overtook me beyond my words to express. My eyes grew heavy and refused to stay open, until my head came to rest on Jason's shoulder. It remained there the entire trip into town. It was too early for the **P**ersonal **T**ransit to swish above the streets below. All was quiet.

Later, Jason nudged me gently when Silas stopped the car in front of the Indian River Apartment building. "Honey, you're home." He kissed me softly on the forehead.

"Home?" I questioned. The word *home* had not been part of my vocabulary for months, only my dreams.

"I know. It sounds strange doesn't it?" Jason agreed.

I leaned over and kissed him tenderly. "I wish you could come in."

Silas said nothing but smiled shyly.

"I wish I could, too," Jason admitted. "But each second is important. You have to be in your apartment and ready to come to your door if Stoner were to show up. I have to be at my house or in my office if he were to go there. We have each given plausible excuses for our apparent absences. You claimed you've been sick and have been regaining your strength. Since we no longer have illnesses, there aren't medications for some of the previous medical problems. Even influenza is a dangerous disease and requires a lot of bed rest."

"I feel like I have a serious illness right now" I sighed. "I know—it's called extreme fatigue." I knew Jason was right, but I was too tired and too frightened where Inspector Stoner was concerned to think clearly.

"Thank God your real condition isn't serious. Just remember, rest will be important," Jason said. "Dahlia helped me support the story that I've been studying a new medical procedure, Orthopedics. Now, with the Length of Days Law suspended, people no longer get points against them for injury or illness, so bones can be set and heal properly when an accident occurs, rather than leaving them untreated with the resulting bent backs and limping legs. I need to come out of my lengthy study time and be available too. My nurse can only cover for me for so long."

"I love you, Dr. Jason O'Reilly," I whispered in his ear.

"And, you as well," Jason replied in response.

I got out of Silas's car and stood on the sidewalk. Leaning in through the car window to embrace Jason, I stroked his face. Then, turning toward the apartment building, I didn't look back. My heart pounded as I walked up the sidewalk and reached for the door handle.

Before I opened the door, I looked around the bushes and trees, and down the street in both directions, for eyes trained on me. I turned the knob and was thankful the hinges didn't squeak. Pushing the door open, I entered the building into the huge entry hall and turned to close the door behind me. I was home.

CHAPTER 2

Home

Once inside the Indian River Apartment building, I realized I had been holding my breath. With my eyes closed, I exhaled slowly. That was when I heard him.

"Welcome home, Lady Applewait," a deep voice announced from the large, common area to the left of the lobby.

My heart raced in my chest and once again, my breath caught in my throat. I grabbed at my shirt and pulled on the fastener to release its grasp on my neck. Could I get enough air? Slowly I turned in the direction of the voice I had never heard before and saw a stranger standing near one of the over-stuffed chairs in the large room.

"I'm sorry," I smiled politely, but inside, my stomach churned, knotted and turned sour. "I'm at a disadvantage. Have we met?" I started to reach out my hand in a gesture of friendship. When I couldn't control the nervous tremors that rattled my body, I quickly put my hands in my pockets.

"No Ma'am, we haven't met."

"Then—" slowly I began again and stopped. I felt trapped. Was the man a member of the Blue Guard? Did he answer to Ward Stoner? I nearly choked.

The man took one step in my direction and spoke quietly, calmly. "I'm sorry. I don't mean to frighten you, Ma'am." The tall, muscular one squared his shoulder. "My name is Tayton Braxton. I'm a friend of Sean's. He asked me to transfer into this district, get an apartment here in the Indian River complex and protect you and Dahlia Zoobamba. Stoner found out I was living here and made my stay a special assignment. I'm supposed to tell him every time you leave and return." He looked toward the windows that faced the front of the building. "We'd better get you off the first floor and into your apartment. Stoner shows up here at all hours."

I said nothing. I was simply too tired. My homecoming could be my undoing if not found in my apartment. Our mission was too great to risk it all. Yes, Judge Bruner had ordered a stay for the Length of Days Law. Death wouldn't come to anyone in the furnaces under Howard Mountain just because they had reached a pre-determined number of years and lacked a significant value to society. But, our work had only begun. Jason and I had crossed borders illegally to get signatures on petitions that would make the stay on exterminations permanent through a national referendum. But, it wouldn't come to a vote for almost two years.

"Hurry," Tayton urged as he checked his time piece. "Stoner has burst in here at 4 a.m. and 4 p.m. He never shows up at the same time twice."

Following him obediently, I stopped at the lift door that opened immediately. The doors swished open and we hurried on. The doors closed again before there was any movement near the front of the building.

"Are we safe?" I whispered.

"Yes, Ma'am," Tayton responded.

I stood rigidly, facing the front of the car and stared at the crack between the doors. Afraid and exhausted, I couldn't force my mind to stay in the moment. At first I wondered why. After all, I was finally home. With a review of the last few days in my mind, even the previous months, the cause of my weariness was no mystery. Jason and I had literally covered the entire country.

"You're a friend of Dahlia's and Sean's?" Finally I asked the big question, as I tried to pull together a measure of safety through questioning.

"I know Sean better. I just met Dahlia recently." He paused as the lift door opened on the top floor. We stepped off and Tayton followed me to my door.

With my hand placed on the door knob, the identifying markers in my palm released the lock. I turned and placed my back to the door, blocking the stranger called Tayton.

"Thanks," I smiled a little and waited for him to back away.

"I know you just met me, Ma'am. I understand that my assurance of trust may not be enough for you. All I can say is time will prove my loyalty to you and to your cause. It is a cause I believe in too." He took a few steps backwards and bowed slightly at the waist.

"Thank you, Tayton." I paused and watched his face for changes of expression that would give away his true feelings and meaning. "If we're going to become friends, Tayton, I must ask you not to bow."

I thought for a moment and cleared my head. What should I tell this stranger? "Tayton, Jason and I started an adventure months ago, one we had not even considered a possibility just weeks before that. I was, and am if I choose to be, Lady Christiana Applewait, a Legacy Citizen, privileged by accident of birth." I searched his eyes to see what clues hid there. "Now, I see myself as an equal to everyone. We met Raymore Goring, Kasamar's father, one of the hollow people of the west; the underlings in the sewers and old subway passageways of the east; and all those who lived in the forbidden zones in-between."

"Yes, Ma'am," the double-agent began again, but I interrupted.

"We each have a job to do, Tayton. And, if you are true to your word, your task will be equal to mine." I still didn't turn my back on him nor open the door. I wasn't ready for that. I would have to talk to Dahlia and Sean first. I stood firmly, with my feet planted, and watched as he backed down the hall, got back on the lift and started down.

With a deep breath, I opened the door to my flat and a life I had left behind came rushing back in. The room was silent. I didn't hear the sweet sound of the coffee maker that was always humming on the counter or the toenail tapping of my little kitten. Then, I remembered I had left the furry bundle with my parents before Jason and I left the Central Zone. Still, I half expected to hear the little feline playing near the window.

First, I needed to empty and stash my carry-all bag on the floor of the sleeping-room closet. I was not going to make that obvious mistake. If Stoner were to come in unexpectedly, he shouldn't find a packed bag, evidence of my absence, when my cover had been a lingering illness with confinement to my apartment.

I hurried into my room and opened the closet door. While there in the wardrobe, I pulled out a lounging suit and slippers, removed my clothes and hung them up. I slid the clothes I had been wearing in place along the pole, inviting a sense of casual organization, and went back into the sitting room. Flinging the window fabric back, I welcomed the rising sun. I even opened the window sash a moment to let the stale air out, and then went into the kitchen to put on a pot of fresh coffee. The morning air was crisp and fresh. I was reluctant to re-close the windows, but wastefully letting out all the mechanically treated air would have been irresponsible.

Over at the bookshelf, I ran my fingers over the books that had gone untouched for months. "*To Kill a Mockingbird*," I read from the book spine as I pulled the volume from one of the shelves. This was one I hadn't read. It was one of the paperbound books Jason had given me from the huge stash of books in the hospital library.

Following the great uprising of the previous millennium, the government banned all books, so I thought the only books that had survived were the ones in the back stacks of a closed section of the public library. The curator of the library and I were the only people who had access to those books. My key to the back room was because I had been working on my Graduate Degree in Library Science. I smiled as I took *Mockingbird* to the couch and lay down with a pillow under my head.

Suddenly, I heard a tapping at the front door. My book fell to the floor with a muffled flop when it landed on a small rug. The intrusion on my greatly needed rest set my pulse racing. I jumped upright with rattled and jangled nerves. My hand trembled as I picked the book off the floor. Would I ever be safe again?

"Stoner," I gasped silently, pronouncing the fearful name with my lips. Then I thought again. *The Chief Inspector would have beaten down the door, if necessary, not gently rapped. But, if it isn't Stoner, who could it be? Who's here?*

CHAPTER 3

New Information

Did I have the nerve to open the door to my penthouse? What if I had forgotten something, a detail left unattended? Was there some tiny leaf, grown only on trees from the Eastern Zone, still attached to my shoe? But, my shoes were in the closet and no time to run in there and check. The crack I permitted between the door and the jamb was minuscule. My hands trembled as I peeked out and then flung it opened. "Mother, Daddy," I squealed, like an Academy school girl with a coarse and raspy voice.

"We thought you might be home." Mom and Dad embraced me as they hurried into my apartment. Mother stood back quickly and held me at arm's length. "Honey—your voice. Are you really sick now?"

"No, I don't think so, just exhausted." I hugged her again. I couldn't get enough of her touch or the fragrance of her hair. Even though I was an adult of twenty-four, she smelled like Mama.

"Well, you look like you haven't slept in days. Let me make you a nice cup of tea." Mother patted my cheek and turned toward the kitchen. "How's Jason?" She asked over her shoulder.

"Resting, I hope," I said as I yawned. "He plans to go to the office today."

"Oh my," Mother said. "He is really pushing himself. I hope he has a nice cup of tea, too."

"I imagine he will." Then I added, "We won't need tea. The coffee pot is already on." I smiled and sat down at the table. Mother was eager to take care of me and I wanted to honor that. I had been gone for many months.

"And—we brought a friend of yours," Daddy offered as he placed a brown paper sack on the floor and then reached under his sweater.

"Shakespeare!" I smiled broadly and reached for the feline that had grown since the last time I saw her. Careful to keep the cat's paws off the table, I snuggled her in my lap. "She seems to recognize me. I can't believe it."

Daddy reached for the sack he had brought in. "You rescued her, Christy. You brought her in out of the winter cold months ago. She was fed and loved," he reminded me. "And, here are her water and food dishes and a box of food only half eaten." He put the dishes on the floor of the kitchen, filled them and put the rest of the food box in the cabinet under the sink. "There cat, enjoy," he chuckled.

Mother took a small plate from the cabinet. "We brought some orange juice and salt crackers. Good food for eating lightly," she assured me. "And, I'm embarrassed to say, we brought some of your grandmother's best cookies. She made them yesterday." Mother arranged the sugary treats in an artful display. "I'm sure the government health department would say they are too rich for healthy eating, but we'll enjoy them anyway." Her chin jutted out in defiance as she placed the plate on the table.

"Mother, you would be amazed by the pastries and other foods I ate while I was away. We had home-made noodles at Martin and Rebecca Spires' home in the Valley of the Keepers, with wonderful smashed potatoes and butter and large chunks of beef." I closed my eyes and could taste the warm melted butter that oozed over the top of the bowl. "In Rachel Claudette's fine dining room on the far west coast, the sideboard was loaded with sweets of every kind, some with names I had never tasted and some I had never heard of. The memory of the platters of meats and other finger foods makes my mouth water." I cleared my throat and smiled at the thought of all that cuisine. Then I remembered I hadn't eaten in a long time.

Daddy's voice lowered and grew coarse. "Do you think that Chief Inspector Stoner knows you're back in town?" he asked. He sounded worried.

"He has posted an officer here in the apartment building," I said as I swallowed hard. "I met him when I came in. He seemed to be waiting for me. He said his name was Tayton Braxton and claimed to be a friend of Dahlia and Sean's. Stoner shows up here at frequent but random times Tayton said. The Chief could bang on the door at any moment."

I was surprised at how confident Mother was as she stated resolutely, "Then we'll do what's natural. If he comes in unexpectedly, we'll be caught being us."

"The most natural thing in the morning is coffee. Would you like some?" I asked as I watched Shakespeare. The little creature wasn't an inanimate replica of a cat as others in the Central Zone had, but the real thing.

Daddy agreed with eager anticipation. "I would love some coffee," he said as he gave me another hug. "We sure missed you, Angel."

"Let me pour the coffee," Mother offered. "If Stoner comes in, I would love to be caught in the act of being a normal family." She also poured a small glass of juice. "Here Christy, drink this quickly for medicinal purposes."

"I missed everyone on this side, too," I responded, exhausted but full of feelings only possible since I started my detoxification. I sat and watched Mother do her motherly thing, while I emptied the glass of juice. "How are Grand-mère and Grand-père? I thought of the dear ones often during our travels to the other zones."

Mother finished pouring the coffee. "They're fine now. Your grandmother had quite an episode when Inspector Stoner told her of your capture in New York and the gunshot wound you received at the time. Your grandma collapsed, but when she found out it had all been a lie, she was too furious at the Inspector to stay down any longer." Mother laughed and added. "Can you imagine your grandmother not seeking the truth behind anything Stoner had to say?"

"I can't imagine Stoner ever telling the truth!" I joined in the fun as I watched her take three cups from the cabinet and pour our coffee. Far below the window I heard the *thunk* of a car door and jumped. All sounds startled me now. There were few vehicles on the roads and I knew that strata cars, of the infamous Blue Guard, were some of them. I had to calm down. I didn't want to alarm Mother and Daddy. I snuggled Shakespeare closer and began to relax a little as I stroked the cat's soft fur.

"We have to tell you what's been going on since you left," Mother said as she took two of the filled cups and placed them on the coffee table in front of the couch near the windows. She went back to the food prep-area and brought the plate of Grand-mère's amazing cookies and the third cup.

Daddy sat on one of the side chairs and Mother joined me on the sofa. "It feels so 'same,' having you both here—and yet so different, like I have been gone for years." I looked around the room with heavy eyes and glanced up at the Bible, hidden in sight near the top of the bookcase. *It's there. Stoner didn't break in and confiscate it. Neither did Tayton. I don't know if I believe him yet.*

Daddy sipped a little from his cup but when it was obviously too hot he drew back. "The Council of Elders met many times while you were gone, to discuss the direction of our country. Christy, you and Jason are close to having enough signatures already to place a citizens' referendum on the ballot at the next election here in the Central Zone. By the time the other three zones have finish canvassing their people, there will be an abundance of names. We will vote to overthrow the Length of Days Law for good on Election Day November 3, 2114."

"Election Day? The Presidential Election should be in 2116," I thought aloud. "I've read the old documents many times."

"The Council is aware of the old documents," Daddy reminded me. "The new Constitution changed the presidential election date. They had to hurry to get everything passed as quickly as they could. Christy, it was a coup. They acted fast."

"A coup d'état," I whispered. "A sudden strike against the State." My stomach began to churn. The thought of an uprising to bring about change was overwhelming.

Mother drank her coffee with excitement. "People will no longer be placed in the never-ending-sleep, ending their Length of Days." As she crunched her cookie, she dropped crumbs onto the saucer. "Everything is coming together so fast, Christy. As volunteers sign up to travel all over the country to put the campaign in place, Sean will continue to keep us all up-to-date with his underground newspaper." She shook her head in disbelief. "Your friends had started to establish a network before most of us even knew there was a need for one."

Daddy added, "And—in Sean's newspapers, the topic of a truly *elected* president continues to be the center focus of the articles." His voice was giddy with excitement.

"No more seizing of power? A real presidential election—isn't that amazing?" My head was swimming with the pace of the life I had returned to.

"That's right," Mother assured me.

"November of 2114 will be the Presidential Election day?" My memory went back to the display cases in the old part of the Library where historical documents had been laid to rest.

Daddy scooted to the edge of his seat, his hands in full expression. "Judge Brunner explained that even the date for the election was changed when they re-wrote the Constitution. Those who seized power had their own agenda and needed to rush things past the citizens in order to accomplish their devilish plans," his jaw ground in anger. "So, the presidential election is now in November of

2114. Actually, that's why Judge Brunner issued a two year stay, to coincide with the next National Election. So, besides voting on overturning the Length of Days Law, we will elect a new president at the end of next year."

Mother placed her cup on the table and clasped her hands together. "Christiana, your name continues to fall on the short-list of candidates for president."

"But, Mother, constitutionally I'm too young to run for president. You have to be at least thirty-five years old."

"Yes, I know," Mother relinquished. "But, it is an honor to be asked." She smoothed the skirt of her dress and brushed the crumbs to the floor again. "The Council pulled the original constitution of 1787 out of storage and—they got rid of the new one."

"What?" I gasped. "They just threw it away?"

Daddy leaned in closer as if there were others around that may hear. "With a careful re-reading of the history of the time, following the great upheaval of a hundred years past, your grandfather discovered that the new constitution had not been ratified."

"It's not legal?" I squealed silently as I mouthed the words with exaggerated movements. "Not binding?"

"No," Mother agreed as she jumped to her feet and began to pace. "It's not legal at all." She swirled around and faced me again. Then, she threw her hands up and buried her face in them.

"What is it?" I asked as I turned and looked out of the large window. Below, on the wide street that ran in front of the building, a strata car hadn't even pulled to the curb. Inspector Stoner leaped from his vehicle where it stopped in the middle of the road. "Oh no!" I felt truly ill.

"We'd better leave," Mother whispered.

"Why?" Daddy questioned. "We're Christy's parents and we're checking on her following her illness. It's perfectly natural. We'll relax and it'll all appear to be quite normal."

Shaken, I stepped back from the window, as if Stoner could see through the tinted glass. So much had happen I didn't know if I could handle more. Morning had started on the other side of Howard Mountain, in the Valley of the Keepers. It was now hours later and I was only half awake. I wasn't sure if I was ready to face Chief Inspector Ward Stoner.

"Go ahead, Mother. Tell me more about the Council's decisions." If rested, I would have refused to be intimidated. In my current state of exhaustion I was just stubborn, and that would have to do for today.

"Okay—the other big news, Christy," Mother continued. "They want your grandfather to run for president. It looks like the current Zone President Nathan Alexander will run in opposition."

"Oh, Mother!" I leaped off the sofa and gave her a hug. "Grand-père has agreed to run?" I sat back down on the edge of the couch and waited for the answer that would change everything.

"Yes, Honey," she said as she sat next to me and threw her arms around my shoulders. "He didn't hesitate a moment."

"What about the primaries?" I asked, excitedly.

"Primaries? What are primaries? Mother asked.

"That's when the citizens vote on which candidate they want to represent their political party," I explained.

"There aren't multiple candidates, Christy," Daddy reminded me. "For more years than I can remember, the government selected a successor to the one in office without the waste of time of an election. They did away with the primary process. And, since there is just one candidate in each of the parties at this election—again, there is no need for a primary."

I thought for a moment. "I imagine the entire election process will have to return to the previous system eventually, or maybe an improved one."

Daddy smiled and groaned at the same time. "There will be a lot of work to do."

"Then—" I said as the truth of what I had heard sank in and recharged my tired body by igniting my spirit. "In spite of Ward Stoner and any of the negative forces that have strangled our country, a rebirth of freedom has begun."

CHAPTER 4

An Intrusion

To my mind, it was both amazing and logical. My own grandfather had become a candidate in the first presidential campaign in decades. Of course, no one could be better.

"What's the plan for getting Grand-père elected?" I asked as I sat back and took in the enormity of what we were talking about that morning in my living room.

Mother was excited as she talked about her own father. "He's filled out and filed the paperwork to register his intent to run and has named Judge Carl Brunner as the chairperson of his election committee," she said in amazement. "Your grandfather is working on a schedule to visit the other three zones. The courts ruled that a candidate for a national office cannot be prohibited from crossing the borders and visiting the entire country in which he is running."

"I'm going to have to sprint to catch up on what's going on here in the Central Zone." My head was swimming with exhaustion. I still had not slept. "Does Stoner know about Grand-père?" I asked, flooded with new information and challenges that seemed insurmountable to my tired mind. There hadn't been a real election in our country for so many years I doubted that the young people would remember it was a normal practice in the past. I had read all the documents in my secluded spot in the back room of the city library. I knew what the founding fathers intended but the re-written constitution had changed everything.

"We—" Mother began. Her words quickly fell on the floor as the door to my apartment banged open and slammed against the wall that flanked the opening.

Startled, I jumped and grabbed my forehead. My nerves, frayed and raw, caused my thoughts to swim frantically like one caught in a riptide. Would I be able to stop the waves of confusion that threatened to overtake me?

"Well, well, well," Stoner drawled, like someone who finally found his coveted four-leafed clover. He strutted through the door and mocked, "The little princess is home, looks well and is surrounded by her loving family. Isn't that sweet?"

"Inspector Stoner," I said and coughed, unable to think of a cleaver thing to say. "Thank you for your concern. I continue to improve."

Daddy extended his arm, a gesture of invitation. "What can we do for you, Inspector?" He asked. "It's really quite early in the morning for you."

Stoner only smirked. "I'm fine. It's you and your wife I'm surprised about. What are you two doing in town so early?"

"Listen to the man, Bob," Mother cooed. She replaced her coffee cup on the table beside her and casually watched Shakespeare cross the room, chasing a stream of sunlight that had managed to stay ahead of her. "We enjoy getting up early. Besides, we wanted to check on our daughter. She's been sick for a long time."

"Yes, so I've heard." Stoner observed the cat for a second and then followed her into the kitchen. He watched her eat from the bowl Daddy had placed on the floor. Popping the lower cabinet open, he mused, "Half a bag of food, huh?" He shook the bag and replaced it where he had found it. "I'm sure you must have run out of food during the time you've been confined to the house."

My stomach churned. My body ached with weariness. As I lifted my cup to my mouth, I couldn't believe how heavy it felt. How could I cover my exhaustion and how could I explain it? The coffee sloshed in the cup and spilled into the saucer.

"I'm sorry," I apologized automatically. "I guess I haven't improved as much as I thought I had. I'm still pretty weak." I coughed again and the depth of the raspy sound and scratchiness in my throat was evident. Was I really getting sick?

Stoner stepped back, out of the path of flying pathogens. "I can't waste my time here any longer," he barked as he stumbled into an overstuffed chair. Quickly, he straightened himself with anger and gathered his dignity. "Missy," he hissed, "you'd better get yourself well real fast. I hear your granddaddy is running for president. He's going to need a smart little lady like you to front for him."

"Lady Christiana is a Legacy Citizen, in line for a seat on the Council of Elders," Daddy said as his jaws grew stone hard with anger. "You will treat her with respect."

Stoner started to speak and then closed his eyes. "You're right. Lady Applewait, please accept my apologies." He bowed deeply from the waist. Then, he raised his brows and darkness like a raging storm crossed his face. "Or is it, Simza Bihari?" he asked. Contempt dripped from his voice, evil from his eyes.

"Who?" Mother asked with a blank expression.

"Ask your daughter," Stoner seethed.

Lieutenant Chalky Boone burst through the door Stoner left open. "Inspector?" she shouted, her breath short and her tone urgent.

Stoner snapped around, his shoulders were taut and drawn up to his ears. "Boone, do not interrupt me."

"Sorry, Boss," she apologized and brushed off his reproach like an annoyance. "I had to let you know that your mother messaged the office. She was taking Christopher to the doctor."

"The doctor?" His eyes flared and his brow furrowed deeply, like ruts in a muddy, warn road. "Why?"

"Mrs. Stoner said Christopher's legs were numb again."

"Boone," he growled. "Hold your tongue. Don't talk about my son in front of others."

"You asked, Inspector," she shrugged and stood tall. "Besides, citizens no longer have to fear every scratch and damage to their body. The government doesn't keep a running tally of life points, until it reaches twenty-five. Defective persons are no longer eliminated."

"A short reprieve in that policy," Stoner snorted. "This obsession with freedom will be voted down at the election. Sanity will be restored soon." He paced across the room with wide, pressured strides. Then he stopped abruptly and spun around with rage pouring from his eyes. "Well, Missy Applewait, is your precious doctor seeing patients again?"

Shaken by his glare and anger, I didn't know what to say or how to say it. My mind raced to the safety of words that would conceal my fear. "He said he wanted to return today," I drew out slowly, like someone searching their mind for a lost conversation. "I'm not sure if he's going to the office this morning or this afternoon." I couldn't help but smile a little as I thought about how tired Jason and I were even hours ago. The only place we wanted and needed to be was in our beds sleeping. Then I remembered his words and knew why I didn't know for sure where he would be right then. *I have to be at my house or in my office if Stoner were to go there.* I couldn't know where Jason would be because he hadn't made up his mind before he and Silas let me out in front of my apartment building a short time ago.

"It's about time he got back to work." Stoner snorted.

"He has been studying orthopedics, Inspector." Daddy spoke with firmness and yet a full measure of compassion. "If there is something wrong with your son's legs, you may be very thankful Dr. O'Reilly has been learning that branch of medicine."

Inside, my muscles froze. Jason may have to put his "study" into practice immediately. He had taken a 281 Palm Device along on our canvas of the country. It projected holograms of orthopedic procedures onto any background that was handy, including the space between Jason's lap and the back of the bus seat in front of us as we traveled through northern California. He studied every available moment with dedication and serious intensity. But, was his time of study enough to learn all he needed? I quickly side-stepped Jason's involvement and focused on the Chief Inspector's son.

"Is Christopher okay?" I asked, intending to speak to Lieutenant Boone.

"How would I know?" Stoner roared. "Boone just got here." I watched his face draw up tightly as he continued to pace.

"Sir, if you think you should leave, we will pray for you and your son." Mother's offer sounded sincere and compassionate.

"Pray?" Stoner thundered. "Madam, do you know you are committing treason? Prayer is a forbidden act. And using the names of God and the Christ is treasonous. If the people were to rely on God, why would they cast their lot and loyalty with the government?"

"Surely, you don't believe that?" I asked him. I remembered when he accidently struck his young son Christopher with his strata car on Gifting Day Eve. Dr. Jason O'Reilly was the anonymous phone number, a physician contact without a name, Stoner had called.

"Do not challenge me, Missy!" he shouted.

"I am Lady Applewait, Inspector—not Missy anything," I stated firmly with my jaw set. "The New Constitution is clear about the need to treat all members of the Council of Twelve, and those who will rise to that position, with respect. I am sure you are aware of your added responsibility to protect Legacy Citizens."

Stoner gasped and gritted his teeth. He slapped his hands together as one would who was brushing the dust from his hands and moving on. As he left, he pounded on the door with his fist and stomped out of the room.

CHAPTER 5

Jason is Back

"O'Reilly?" Stoner bellowed as he burst into the doctor's waiting room. He pressed the heels of his hands to his temples that pounded with hours of anger and thwarted determination.

"Yes?" Dahlia Zoobamba hurried through the door that led from the back hall. She stopped abruptly and stared at the Chief Inspector, her eyes wide. "Oh, it's you Inspector. What can I do for you?"

He worked his jaw in anger; his eyes flashed. "Nothing! I believe I called out for O'Reilly if you were listening." He marched back and forth a few more steps. "I hate to repeat myself."

Nurse Zoobamba swallowed hard. "Sir, I'm sorry. I was in the back office."

"What were you doing back there? What if a patient were to come in?"

"I know the morning's schedule, Inspector. There are no appointments until after lunch." She stepped around the partition from the waiting room and into the receptionist's area.

Stoner sneered. "Do you need a wall between us, Nurse?" He lowered his voice to a whisper, placed his arm on the opening's wide writing surface and leaned into her space. "Are you afraid of me?"

She straightened up and crossed her arms. "Should I be?"

Stoner grinned but his joy soon faded. "Have you heard from my mother?" he questioned as his eyes darted to the entrance.

"Inspector?" Dr. O'Reilly asked as he breezed through the door. "Was I expecting you this morning?"

Stoner's mouth dropped and his eyes bulged. "Doctor—you've finally arrived."

"Yes, Inspector—this is my office." Jason reached out his hand in greeting with a self-satisfied expression on his face. "I'm glad to be back."

"What's the smug expression for?" Stoner scoffed and flipped his hand at the doctor's offering of friendship.

"It seems like a glorious day," Jason said with measured enthusiasm. "Wouldn't you agree?"

"I know this is your office, Doctor. I wasn't sure that you knew it." Stoner ignored Jason's positive attitude. He preferred to intimidate and dominate. That's not possible with someone with a smile on their face.

"Did you want something?" Jason asked the inspector as he reached through the receptionist's window and handed Dahlia his briefcase.

The outer door opened again and Inspector Stoner's mother hurried in carrying his son Christopher in her arms. "Thank God you're here," she mumbled under her breath.

Stoner's eyes darted toward her, then to the doctor. He said nothing, unspoken surprise written on his face. He had never heard his mother evoke the name of the old Deity before. He wondered if the other two heard her.

"Ward," Mrs. Stoner gasped. "Take him." She smiled at the child, but concern was evident in the drawn lines on her face. "You're a big boy," she said. "And, heavy," she added as she kissed the recently turned six-year-old on the forehead as she passed him over to his father.

Stoner grabbed Christopher and drew him close. Since his wife died, Christopher was all he had. "What's wrong, Son?" he asked gently. Turning to Jason he flared, "You're lucky you decided to come back into the office."

"My leg doesn't want to work," the child said, a look of wonderment on his face.

"Did you fall again?" Jason asked him as he ignored the Inspector's prodding. "Remember when you were hurt on Gifting Day Eve?"

"No, he didn't fall," his grandmother said, her eyes searching for answers.

"Yes, I did," Christopher corrected her.

"You did?" she questioned.

"Yes, I fell on the front steps when you were in the house," the little one explained.

"Well, we'll have a look," Jason offered and continued into the inner hall. "It could be as simple as a pinched nerve. Follow me." As he held the door open for the three to pass, he finally answered Stoner's intended question. "I was out of the office long enough to learn new procedures to treat your son, Inspector." Reaching out, he patted Stoner on the back with a firm and confident slap. "I'm sure we are all happy about that."

Stoner was silent but in his heart, contempt festered like a seeping wound. *Well, well, well—the rats have crawled back to their nests.*

CHAPTER 6

May 2113

"Are you ready for this?" Jason asked one evening in May as we hurried from my apartment building and got into his car.

"Yes, I guess I'm ready—why?" At first I thought it was a strange question. I follow my agenda carefully. The meeting that evening was the next event. "Holly reminded me."

"Holly?" Jason asked.

"Holly," I stated. "That's what I call my holographic avatar. I programmed her to appear to me when I have upcoming appointments. I have her set to not appear if there are others around."

I watched the colors of spring pass by as we drove toward Oakwood and my grandparents' home. I didn't want spring to be so busy that I'd miss the pastel daisies, pink snapdragons and the opening leaves on the budding trees. I missed the end of winter crawling around in the old subway system and sewers of New York. Not that I minded helping all the underlings. Tricked out of their homes, they lived underground for decades. It was just that time had slipped through my fingers like the sands of the desert and I didn't know where the months had gone.

"You didn't answer me, Honey," Jason urged as he started the car and pulled onto the street. The solar powered vehicle hummed as we moved into traffic.

"Did you think I might be anxious about the meeting?" I asked and then added. "Are you asking as the man in my life or my physician, Jason?" I was still in doubt about what he was getting at.

"I'm asking as the man who loves you, Christy." His eyes revealed both concern and a little disappointed.

I nuzzled in closer to him and felt his warmth. "I love you too, Jason," I said as a new reality sank in. "You know, this year could be hard on us, at least on me."

Jason rubbed my knee gently. "Why?"

"All of this political stuff is flooding in faster than I can possibly hold back the waves. If Grand-père asks me to help him on his campaign, I could be gone a lot," I whispered as I watched the passing scene. I couldn't take in enough of the glowing colors as the setting sun cast golden rays on the greening grass.

"*If* he asks you?" Jason chuckled in a teasing tone. "He will definitely need you—and he will certainly ask you," he said as he took my hand. "Christy, do you not know that it was your brave confrontation of President Alexander and your willingness to believe Silas Drummond that started this drive to overturn the Length of Days Law and openly elect a new president? If your grandfather wins the election, you will be single handedly responsible for our return to the original Constitution and a rebirth of freedom."

"Oh, Jason," I protested. "I'm a librarian, not a revolutionary."

He squeezed my hand warmly. "I think it's wonderful that you're naive to the impact you have on the events of the day." Jason sounded serious. "But, Honey, you will have to be aware enough of your importance to the cause, to stay safe."

"I'll remember," I said. "We all went through a lot in the other zones. We just got back, so I do remember the gripping fear and my pounding heart. But, the Lord was with us."

"Yes, he was," he agreed. "But, he gave us the ability to sense danger. We have to use our heads too, Christy. And—I won't always be there with you. I used a plausible excuse to be gone before, but I won't be able to convince Inspector Stoner of the same need this time."

"But, Jason," I sat up straight, "it's not going to be illegal to travel into other zones for purposes of campaigning, so we won't have to sneak out of this one. We won't need excuses."

Jason laughed and added, "And—you have Holly." The smile in his voice sounded sweet. "I'll have to program my Hank to keep me straight about where you are—when you aren't here by my side."

"Hank and Holly, I like that." I laughed at the thought of two holograms crossing beams in the night. Before we went into Grand-mère and Grand-père's house, Jason pulled me to him, kissed my face and brushed back my hair. I felt his tender lips on my eye lids and melted in his arms. Though loved all of my life, by my parents, my grandparents and all those around me, with Jason it was so much more. He filled in the micro-slot of my life that had been incomplete. Not that I wasn't strong on my own. I was—and I am. Jason completed the love-particle, that earthy completion that God had intended. We were almost as one.

• • •

Jason pulled the car into the driveway at my grandparents' home. The stately, turn-of-centuries-past, two-story house had beds of yellow tulips around the porch, like colorful lace at the bottom of a fine lady's skirt. I didn't knock but walked in, my usual custom for many years.

Judge and Mrs. Brunner had already joined Grand-mère and Grand-père. Even the Brunner's son Michael had improved enough following his accident to be able to enter with the aid of two canes. Sean, the underground newspaper publisher, and Dahlia, Jason's nurse, Silas Drummond, my parents—Elizabeth and Robert

Applewait, and Jason and I all gathered around Oliver and Constance Richly's ample, oak dining room table. An assortment of doughnuts, artfully arranged on an old bone china platter, sat next to a tray holding a coffee pot and last mid-century pink Depression-glass cream pitcher and sugar bowl. Each place setting boasted a matching china dessert plate and a small crystal glass filled with orange juice.

"Christy, dear," Grand-mère stood up and gave me a hug. "I am so glad you are back safely."

Grand-père took my hand as I walked by. "Welcome home, sweetheart."

"Thank you, Grand-père," I said and kissed his forehead. When I saw Silas, I added, "It's so good to see you, too, Silas." I reached over and gave him a little hug. "You have a small bandage behind your ear. What happened?"

"I was bitten by a bug," he whispered as he looked around, his eyes darting from one person to another.

"Do you want me to look at it?" Jason offered.

Silas covered the small spot on the left near his hair line with his fingertips. "No—no, I'm fine."

"You're looking tired," I said as I observed the circles under his eyes.

Silas's gaze fixed on the large cut glass platter in the center of the table. "Thanks for your concern, but I'm okay."

Before the meeting began and each one around the table had their turn at the huge doughnut plate, Judge Brunner bowed his head in reverence. He raised his eyes and studied each member seriously. "Good evening everyone, and especially you two, Christiana and Jason. We are so glad you've returned safely and without detection. Your venture into the three other forbidden zones was amazing and your safe return, a miracle. I am convinced of it. Bless you both."

The judge turned to Sean. "It wouldn't be safe for you to write about their silent movements right now. The network of freedom-loving people they have established to secure the signatures necessary to overturn the Length of Days Law, freely elect a new president, and place freedom at the heart of our country again is vital to our future."

"Absolutely!" Sean agreed. "I've started writing rough drafts of articles, and in-depth stories about all they did, so it will be ready when we do want them published."

"Perfect," Carl Brunner agreed. Members shifted their feet as they leaned forward, their arms rested on the edge of the table.

I saw Silas open his mouth to speak and then close it again. "What were you not saying?" I teased him.

"Nothing really—well—" he said as he stumbled through his thoughts. "I just wondered why we can't brag a little about your adventures."

"It's for their safety, Silas," Carl assured him. "Christy has some arena speaking events and a big trip east coming up."

"East too? Again?" he asked.

I smiled but felt nervous inside. "New York and Maine are some of the venues on my grandfather's agenda."

"Perhaps some added protection would be in order," Silas suggested as he sat back and seemed to relax a little. Still, I worried about him. He looked tense.

"Carl," Grand-père began, "I'm sure we're all anxious to hear what you've found out so far. How do we stand in the process of identifying zone chairpersons?"

Carl placed his elbows on the table and rubbed his hands together briskly. "It's amazing, Oliver," he said as his eyes flashed. "We started by contacting the Western Zone, since Christy and Jason had gone there first. Within a few days after they left the coast, Rachel Claudette, the head of Claimed-International, contacted me and volunteered to spear-head that zone's efforts to place Oliver Richly in the office of the president."

"Claimed-International?" Silvia Brunner asked. "What's that?"

I looked around for someone to answer Mrs. Brunner's question. *Of course they don't know,* I thought.

"Since the four zone borders were sealed years ago, none of us knew of the work of C-I until we arrived," I explained. "In our Central Zone there is a 'two-child-per-family-law.' If a couple accidently has a third child, the parents can choose any two of their children to keep. They have up to two years to decide which two they want. The rejected child is sent to the furnaces under Howard Mountain for extermination."

"Oh, no," Silvia gasped. "It can't be." Her face wore the same grief I had seen when her son Michael was injured.

"Yes, Mrs. Brunner," I insisted kindly. "I'm sorry, but it's true. We have met many of those children. When they are delivered to Howard Mountain—Silas Drummond here," I gestured to Silas, "the furnace keeper, spirits them away on weekends in the dark of night into the Valley of the Keepers, on the other side of the mountain. From there, Martin and Rebecca Spires find homes for them. Some families may already have two or three children of their own, but they 'claim' at least one bright, precious child from the cast-aside ones, and cherish them as their own." I was so excited about Silas's work with the kids, my voice trembled with emotion. "Now, the Keepers' village has grown so crowded they transport many of the Claimed Children to the West Coast and even cities out of the country. Rachel Claudette, a very wealthy Western Zone woman, has chosen to dedicate her life and fortune to these children."

"They are beautiful, bright, and loving children," Jason added. "They're healthy in body, and in spite of everything, their spirit isn't broken, even though their first parents try not to bond with the third child in case they don't want them."

I couldn't hide my smile that spread so wide I thought my face might crack. "One of the children told me proudly, 'I am not rejected. I am claimed and Father Silas is our lead wayfarer.' She was so beautiful, and I told her so. She said shyly, 'Thank you. All are beautiful in the sight of God.'"

"Ah!" Silvia gasped. "Then, somehow, someone has told those children about God, the Holy One. Here in the Central Zone the name of God has not been spoken for so many years!"

Silas was silent but then spoke. "I didn't know God's name either, since there was no one to tell me. But, forced to work in the vilest place on earth, beneath Howard Mountain, I had to hold onto the hope of a God who cares and loves and forgives, or I would have withered and died."

"Bless you, Silas," I offered as I patted his arm where it rested beside me on the table. "Once Silas rescued the rejected children and took them to the Keepers, the people of the Valley taught them about God."

Jason smiled at Silas and added, "It was through Silas's work of rescue, that we met Rachel and stayed in her beautiful home in California."

Mother was sitting beside me. She straightened and put her arm around my shoulder. "So we have Christy and Jason to thank for Ms. Claudette's quick response," she boasted.

"That's true," Sean agreed. "I was there when Christy spoke to a huge group during a church meeting."

"You were there?" I gasped in amazement. "How did you get there? I didn't see you." I couldn't believe what Sean was saying. Forbidden to cross zone borders, there was no mode of travel.

"I go to the other zones all the time," Sean smiled sheepishly. "I have newspapers to sell."

"At the rally, were you dressed in a disguise?" Jason asked Sean.

Sean laughed. "Simza Bihari was the only one there in a costume."

Dahlia's nose wrinkled in surprise. "Simza Bihari? Who's that?"

"A woman in a gypsy dress and veil, as all women in the Romani culture must be when they're in mourning." Sean was serious. "What do you say, Christy? Do you know who Mrs. Bihari is?"

I laughed and blushed. "Yes, Sean. I am Simza Bihari. Covered in black clothing and wearing a veil was the only way I could speak to the people and go undetected. My face, spread across the Jumbotran, would have been recognized if anyone were in the audience."

"And, someone was in the congregation," Jason chuckled. "Stoner's right-hand assistant, Chalky Boone and her thug, Daniel Washington, were in the back of the arena-turned church."

Grand-mère threw her hand to her mouth in astonishment. "Didn't she recognize you?" she stammered.

"Lieutenant Boone questioned me, or I should say questioned Mrs. Bihari, about my veil. Grace Small, the pastor, explained to her that a Romani widow woman must hide her face in respect for her deceased husband. If she doesn't, a year of shunning would be her fate," I explained. "For that Sunday morning, I was a Romani—or a gypsy widow."

Silvia put her hand to her chest. "Sometime, I want to hear all about your trip around the country. I'll look forward to Sean's newspaper articles."

"Certainly, when all of this is over we'll have long talks," I agreed and then turned to Grand-père. "Now, as I understand it, you have filed out all of the papers necessary to be a legitimate candidate in the next presidential race."

"That's right," Grand-père said and smiled. "It's hard to believe that we will actually vote on a president again, just as the founding fathers intended more than three-hundred years ago."

Judge Brunner wiped doughnut filling on Grand-mère's colorful napkin and sipped his coffee. I smiled because most people didn't use cloth napkins in 2113. But, Grand-mère is not most people.

"Christy," the Judge began, "as we said, Rachel Claudette is heading up the Western Zone election committee for your grandfather. Edward Musselman is in charge of the Midwestern Zone. And, that's very dangerous for him."

Jason agreed. "The Musselmans are one of the few families that didn't have their farm confiscated through laws designed to confiscate every crop-growing acre. The government owns the farms in the Midwestern zone. Edward and Maud managed to keep theirs by staying out of the spotlight, by hiding in plain sight as they called it."

"And, if Ed steps out of the shadows to spear-head the election committee in their zone, his family could lose their farm?" Mother's expression fell as she put it all together.

"He knows that," Daddy spoke up.

"Like the underlings in the bowels under New York City, believing the lies the elites told them, they lost everything. They crawled into the old subway and sewer systems under the city and didn't come out for decades." My eyes filled with tears that spilled over the rims.

"We were really clear about the dangers involved when Ed contacted us." Carl rolled the corner of the paper he had written notes on. "He insisted he wanted to stand and be counted this time."

"That is so brave," Dahlia whispered. "I don't think I could do that."

"Dahlia," Jason's jaw dropped, "you were the only one in the office every time Inspector Stoner stormed through the door. You had to stand firm, to take his insults and questions and act as if I were a 281 Palm Device hologram away. If he had demanded that you contact me, he would have seen that I wasn't within reach. Now, that is brave."

"I hadn't thought about that," she mused.

Daddy listened and then offered, "Oliver will need all the time we have left until the election, just to get into the other zones and meet people. No one even knows who he is in the rest of the country, although they should be aware of the Council of Elders in general. He'll have to canvass every major city and all the small hamlets in between."

"Do you have a leader for the Eastern Zone yet, Dad?" Michael asked the judge. "There's a lot to do," he observed. "This is the spring of 2113 and the election is November 3, 2114. How will Oliver be able to get to every region?"

"I'll get to the large venues," Grand-père said slowly, "but the entire election team will have to help out. There will be a committee in each zone to set up speaking opportunities, interviews—all the things that candidates for president used to do. They can't rig this election. We will carefully monitor it. The people will have to get to know me fast so they can make an informed decision regarding their vote. Christy, the people like you. You will be able to make speeches where I can't go."

Sean tapped his fingers on the table and jumped in. "A hard part of getting Sir Richly's message out to the people, will be designing the logistics for travel outside the zone. I know because I've taken my newspapers to distributers all over the country. But, this campaign is different. We have no connections, no trans-zonal airlines, not even maps from the other areas."

"Yes," I smiled as I remembered. "But, there are maps within the other zones outside of ours." With the sound of bus wheels and Raymar Goring's deep voice in my ears, I added, "Even the children on board the bus that wound along the beautiful stretch of highway between San Luis Obispo and Atascadero, California poured over the maps they had along with them. It is just this Central Zone that has no maps since most people no longer have cars, and the Public Transit only runs up and down the rail."

"There are ways to connect with people, "Carl said. "And, where there are none, we will create them." He folded his hands on the table and took a deep breath. "Michael, to answer your question, we have a volunteer for the eastern zone; the woman Christy and Jason stayed with at the Citadel–the Cornwall Citadel on Park Avenue and Fifty-Seventh Street. It's the home of Richard and Barbara Cornwall. Barbara is the one who volunteered." He paused again and looked around at every face at the table. "Since we are so isolated here in the Central Zone and forbidden to travel beyond the closed borders, we have no idea who some of these people are. I don't know who

Barbara Cornwall is. What do you think, Christy? You and Jason stayed with the Cornwalls; you know them. What is your opinion of her?"

"Barbara and Richard were wonderful to us and to those less advantaged," I said slowly, articulating each word carefully. "They took in some of the moles and underlings when they came out from below the city after years of living beneath the feet of the elite ones who lived above. The Cornwalls filled the rooms in their mansion with people they had never met."

"It was Mrs. Cornwall who volunteered to head up the process in the East. When she contacted me, she didn't say a lot. She did tell me that her husband would join her as co-chair when he recovered from an accident. Mrs. Cornwall insisted that she had to be of service. She said she has a debt to pay. Christy, will she be strong enough to do this?"

"Yes," Jason offered. "I'm sorry to interrupt, but, as a physician, I observed Barbara a lot. She is strong enough to do anything she chooses to do."

The Judge paused, his eyes focused on the ceiling. "Jason, did she do something that she needs to pay penance for? Will her former actions come around and embarrass our efforts to elect Oliver as president?" He looked at Jason and then at me. "Now is the time to tell us of any possible legal action against her."

I chuckled silently. Barbara Cornwall—in trouble with the law? "No Carl, there are no charges against Barbara. She has no criminal record. She is a very strong person. She stands up to her father often, and she does it with a straight back and clear eyes."

Carl breathed deeply. "Standing up to one's father is not necessarily a brave thing to do. Does that account for her need to pay off a debt?"

I looked around at all those gathered there. Then I lingered on Silas for a moment. "It is not her debt," I explained. "She is trying to repair the moral obligation of her father, to restore a measure of respectability to the family name."

Silas adjusted his position in his chair and continued to hold his eyes on me. "My Lady—Christy—who is her father and what did he do?"

"Silas, I know what you have been through." I patted his hand again and tried to reassure him, as his eyes darted left and right like a trapped animal. "The evil under the mountain and the museum of horrors you had to live with down there were unbearable for Jason and me to see—and we just passed through. You had to live with it all." I lifted his hand and kissed the top of it. "Silas—Barbara Cornwall's father—is Alister Bedlam, the richest and most evil man in the world—and the source of all your fears and sorrow."

Tears rolled down Silas's cheeks. "Then she has been in more pain than I. She's a perfect zone leader," he stated as he slapped the palms of his hands on the table.

The judge folded his hands and looked at me intently. "Christy, with a line-up like that, we are going to need you in Oliver's campaign office. You'll need to travel with him to be his liaison with these people in the other zones. Are you ready for this?"

Then I really knew why Jason had asked me the same thing on our way over to Oakwood. He was preparing me so I could answer the question when the judge asked it. I didn't have to think about it.

"Yes, sir, I'm ready," I said without hesitation. "And, where I'm not, the Lord will go before me and prepare the way."

CHAPTER 7

June 2113

The lettering was bold and black–*1787-Constitutional Party*–with red, white and blue stripes and full fans of bunting surrounding it. I knew the signage hanging over the door was a little too ostentatious for Oliver Richly's liking. It must have been a decision made by the Richly Election Committee. In the window of the storefront-turned massive office space was a two by three foot photo of Grand-père with the caption, OLIVER RICHLY FOR PRESIDENT.

I opened the door and walked in to more bustling energy than I had seen since the Claimed Children bellied-up to Rachel Claudette's dining room sideboard. People were laughing, having discussions in small groups, some had pulled their small ear deflectors out of their pocket to work quietly and independently.

Spring had dripped into early summer and still the rains continued. Water droplets gathered on the window panes Rand together formed a stream that ran down the glass to the sill below. Someone had placed a bucket beneath the double-hung sashes to prevent puddling on the floor. I watched a young man swap out a half-full pail for an empty one and smiled. Grand-père would never have had such a make-shift scene in his own home or office, regardless of the need for election funding.

"Lady Applewait?" a thirty-something woman with bouncing curls questioned as she approached me.

"Yes, I'm Christiana Applewait." I watched the room with excitement. Before the government removed the anti-emotion chemicals from our water supply, no one would have had the energy or interest to forge up this much enthusiasm.

"I see you are amused by our antiquated building," the woman who had greeted me said. "Starting yesterday, rapidly awakening campaign contributors started to drop off fists full of money for this renewed concept of free elections. The people want full freedom. We might also be able to make a few needed repairs to the building with some of the campaign money."

"What is your name?" I asked as she led me to a vacant desk behind a glass partition.

"My name is Ivy, Lady Applewait," she answered. Then she turned to the area in front of us. "This is your desk—if you want it."

I looked around and sized up the space. Complete with a small vase of flowers and a few books on the desk top, it looked homey. I would be able to help my grandfather from this small cubby of an office. "Yes, Ivy, thank you. I believe I do want it."

"I understand you will continue to monitor the progress of each zone campaign organization. That's great," she looked around the small space again. "And—I heard the signatures are all in place for the bill to come to a vote to overturn the Length of Days Law. It has secured a spot on the election ballot."

"Yes, Ivy, that task is complete. Now—" I paused and took my place in the chair behind my new desk. "Those same volunteers are working on the Richly Election Campaign Committee."

Ivy smiled as she sat in the facing leather chair. "We have a full agenda for you, Lady Applewait."

"Christy," I corrected her. "If the office is going to run smoothly, let's not complicate the conversation with cumbersome titles. Please, call me Christy. Everyone does."

Ivy blushed a little with cast down eyes. "I heard that. But, I didn't want to assume anything. I—I was in the crowd on Gifting Day Eve. I heard it all. I saw it all—and it filled me with awe. You are—"

"I am a campaign worker, the same as you, Ivy," I protested.

"You are the seer, Christy," she beamed. "I heard you described as a disciple of the Holy One. The Lord has blessed you with—"

Crack! The moment was shattered and the glass partition fractured by something that whizzed past my head.

Screams rattled through the air as everyone in the outer office hit the floor in self-protection. But, I was frozen. I experienced no shock, helplessness or hopelessness. I wasn't confused or disoriented. Rigidly fixed in a state of focus I had never known before, I didn't move. The last months raced through my mind like the fleeting images of a drowning person. Jason and I had experienced dangers of many kinds, under filthy city streets or crawling along frozen ground in order to avoid detection. But, we had never been the target at the end of a firearm, actually fired on in broad daylight.

Ivy flew across the desk, threw me to the floor and dropped her body on top of me. Pinned down and dazed, I waited for an all-clear signal.

"Is everyone out there all right?" Ivy shouted to the pool of volunteers in the front office.

Ivy and I scrambled to our feet. She started out of my office and I followed close behind. We both were on a mission to determine what had happened.

"Yes—I think we're all okay, just scared spitless," one volunteer gasped as we approached. Others just stared with wide eyes.

In the larger staff office, Ivy began at the windows where she slammed heavy storm shutters closed. The room grew eerily dark without natural light pouring in. She inspected the area all around the broken glass. "It appears that a long range rifle round pierced the street window," she began as she walked through the room, "lanced the tight spaces between campaign workers here in the outer office," she continued as we walked back into my small space, "and then embedded its lethal projectile in the wall just over your left ear," she concluded.

Then it occurred to me as I stood behind her, Ivy hadn't dodged any flying projectiles by falling to the floor like the rest of us. She had actually leaped onto my desk and placed her body between me, any additional bullets and the flying glass from the window that divided my office from the outer general work area.

From behind her, I could see something in her hair. I placed my hands on her head and felt hard, sharp fragments that nicked my hands. "Ivy," I gasped as shards fell from where they had clung to her curls. "Here, let me help you."

I guided her back to the chair she had been sitting in and carefully parted portions of her hair and began to remove the glass. At first I worked silently, my mind full of possibilities. Who would have shot at me? Stoner had many opportunities to murder me in cold blood if that was his intent.

"Christy!" Grand-père shouted as he dashed into my office, with both arms spanning the entry. His eyes quickly darted around the small space and then rested on the gaping hole in the wall. "Are you all right?" He hurriedly put his arms around me as I stood over Ivy.

"Ivy, how are you? Are you hurt?" he asked when he saw the broken glass.

"I'm fine. Just itchy with fragments in my hair I don't want to scratch." She carefully picked at some remaining pieces that had eluded me.

"If you're sure you're okay, I'll check out front again on the rest of them," he said as he headed back out the door. I could see him going from one volunteer to another.

Ivy started to get up from the chair, but I touched her shoulder and asked her to stay, gently running my fingers through every blond wave and curl. "Your hair is very thick. It looks like the depth of your curls caught some of the glass and wouldn't let it slip away."

"I always knew my thick mane, that I can hardly get a comb through some days, would eventually cause a problem." She patted my hand and inched to the edge of the seat, her eyes fixed on the hole in the wall. "Thanks, Christy." She didn't look at me but crooked her finger for me to follow her direction. "Look at this," she whispered as she inspected the end of the failed attempt at murder.

"What?" I asked but eagerly followed her lead.

"This is not the projectile from a 750-Z or any of the other Blue Guard weapons," she mused as she fished in her pocket. She pulled out what appeared to be an old fashioned pocket knife I had seen pictures of in some of my books. With determination, she opened the blade and began to dig out the lead.

I watched as she pried at the shattered area, seemingly careful not to damage the bullet. "Ivy," I finally began slowly. "How do you know about a 750-Z and any of its ammunition?"

"Oh—I read a lot," she answered as she worked on the spot.

I continued to watch her extricate the bullet. "You probably don't know, Ivy, but I have a master's degree in library science. With book burnings in decades past and book banning of our current era, there are no weapons of any kind or pictures of weapons in the current literature. That information was eliminated a very long time ago."

As Ivy pulled the bullet from the wall and inspected it in her hand, I asked, "How could you have known about any of this—and where did you get a pocket knife? They aren't manufacture anymore?"

"Christy—there are some things you don't know," she began, stumbling as she searched for words—"yet."

"Okay," I said as I sat back down and motioned for her to return to the chair. "Let's talk."

"Well—your grandfather—"

"Grand-père? What does he have to do with this shooting?" Now, I was really confused. But one thing I did know, "That bullet comes from an antique long rifle. I do have access to books of all kinds and that round looks familiar."

"I won't lie to you, Christy. You're right. I have never seen ammunition like this. Where would it have come from?"

"I once overheard Ward Stoner say, 'We have a well-stocked arsenal of weapons and instruments, both new and vintage.'"

My head was swimming with dreaded possibilities. "I still say, Stoner would never attack me or Grand-père. He would chase me to the ends of the country, but he would never attack me. He's too loyal to his precious rule book and wants to carry out every new law that was created under the New Constitution."

"Then, there has either been a breach of security at the Federal arsenal—or there is a rogue Guardsman who can get really close to us," Ivy thought aloud.

"Ivy," I began cautiously, "just who or what are you? And, tell me now, what does my grandfather have to do with all of this?"

"Sir Richly hired me to pose as your assistant—but in reality, I'm your bodyguard." She winced as though she expected me to reject her.

"Sounds like a good idea to me," I agreed. "I hope I never need you to protect me with your own body again. "And—" I began as I looked into her eyes. "I want only honesty between us," I insisted. "I know I'm young, but I'm not a child. I have proven that I can help implement changes and take care of myself. I will allow you to be my partner-in-safety. Today has proven that life has become even more dangerous than before." I reached out my hand and eagerly shook hers as a gesture of warm, equal friendship. Then I added confidently, "We're in this together—as friends."

CHAPTER 8

The City of Angels

October 2113

Unable to take my eyes off the ground below us, I watched as our plane closed the space between the landing gear and the runway. "Look at the colors on the tree tops below us. I can't believe this is early autumn already."

Months ago, Jason and I were smuggled into the Western Zone on a cool winter day. It was early evening this time, bright enough to see the landscape below and dim enough to bring up the sparkle of the night. The lights of the bright City of Angels glowed in multi-colors, with shimmering hallows around the beams. Gray Fox and his wife Little Feather weren't here to guide us this time, but that would have to be okay.

"Grand-père," I began, slipping my arm through his as the plane descended, "you won't meet Martin and Rebecca Spires on this leg of the campaign. There're wonderful, and I really want you to meet them, but—they'll be with us in New York."

"Martin and Rebecca—keepers of the Bible," he nodded, remembering what I had told him.

Ivy mostly remained silent and stayed in the background, ever present, ever watching. Not this time. "I'm sorry to interrupt, but what are the keepers of the Bible?"

I smiled as I watched Ivy lean in and listen to the story of the wonderful people of the valley on the other side of the mountain from Capitol City. "Their valley was hidden after an earthquake but not destroyed as people on both sides of Howard Mountain believed. All the families in the Valley of the Keepers are responsible for different books the ruling elite tried to erase after the great uprising of the previous epoch. For four generations, every man, woman and child in the valley have carried a verbal account of the history of this great nation. Because their existence in unknown to the rest of the world, they can live in seclusion and their secret activities go undetected. Different families have in their possession certain books and volumes which they have guarded and memorize in case the books are confiscated. You're right. The Spires family is the keeper of the Bible, the story of all of us."

Ivy's jaw dropped. "Families memorized whole books?"

I was thrilled to say, "Yes, they did," as if the knowledge of it was as stupendous as the act of it.

Ivy began to gather up her belongings as the plane taxied. "I have recently heard of the Bible, but I've never read one, or held one in my hand for that matter."

Not sure of how much to tell her, since the confiscation of Bibles happened years ago, I wanted to say something, since she seemed interested. "I think we can get you one out here in the Western Zone while we're in the area. This zone follows the rules they agree with, not the rules written down. The Western Zone is the new Bible belt."

"That would be great," Ivy beamed. Then, as if she had just noticed, she asked, "Why isn't Jason with you, Christy?"

My last moments with Jason when he dropped us off at the airport, flooded back. I felt my cheeks grow warm, and I hoped my blush wasn't evident to others.

"I love you so much," Jason had whispered in my ear. "I'll miss you more than I want to think about."

At the gate, checking out my grandfather and Ivy Trudeau's diverted gaze, I leaned in and kissed Jason goodbye. "I didn't think I could do this without you."

"You are so strong, Christy. I know you can," he assured me.

"I love you." My lips formed words I shared only with Jason.

I smiled again as I thought of him, picked up my cross-body satchel and slipped the strap over my head. "Jason was out of his office for so long when we were gone during the winter, he thought he had better stay in Capitol City. He'll join us in New York."

"I may be a member of the Council of Elders, but I have never been to New York—or L.A. for that matter." Grand-père reached under his seat and pulled out a leather bag. "Odd, I'm willing to come to the coast, but my worthy opponent, President Alexander, chooses to call his presence in from Capitol City."

Ivy thought for a moment. "Alexander is a zone president, now he wants to be president of the whole country."

I chuckled a little. "He's afraid to have his face enlarged to gargantuan size. Everyone will see what he really looks like," I said as I rolled my eyes. "They'll use the Jumbotron. He'll be bigger than life. When you see your own face enlarged by tens, you get a sense of your own presence. It will be the same for Alexander," I added as we began to disembark the plane.

"Jumbotron is it?" Grand-père asked, but it sounded more like a statement than a question.

"Just remember, Alexander may be the Zone President but you are on the council, and that's national. They will recognize your position, if not your face."

I paused when I arrived at the cabin door. A jetway from the previous century was still in use and waited in front of me. With travel between zones, even from town to town, forbidden, lack of use ensured that most of the equipment of air travel would never wear out.

Now, here we were, legally flying into the Western Zone. I smiled at the miracle of my awakening country and then thought of my grandfather's participation in it all. "Regardless of Alexander's size on the huge screen, the image would still just be little-old-him."

Grand-père hoisted up his bag, like a man intending to make a point. "Maybe that's why he will only be present electronically. He needs to feel larger than he really is."

We walked quickly down the jetway ready to take on all that the west had to offer. "Raymar!" I shouted to the man who waited with a small American flag in his hand. He was the only one in the terminal with a flag. When they partitioned the country into zones, they banned Nationalism. The American flag was one of the first emblems to go. With so many nationalities coming to our country, the immigrants were offended that they could not fly their own flag. Therefore, to be fair, none was visible.

Raymar stood there—clean shaven, dressed in appropriate clothing, with a calm and peaceful expression on his face. "I didn't know if you would recognize me," he blushed. "They tell me I look different."

"You look wonderful, old friend," I smiled as I reached up and gave him a hug. Then I turned to my grandfather. "Grand-père, I'd like you to meet Raymar Goring. He is a man of many identities. He was one of the hollow people. But, he is also, the famous author, Robert Gross."

"I'm still one of the hollow people. The government said the hollow ones will always be second class citizens until a law is written, specifically overturning the previous law." His expression was dark and defeated.

"I am so pleased to meet you," Grand-père assured him as he shook his hand. "I've read your books. As Robert Gross, they can't call you second class anything." He gave Raymar's shoulder a hearty pat. "And, as to creating a new law, we are going to overturn the entire New Constitution and reinstate the original one. A plan is already in place." He gave him a friendly slap again. "There was no mention of the hollow people in the Constitution of 1787, and to be precise, there is nothing in the new one about the hollow ones either. Some may treat you like a second-class citizen, but you are equal under the law. And, all of you can vote—so get out there and register everyone."

"Thank you, Sir," Raymar said with sincerity. "Come," he stated briefly. "Rachel Claudette will have a late supper ready for us when we get there."

"Wonderful!" I said out of appreciation and a hungry stomach. "It will be good to see your daughter, Kasamar, again." Then I paused. "I hope she'll be there."

"Rachel had me drive one of her cars. It's this way." Raymar directed us toward the door that led to the parking structure. "Indeed Kasamar will be there. Rachel has put her in charge of Claimed-International. Since Rachel will be heading up the Western Zone committee for your election, Sir Richly, she knew she would need dependable help."

Grand-père stopped in mid-step. "Raymar, there will be no class-system in the renewed USA. Call me Oliver."

Raymar smiled. "I will try to remember. But know, in my heart, you are my friend."

"Stated like an accomplished writer," Grand-père bowed at the waist, laughed and preceded out the door.

Since the sun had set, the parking structure was dim and full. The west wasn't like the Central Zone where the government prohibited citizens from owning personal transportation. Those in the Western Zone would kick and scream if anyone were to attempt to take their car, so every parking facility was crowded.

I watched with caution as my grandfather and my friend bonded—and smiled. I wasn't cautious because I feared Raymar, but there was something eerie about the surroundings. The smell of the old gasoline engine cars that dotted the garage reminded me of the wonderful time we spent in California just months previously, and yet it was so different. Something was wrong.

I tried to brush off the feeling of danger with conversation. "Did Rachel send her personal flash-car?"

"Rachel had me drive her last-century minivan." Raymar laughed as he approached a funny car that looked to me like a pointy nosed sausage. "She said we would all have more leg room." He smiled at Grand-père. "I guess she already knew how tall you are." I watched him measure Grand-père's six foot five inch height with his eyes.

"Sir," a large man in a black suit and white shirt intruded in our small group as he took Grand-père by his elbow and tried to lead him aside. "I must speak with you, Richly."

"Not now," I urged the man to move on, acting as Grand-père's handler.

"No, he will come with me this minute," the man insisted with a near tourniquet grasp on Grand-père's arm.

"Release him, mister," Ivy said as she stepped between the man and me trying to reason with him.

With his free hand, the robust one drew back his fist and delivered a direct punch to Ivy's face, knocking her down and out. He tightened his hold on my grandfather with white knuckles and tried to pull him away.

Raymar snapped around with a hollow stare and faced the man. I saw him try to conquer the man with the same mad-dog eyes I had seen when I first met him, when Raymar was still a hollow man. He moved in close to the man's space with no fear or hesitation, his teeth bared, a sign of unspoken but fierce aggression.

The man in the suit withered and averted his eyes, but he did not back away without one last word. "I have a message for you, Richly." He raised his eyes and cast a hostile gaze at Grand-père, holding his ground. "We have certain information you wouldn't want shared. Drop out of the race or drop dead."

Raymar grabbed the man's throat with one hand and pried his grip from Grand-père's arm with the other. Raymar didn't use words, but throwing back his head and growling like a rabid wolf, he headbutted the assailant. Then, like a nasty piece of spoiled fruit, he flipped the assailant to the ground. With one last evil glance at the three of us, the suited man picked himself up, limped and stumbled off.

I wished Jason had come with us. I felt safe with him around. Raymar and Ivy would have to fill in for him until he arrived. Turning to Ivy, I bent over and helped her stagger to her feet.

"Are you okay?"

"Yes," she said as she shook her head and reached for her sidearm. "Did you see where he went?"

"No," I said as I looked off in the direction to which I thought he escaped. Overwhelmed by the danger, the attack on my grandfather, and the instantaneous change in who I thought Raymar had become, the truth was, I couldn't think about anything.

Now, with Raymar's return to the screeching persona of a hollow one, I wasn't sure what he was capable of. Torn between fear of the possibility of Raymar's actions and relief that he was able to turn the man away with the power of his will, I reached out and patted Raymar on the shoulder.

"Thank you, my dear friend. Are you all right?" I was worried. I didn't know if he would be able to drag himself back from the edge of the dark abyss again. Could he step in and out of his hollow man behavior?

Raymar had lived in the world as a wild man all of his life. Along with others like him, a hollow one was his label. Seen as half animal, people supposed the hollow ones had little civilized nature within them. It was only Raymar's relationship with his wife and then his daughter that cooled his savage fire.

Then, there was his other side, his inner life as a beloved philosophical author that the world loved but did not know. Who would win this new battle between the light and darkness?

Raymar straightened his hunched shoulders and rose to his full height. He shook his head like one would shed lake water after a swim. Then, he smiled a smile that filled his face. "I'm okay, Christy. Thank you for worrying about me."

"You are really in control!" I marveled.

Grand-père followed the suit-man with his eyes until he was out of sight. "That one was not in control," he said as shades of anger crossed his face like I had never seen before. Grand-père did not get angry—ever.

"And, thank you Ivy for your efforts to protect me," he added.

Her jaw was red from the fist jab and set rigidly in disgust. "But I didn't protect you."

Grand-père patted her shoulder, "But you stepped into harm's way. That's all anyone could do."

She muttered as she walked ahead to the car. "But it wasn't enough."

As we hurried into the safety of Rachel's vehicle, I wondered aloud. "What did he mean about having information about you, Grand-père? I cannot imagine anything negative about you. What do you think he has?"

"I have no idea," he shrugged off the question. "I do know I have nothing to hide."

• • •

"Rachel, I'd like you to meet my grandfather, Oliver Richly," I said as Rachel Claudette led us into her beautiful home in Los Angeles. "It is wonderful to be here again."

"I'm happy to meet you, Sir Richly. I recognized you from the posters that are already dotted around the city."

"Please, call me Oliver," Grand-père urged.

"If you'll call me Rachel," the movie producer and director of Claimed-International said as she showed us into the dining room.

The table, covered with a cream colored cloth with hand painted golden birds of paradise artfully placed on it, already boasted a wooden server with a huge loaf of steaming bread on it. White porcelain dinner plates, placed at each setting and flanked by shinning silver flatware waited for us.

"Oliver," Rachel directed, "please sit at the head of the table. I'll take the foot. Christy and Raymar, please sit facing each other. Ivy, please take the seat beside Christy."

As we sat down, I noticed there was still an empty seat beside Raymar. "Your home is as lovely as I remembered it," I admired as someone came through from the kitchen with a platter of steaks.

"Kasamar!" I said as I jumped up and hugged Raymar's daughter as soon as her platter touched the table.

"Christy!" Kasamar squealed as she turned and embraced me. "I'll be right back with the rest of the food," she said. "Then, we'll catch up."

I started to follow her into the kitchen. "Let me help you," I offered.

"No, My Lady," she protested. "Let me serve you."

"Kasamar," I chuckled and followed along behind her. "I went from Christy to My Lady, practically in one breath."

"I'm sorry, Christy," she apologized. "With your grandfather's campaign for president and his presence here, I guess I'm a little star-struck."

"No stars here," I said and laughed. "Just us."

In the kitchen, the large six burner stove held several pots. She hurried over and ladle out a serving bowl full of small red potatoes. She dabbed a large dollop of pure creamery butter in the middle. I watched it melt and soak in. Into an oblong serving dish she placed long spears of asparagus to which she topped with more butter.

"In the Central Zone, the dietary police would arrest you for butter indulgence and throw you in jail without a trial." Laughing again at the silliness of it all, I marveled at how good it felt to just laugh. "Okay, what can I do to help?"

"Well Christy—I think I may have forgotten the steak knives," she nodded her head in the direction of a cutlery drawer that remained open from the last piece she removed. "It would be wonderful if you could take them in. There's a narrow basket there on the side counter. It would look better if they were passed around rather than plopped down." Kasamar picked up the vegetable bowls and turned to me again. "Thank you, my friend."

Picking up the small basket and placing the knives inside, I couldn't help but anticipate the hot juices running into the bottom of the meat platter that already sat on the table. My mouth began to water and I wondered when I had eaten last—perhaps a breakfast bar and a half cup of coffee in the morning?

As I went back into the dining room, I saw Grand-père's eyes, still widened, as he continued to fix them on the meat platter. "Oh my goodness, Rachel, those steaks look amazing." He sat back in his chair and patted his stomach. "Wouldn't Jason love one of those, Christy?" he sighed. "Your grandmother would say, 'Now Oliver, remember your heart.'"

I stopped abruptly as I placed the knife basket on the table. My words caught in my throat. "What's wrong with your heart?"

"Absolutely nothing." He grinned as he continued to eye the meat.

Rachel rolled her eyes and smiled. "You're healthy because your wife continues to be proactive and reminds you—before you eat."

We all laughed at the logic of her simple statement. "I was contemplating a diet that would eliminate meat," I said as I looked again at the platter. "I'll consider it again sometime in the future."

Rachel placed her elbows on the table and folded her hands. "Many here in California were vegetarians in the distant past." She shook her head slightly and a faint smile crossed her lips. "Then the government changed, and they re-worked all the facts about nutrition and how certain foods act on the body. Most people decided to go back to the plain eating of our farm ancestors, only we eat in moderation. Common sense people—common sense." With her hands still folded in prayer, she turned to my grandfather. "Oliver, would you please bless our food while it's still hot?"

Grand-père bowed his head and reached for my hand. Then I reached down to Rachel and took hers. Around the table, we held the warm hand of the one near us while Grand-père lifted up words asking God to bless our food, gave thanks for our safe trip and the profoundly important assignment we had been tasked to accomplish.

"Eat up," Rachel encouraged after the Amen, "and then we'll talk about the political rally at the arena tomorrow. There will be thousands present. The Jumbotron will pick up President Alexander in the Central Zone and send your images out across the old public airwaves of previous years."

"Who will ask the questions?" Grand-père wondered aloud.

Rachel passed the meat platter and then cut thick slabs of yeasty smelling bread. "I will, Oliver."

"Great—I guess," I said as another thought rushed in. "Will anyone wonder if you had fed Grand-père the questions ahead of time? You are managing his campaign out here."

"They shouldn't," she stated flatly. "Actually, I haven't seen the questions either. A committee, made up of three political analysists, created the questions. They are in a sealed envelope and will be presented to me at the debate."

"That's a relief," I sighed. "It's been so long since there has been a presidential debate, I wasn't sure how that would be handled."

"I'm glad they chose you," Grand-père said as he began to cut his meat into bite size pieces. "I'll welcome a familiar face."

"They didn't actually choose me," she smiled sheepishly. "I own the production company, the communications network and the studios."

Grand-père placed his steak knife and fork on his plate and beamed. "I'm glad to know you, Ma'am."

"Don't Ma'am me, or I'll Sir you," she said and laughed.

It was a good supper and a great evening.

CHAPTER 9

Suddenly

The next evening, the Los Angeles Memorial Coliseum sparkled like a precious jewel in the night. It was full to capacity. Increased two decades back, the seating capacity now held over one-hundred thousand spectators. The Central Zone had no such arena, so I was taken aback by the shining bowl that glowed with multi-colored flood lights.

Capitol City would not have drawn one-hundred people, let alone thousands. With the chemically treated water, citizens simply wouldn't have had the energy to go out again after work. Since emotion-numbing chemicals no longer cloud the old water supply, I'd seen a few people out walking in the evening and tossing a ball with their children.

Ivy and I stood at a distance to the center of the arena and watched. "This is astounding," Ivy gasped in awe.

"As compared to the Central Zone, where it is illegal for more than two or three to gather in one spot, it is indeed astounding. I agree."

"I am amazed," a voice whispered in my ear.

"Jason!" I yelled as I turned and threw my arms around him. "I thought you couldn't get away," I gasped.

He kissed my forehead and held me close as Ivy smiled and stepped a few paces behind us.

"I couldn't stand not seeing you." The fire in his soft eyes said it all. "Besides, it's Friday evening and the weekend is ahead. I would have had an intern on-call for me anyway."

I took his hand and didn't let go. My heart felt full to overflowing. "Rachel asked about you. She'll be happy to see you when we go back to her place later."

"Ladies and gentlemen," an announcer interrupted as he bellowed across the booming speaker system. "Please greet our moderator, Rachel Claudette."

The crowd jumped to their feet and cheered as Rachel came into center field. She turned to face the four corners of the massive arena and eagerly waved to everyone. Her smile lit up the Jumbotron.

"Now, please welcome President Nathan Alexander, who is with us on the screen," the voice announced and waved in the direction of the Tron. There was relative silence from thousands of spectators. Alexander cast his eyes down in embarrassment and then shot them back to the camera in a defiant smirk. A few called out questions I imagined he would rather have not heard.

"Why aren't you here?" a man yelled on the clear evening air.

"Are you afraid to show up in person?" another shouted. Loud, inaudible mumbles followed, along with the sound of those who shifted in their seats and shuffled their feet in discomfort.

"And now," the voice drew out slowly, like a pitchman for a new kind of communications device that customers had to rush to purchase immediately, "please show your appreciation to Sir Oliver Richly, who traveled all the way from the Central Zone to our sunny coast."

The stands went wild, cheering and clapping and throwing their hats in the air. "Richly—Richly—Richly!" they chanted feverishly.

Grand-père walked briskly and confidently out to the middle of the arena, where all attention focused on him. Turning, he waved to all those present. The cheering didn't stop for eleven minutes. On the Jumbotron, the producer had split the screen, with Grand-père's smiling, strong, humble image on the left, and Alexander's scowling, bitter face glaring down on everyone below on the right. The cheering turned to laughter when the crowd watched and then pointed at the vast difference between the two expressions.

The contrast between the image on the screen and the miniature size of the one person in the middle of the excitement was powerful. Grand-père didn't have to puff himself up. Even though he appeared small to those in the upper seats, he filled the arena with his presence.

"The order of speaking has been determined by a toss of a coin," Rachel began. "Our first question begins with you, Sir Richly." She touched the air in front of her and read from the screen that was invisible to everyone else.

She paused, "This question is about the Constitution. Sir, your campaign slogan is the *1787-Constitutional Party.* Exactly, what is the 1787 Constitution?"

"I'm glad that this is the first question because it will set the theme for everything else I say." He raised his arms to the sky and clasped his hands as a sign of triumph. "My friends—this country of ours was a miracle from its making." His voice echoed off the bleachers, high in the stands. "People had left their homeland for the promise and hope of freedom here in the new world. When the time was right, our forefathers wrote a Constitution, creating a government like none other in history, a place of equality. It took many years for all of those who lived here to secure that freedom for themselves—but it happened when those flaws were rectified.

"We as a people were the shining light in a dark world—an experiment in freedom never experienced before. When the chaos of the previous millennium created a security gap through which the revolutionaries sneaked through, like thieves in the night, they sat at the desk of our forefathers and wrote a new Constitution. In that new document, they stripped freedom from all of us. The government took over every decision in our lives.

"Your own Western Zone banished a group of people to the forests and caves of the mountainous regions. As those people languished in exile, you began to call them the hollow ones."

Murmurs of unease and discomfort rose up from the assembled body. But, the crowd saw Grand-père's eyes of love and forgiveness on the huge image of the Jumbotron.

"Some of you are loving them back into the human family." Shouts of joy floated across the air like the melodic sounds of music. Grand-père started again.

Alexander's face appeared on the right side of the split screen. He looked hard and red with anger when he interrupted. "Wait a minute. How long does he get to talk?"

"There is a ten minute limit on these introductory remarks, Mr. President," Rachel Claudette soothed. "Sir Richly, you have more time on the clock if you want it."

"Thank you," Grand-père bowed to Rachel and ignored the interruption. "In the Midwestern Zone, they confiscated all the crop-growing acreage, and made the farmers tenants on their own land. In the Central Zone, they drugged the water so the citizens didn't really care about anything nor have the energy to rebel."

He paused while the crowd jeered the audacity of those currently in power. "And, the Central Zone obeys the Length of Days Law. When people reach a prescribed age, based on a formula that is determined by their value to society, they are taken to the extermination center and placed in the never-ending-sleep, thus ending their Length of Days."

"What?" angry voices belched from the distant seats.

"It is true," Grand-père insisted with his arms lifted in power. "My granddaughter, Christiana Applewait exposed the atrocities under Howard Mountain!"

The crowd erupted in chants and cheers, "Christy—Christy—Christy!"

"Thank you—thank all of you," he shouted and waved his hands in the air.

Still he continued. "In the East, the elites told the citizens that there were roving bands of marauding plunderers who would steal everything they had and kill them and their families, just for the thrill of it. Thousands of the citizens escaped to the sewers and old subway systems under the streets, thinking that would save their lives. For generations, those fine people lived in the filth and utter darkness of the caverns beneath the feet of those who lived above. Called the underlings, just recently they have been set freed." Again, those in attendance jumped to their feet and shouted for joy.

"When I am president, the first thing I will do is overturn the New Constitution and reinstate the original one, the Constitution of 1787, which will also completely erase the Length of Days Law." Thunderous applause and cheers rose up from the stands and they pounded their feet on the floor, creating the sound of thunder.

"I'll have to admit, he does look like a powerful man," Inspector Stoner grudgingly admired from behind us.

At the sound of his voice, I jumped and grabbed Jason's arm. "Inspector, you startled me." Then the impact of his words caught up to me. "Is the head of the Blue Guard admiring my grandfather?"

Stoner didn't look in my direction but kept his eyes on center field. "I would not have believed it, but there is something there." He planted his feet squarely and firmly beneath him. "I always admire power," Stoner rumbled, his eyes narrowed.

Jason crossed behind me and stood between the Inspector and me. "What are you doing here?"

"I am tasked with protecting Sir Richly and, by association, both of you." He folded his arms across his chest like one with no intention of moving from the spot.

"How can you protect him in the middle of all these people?" I asked, genuinely worried about the number of followers and fans in the arena and the thunder of the applause. I remembered the man in the parking structure at the airport.

"There is a force field around him, Lady Applewait." Stoner looked around the mammoth structure.

Then, in a strange comparison, the gently moving air blew in a sweet autumn fragrance on the evening breeze. The aroma reminded me of the orange-red serpentine columbine that grew in Rachel's flower garden. I smiled. It was a stark contrast to my own perception of Ward Stoner—a black rose.

"He is protected," Stoner insisted.

I thought for a moment and wondered if I could trust him. Stoner was a conundrum and I didn't know what to do. "If you are truly here to protect my grandfather…."

Jason seemed to know what I was going to say. "It's all right, Christy. Tell him about the airport."

"What about the airport?" Stoner asked, his brow furrowed and his face was deeply lined.

I watched as the crowd continued their loud agreement with all that Grand-père said. Finally, I explained, "After we got out of the airplane terminal and entered the parking garage, a man approached my grandfather and threatened him. He grabbed his arm and told him to drop out of the race or he would reveal certain information. Grand-père had no idea what he was talking about."

"Yesterday, right here in LA?"

"Yes, Sir," I said as I turned to hear the question posed to Alexander.

Stoner spun around and looked at me intently. "You mean a man was able to get close enough to accost the Center Chair of the Council of Elders?"

"Yes, that's exactly what happened," I agreed. I worried more for my grandfather's safety now after I saw how concerned the inspector was. "Ivy tried to stop him but got knocked down. Raymar's near rage chased the man off."

Stoner bristled. "Where are Raymar and Ivy now? I thought Ivy was assigned to protect you, Miss Applewait."

"Raymar is just out of the spotlight near Grand-père." Then, I smiled and nodded off to my left. "Ivy is right there. Near me and yet giving Jason and me some space."

Stoner sniffed and rubbed his nose, seeming indifferent to anyone's need for privacy. "Tomorrow, at first light," Stoner shouted to me over the crowd, "I want a full description of the man from the parking garage. Write down everything you can remember, his facial features, his possible age, what he was wearing—everything."

The loud speaker squawked open again as Rachel's voice filled the air. "And now, President Alexander, your first question." Again, Rachel touched the open space in front of her and read from the invisible tablet. "Please tell us your theme for this campaign and for the first months of what would be your administration. What will you hope to accomplish by this advancement from zone president to national president?"

"Theme? I need no contrived message," he spit out. "My theme is to continue to maintain this great country just the way it is." The veins in his neck began to bulge and his face reddened. "My army will not allow an insurrection." His cheeks glowed like two blotches of over-ripe purple plums. "And, I will defend the New Constitution from all those who would attack it. The New Constitution was written to provide food for the workers, love and guidance for all of our children, protection from one's emotions and sexual appetites, and to maintain a lean census by discarding those who cannot or will not work and those who have outlived their usefulness to society." He thumped his fist on the desk in front of him. "These are noble causes." He straightened the front of his suit and pulled himself up as tall as he could reach. "The next question please."

The crowd said nothing but sat in stunned silence. Stoner said little more.

"Who is protecting Alexander in Capitol City?" Jason asked as his eyes scanned the thousands of restless people in the seats.

"His bodyguards," Stoner said as he gritted his teeth. "And, the strength of his entire Zone Guard."

"Since he has nothing to offer," I breathed out slowly, "I doubt he has anything to fear."

"Oh no, Ma'am, he has everything to fear," Stoner said as his eyes scanned the angry faces of thousands of people. "With your grandfather, it is the man in a parking garage and those like him that he has to fear."

I pondered deeply the words Stoner had just used. Fear for Grand-père's safety flooded my heart. But, there was something else Stoner said. He referred to Grand-père as 'your grandfather,' not just a name or title. He didn't keep him at a distance. He drew Grand-père closer, and made him real. I felt better, more hopeful. Perhaps Stoner would put more effort into his task of protecting us.

"Hey, Richly," someone yelled from the stands with the help of an old megaphone. "The Council of Elders is powerful. Why didn't you stop the Length of Days Law?"

Grand-père didn't apologize or hesitate to answer. "The Council doesn't make laws. They only interpret them."

"Isn't it true that a change in that law would mean that you and your wife will get to live longer? Weren't you and your wife scheduled to surrender your Length of Days? Why didn't you just change the law?"

"As I said, we don't create new laws nor amend the old ones. The Council only interprets the laws."

"Interpret this," the man yelled.

Suddenly **ka-pow, pow, pow, pow** echoed across the top of the arena. Stoner reached for his holstered weapon and ran in Grand-père's direction.

I grabbed Jason's arm and buried my head in his shoulder. "Is Grand-père okay?" I gasped. My body shook in terror.

Ivy ran to my side and grabbed my arm. "Come Christy. Let's get out of the open." She tried to pull me off to the side.

"No, Ivy! I have to see how my grandfather is." My hands trembled and my throat tightened.

"I know, but we have to move—now!"

"Wait," I demanded, looking to the infield and then back at Jason. "What do you see?"

"I can't see anything," he said, his breath short and choppy. "There's like—smoke—in the infield."

"Smoke?" I asked as I flipped back and forth to see the chaos in front of us.

The people in the stands didn't stampede as I feared would happen but sat stunned where they were. A few screamed, but for the most part, the thousands of Richly followers and fans only seemed to hold their collective breath while experts assessed Grand-père's safety.

Blue Guardsmen streamed out of the side entrances and flooded the grass with weapons drawn. From our distance, they looked small but mighty, ready to devour everything in their path. Some of their number came out of the box-seating area and ran in the direction from which the gunfire came.

"Let's go!" I yelled and grabbed Jason's hand.

"No, Christy!" Ivy ordered and took my arm again. I wiggled free and stared back at her in disbelief.

"Wait!" Jason protested and tried to rein me in.

"Why?" I turned to him and stammered. "Grand-père may need me."

"You cannot put yourself in harm's way. That won't help Oliver." He stopped and look toward the field. "Look, Christy," he said as he pointed to the middle of the arena.

The smoke was clearing enough to see a transparent dome over Grand-père. The pungent odor of Nitroglycerine hung in the air. Dust particles that landed on it defined the dome.

"There is a force field around him." I said as I stood and gazed on the scene in amazement.

"Christy," Jason grabbed me and pulled me to him. "Honey, if you go down there, you could be in the sharpshooter's crosshairs too—and without a bubble to protect you."

The Jumbotron revealed an encapsulated Oliver Richly on the left side of the screen and a smirking Nathan Alexander on the right. Finally, the president asked weakly, "Is Sir Richly all right?"

At first there was silence. Then, the announcer assured everyone. "Ladies and gentlemen, Oliver Richly is safe. Blue Guardsmen pursued, found and eliminated the gunman. Everyone is safe. We will continue."

I looked down at my grandfather. His posture was now relaxed and calm. His huge image on the screen told me a lot. His face was neither drawn nor strained. Then I noticed something. He winked, as he often did at me, and mouth, *I'm hiding in plain sight.*

I laughed and wiped tears from my eyes. "'I'm hiding in plain sight,' he just said, and winked at me." Turning, I grabbed Jason's jacket lapels. "It was a code, a secret message."

"Code?" Jason questioned.

"When he gave me the—" I looked around to see if anyone was near enough to hear me and lowered my voice to a whisper. "When he gave me the Bible, he told me to hide it on a shelf, *in plain sight.*" I turned back to see Grand-père smiling and waving at the crowd. "He means he is fine and can continue. He told me—he is trusting in God."

CHAPTER 10

January 2114

The campaign continued through the Christmas season, or Gift Giving season as we were required to call it in the Central Zone. No one mentioned the name of Jesus Christ, Christmas or God the Father.

Gifting Day Eve of 2112, a little over one year ago, was the day we challenged President Alexander with a march to his home. We delivered thousands of petitions, signed by most of the citizens in the Central Zone. When all zones had the required number of names they would place a citizens' referendum on the next election ballot to overturn the Length of Days Law. Thousands sang the Christmas carol *Silent Night* though they had never heard it before. The longing of their souls knew the words.

I couldn't believe it. With all of our travel and speaking engagements, I wasn't totally fexhausted. The harder we worked, the more energy I had. I felt the Lord with me at every turn.

Now, Jason and I were in New York City again. Ivy had accompanied us as my bodyguard. We had all been staying with Richard and Barbara Cornwall at the Cornwall Citadel; it felt comfortable and homey. Richard's broken hip had mended and the limp would eventually work itself out. The truth is Richard's injuries occurred when he helped a woman crawl up out of the sewer through a manhole. The heavy cover had fallen on him. He considered it worth the price for the underling to see the light of day, even for a short time.

"Richard, no wheelchair?" I marveled the next morning at breakfast.

"I am free at last," he said as he laughed. "Now, come. Let's eat."

The table was set with steaming mugs of coffee and the most delicious looking coffee cake imaginable. Cinnamon and butter oozed from the pastry and puddled on Barbara's yellow-handled California Art Pottery serving platter.

"Barbara, this serving plate is amazing," I admired. "In the Central Zone, no one cares about fine dining or how food looks."

"The platter is very old, but I love using it. Mother had it before me," she said.

"Does she still live up stair?" I asked.

"Yes, but she is visiting family in California right now. She will be so sad she missed you."

"Hence the California connection?" I asked and nodded at the serving platter.

"Exactly," Barbara agreed with a big smile. "I'll cut the pastry while it's hot but save room for scrambled eggs and sausages."

At that moment, Maisie, the surface mole we had met when we were guests of the Cornwalls months before, brought in a large bowl of fluffy eggs, moist and scrambled to perfection. "It's so good to see you two," she squealed. "I'll be back with the sausages." Then she added, "We'll catch up."

She whisked back in with mounds of deeply browned sausage patties, sat the platter on the table and then whirled around to collect a hug from me. "Christy, you look wonderful!" she said as she stood back and studied Jason and I. "Dr. Jason, you always look good." She laughed out loud.

"Maisie, I'd like you to meet my friend, Ivy Trudeau. She's traveling with us."

Maisie put a generous spoonful of eggs on Ivy's plate. "I'm happy to meet you."

"Thank you, Maisie," Ivy beamed as she looked at her plate.

"Speaking of doctors," Jason teased, "how are your medical studies going?"

Maisie talked with her hands and drew out an emphatic, "I am loving it."

Barbara patted Maisie on the arm as the young woman served her and then she waited while Maisie sat down opposite me. "She is working hard and doing great," Barbara said as she beamed.

I could barely believe all I had seen as we drove in from the airport yesterday. "I noticed lights were on in the apartments above the street-level businesses. I hope that means the moles, the underlings, have reclaimed their vacant family homes and apartments."

Richard started to reach for his fork and then stopped. "I am so excited about what has happened. The underlings not only relocated from the sewers and old subway system when you were still here in New York, the elites accepted them aboveground. Even Alister Bedlam put up the money to make it possible for those who wanted to reopen family businesses to do so."

I stuck my fork effortlessly into the lightest eggs ever placed on my plate. As I took a bite, they melted in my mouth, if eggs can melt. Turning to Barbara, I began hesitantly, "Your fa—"

"Yes, my father, although I'll have to admit the title 'father' still doesn't really apply to him. But—we have found a measure of peace." She cut her sausage patty with the side of her fork, closed her eyes and seemed to savor the richly browned flavor.

Richard smiled and reached for his wife's hand. "I am so proud of you, Sweetheart," he said. Then he turned back to Jason and me. "Her father has even been coming to the church services Barbara and I started over on Fifth Avenue, where the old Cathedral had been."

I thought of Barbara's mother, hiding in safety in her upper floor apartment. "What about your mother? It sounds like she is coming out of her apartment to be part of the world again."

Barbara's eyes welled up with tears as she put her fork on her plate. "Yes and no. No, Mama won't come out of the tower, under most circumstances. But—her sister Rebecca is dying—so—we arranged for a private flash-flight to California." She sipped at her coffee and then added, "I hope her stay in the attic apartment isn't permanent. She has been traumatized by my father's previous activities and doesn't trust that he has changed." Replacing her cup on its saucer, she added, "She may never return to any normal life. Perhaps, as the wife of the richest man in the world, she never had a normal life."

Richard blinked and swallowed, obviously concerned for his wife's pain. "Christy, tell us a little about what you plan to tell Oliver's supporters and fans tonight."

I wiped my hands on the linen napkin and paused for a moment. "Since the borders to our zones have been closes for decades, no one in the other areas of the country has heard of Oliver Richly."

Jason smiled and added, "The most time consuming part of Oliver's campaign is introducing himself to the people as one of the candidates." He reached over and massaged my shoulder. "That has been Christy's job—since she knows him the best."

"Part of what I'll be doing tonight is taking the starch out of Grand-père's title. Because he sits on the Council of Twelve, he is Sir Oliver Richly. It is the 'Sir' that might frighten people. They may think his elite status sets him apart from the average citizen. That's not true. Grand-père isn't rich, and he doesn't live in a mansion. His elite status just affords him protection by the Blue Guard and keeps him safe from harm."

Jason shook his head in a gesture of disbelief. "In California, a gunman fired at him from the stands at the Los Angeles Memorial

Coliseum. Oliver was in the center of the field—surrounded by an electronic-vapor force field, so he wasn't struck."

"The gunman got away, but—so did Grand-père."

"I thought they said he was 'eliminated.' Is that not correct?" Richard asked.

"He got away," Jason repeated. "They were careful with their words. Because they eliminated the danger when the gunman got away, they borrowed the term and stretched it to include the physical presence of the shooter."

Richard thumped his index finger on the table. "Certainly, the people must know that all candidates will receive ramped up security after that attempt."

"They know," I sighed. "But knowing and being inside of the knowledge are two different things."

"I understand," Barbara admitted. "People see all that my father is doing for the previously oppressed people in New York, but they don't seem to own that knowing."

I smiled at her and tried to place myself in her shoes. Her father had been so evil it was hard for me to believe he had changed, just like the others who hear the story. "When someone has broken a trust, it takes years of exemplary behavior to rebuild that trust." I broke off a corner of the coffee cake and pierced it with my fork. How could I not think about the grotesque private museum Bedlam hid under Howard Mountain—taxidermied bodies of the deceased leaders and elite of the Central Zone—when I had already seen them? Those images seared a brand in my mind. "It will take time, but if your father is truly sincere, he will take joy in doing what is right, even without the recognition and approval of others."

Barbara placed her hands in her lap and looked deeply at me. "I hadn't thought of it that way. You know, he does seem happier now." She picked up her cup and added. "Time will tell. Is he truly a changed man or is he duping the people—and his family again?"

• • •

Jason, Ivy and I joined Barbara and Richard in the library after our brunch where we relaxed and listened to music. Since the government banned all music in the Central Zone years ago, I closed my eyes and soaked up the beauty of the melodic themes that had the power to lift me out of myself. I thought about how our government believed that people would not be able to keep their emotions in check when under the influence of music. They thought, since music had the power to stir one's soul, the government would control the people's emotions by silencing the music. How silly, how very sad and silly.

Finally, Jason woke up from a brief nap, rubbed his eyes and said, "Christy, how about a walk? Maybe some shopping?"

I couldn't belief the suggestion. I rarely went shopping in Capitol City. Now, he was offering a chance to shop in New York City.

Barbara sat straight up in her chair, her eyes wide. "Do you think it would be safe to go out on the streets after your grandfather was fired on a few months back?"

"But, I'm not a candidate," I said as I brushed off Barbara's concern.

She nodded in agreement. "I know, but you're the granddaughter of a candidate. Someone could try to get to him through you."

"I hadn't thought about that," I denied.

Jason looked at me in disbelief. "Christy, you were shot at in Campaign Headquarters last June." He shook his head. "I should have thought before I spoke."

"Not exactly," I corrected him. "The office was shot at, not me personally. It just happened to go past everyone else and get embedded in the wall beside me."

"But—"

"Jason," I stood my ground, "I wasn't targeted. I know I wasn't." I had to believe that. If I didn't, no place was safe.

"Okay," he agreed, "technically you're right. But, a few more inches and you would have been hit, target or not."

"Factually I'm right," I insisted and stood up. "The bullet was embedded in the wall."

Ivy rolled her eyes. "I was there. Everyone in the office was targeted, Christy. You are a member of Oliver's campaign team. You're the warm-up act to his major attraction. Maybe going out isn't the best thing to do."

"Well, come with us if you want to, Ivy. But, I refused to be a prisoner, regardless of how beautiful the prison." I turned to Jason. "Let's go." As I grabbed Jason's hand I said, "Barbara, would you and Richard like to join us?"

"I don't think so," she answered slowly, indicating she may still have concerns about our leaving the Citadel.

"How about you, Maisie?" I asked. "Would you like to go shopping?"

"Maisie," Barbara chimed in enthusiastically, "that might be nice for you. You have had your head in your books for months." She turned to Ivy. "If you think it will be safe for them to go out, Maisie would benefit from the walk if not the shopping."

"Thanks, Christy," Maisie said. "If you don't think I'll interrupt your time with Dr. O'Reilly, I would love to go."

"Ivy is going too, aren't you, Ivy?" I teased. I knew she would have to. A bodyguard would have to be with the body they were guarding. The plan was set. The whole city waited just beyond the front courtyard.

• • •

We put on heavy coats, hats and gloves and went out the front door. The previously manicured front courtyard now boasted a light dusting of snow. I had brought the same winter cape I wore last year and pulled it around me as the winter chill whistled up under the folds of the unique fabric.

Ivy went out to the gate first and checked the street for anything or anyone that looked suspicious. With a wave of her arm she motioned an all-clear signal and gestured for us to move forward. I felt free as we walked through the Citadel gate, left the grounds and walked along Fifty-Seventh Street over to Fifth Avenue where we stopped for coffee at Trump Tower, a mid-century old building from a hundred years past. Jason stood back and let us enter first. It seemed hard for Ivy to not pull up the rear, but she acquiesced.

As we went in, Jason started laughing. "Honey, this is not our quaint coffee shop at home."

I took his arm and snuggled close as I remembered happier, simpler times from a year past. "The Demitasse Coffee Shop," I said as I smiled to myself.

Inside the Trump Tower, we sat at a small table. "Maisie," I included our young friend, "the little shopping area where our Demitasse Coffee Shop is located looks like something out of a Dickens novel. Ivy, you know the Demitasse don't you?"

"I love the place," she answered.

Then I paused, "Maisie, do you know the writings of Charles Dickens?"

"Yes, of course," she said. "I've read many of his books."

"Somehow, I knew you had," I said as I ordered a chocolate flavored mocha. We looked around the room. "I wonder if this place looks the same as it did when Trump built it."

"Builders don't put this kind of marble and brass in today's buildings," Jason observed as his eyes caught the details of the place. "The floors are foot-worn, like all elegant antique buildings, but buffed to a high sheen. My guess is the finishes are original to the building."

"They are beautiful," I admired. "Everything gleams and shines. We have nothing back home like this."

"O'Reilly," the lady behind the counter signaled that our order was ready. Jason went over and brought back the tray with four cups.

I took mine off and placed it in front of me on the table. First, I inhaled the perfume of the chocolate in the coffee. "I think God created chocolate just for me." I blew across the steamy surface and then took a tiny sip, waiting for it to cool. "Now, tell me about the shops we'll find along Fifth Avenue."

Maisie tipped up her mug to savor the cup. "Jewelry stores, high-end fashion clothing, so much to see, and so much to buy."

Ivy's expression was serious. I smiled and wondered if she was a no-nonsense shopper. "What is security like in the city?"

Maisie started to speak and then seemed to gather her thoughts. "While only the elites lived above ground, physical safety was not an issue. But, their haughtiness caused financial corruption and defamation of the character of others."

I was saddened by what I heard. "It sounds like the underlings have created a problem now that they are above ground."

Ivy listened intently and asked, "Have they become dangerous?"

Maisie sat back in disbelief. "Oh no, I'm sorry. I didn't mean that. Actually, the elite only thought the moles would be dangerous when released from their purgatory so they hired more guards and police. The underlings are very honest. They had to be above reproach. Living on top of one another underground, they would have killed each other if they weren't trustworthy."

Ivy smiled and concluded, "So you're saying, it is even safer than before."

"Yes," Maisie laughed, "stated succinctly, the city is safer."

"Of course," Ivy added, "bad things can happen. Christy, you have inherited the target that is now on your grandfather's back."

"I understand," I agreed, although deep down, I'd have to admit, I didn't want anyone telling me what to do. I tipped my cup and watched the last drop flow to the rim.

Jason also polished off the rest of his coffee and stood up. "Lead on, Miss Maisie," he directed.

We were having fun for the first time in so long, I smiled and my face muscles hurt from lack of use. I walked out onto the sidewalk backwards, laughing and talking to Jason and Maisie behind me. The sky was a winter blue, so bright I wished I had worn dark glasses. My joy was so great I wanted to dance in circles. "Oops," I said as I nearly fell over backwards when I felt someone grab my shoulder. It could have been a masculine hand or a very strong woman, I couldn't tell. They spun me around fast, and I saw a man in a knit face mask for just a second. He gathered me completely off my feet and headed to a waiting large vehicle at the curb, with me forcefully thrown over his shoulder like a bag of trash.

"Hey!" Jason shouted. He slid low in the abductor's direction and swept the man's lower legs with his feet, knocking us both to the concrete. Ivy and Maisie piled on top of the man and started pounding him with their fists. Suddenly, I heard the sound of a strata car's siren. Even though I needed help, I hated that sound. I felt my eyes grow large as Inspector Stoner pulled in front of the large van, blocking the driver into the curb. Stoner jumped out like a blue beret trooper on an assault mission.

My abductor tried to get to his feet as I lay in the scrambled mess. The concrete of the city sidewalk was hard and rough. I felt the crunch of every bone in my body.

I lifted myself up on my elbow there on the sidewalk and reached out my hand in a blessing. "May the Lord forgive you," I called after the assailant. Surprised by the weakened sound of my own voice, I sank back down again.

The man turned back and looked at me with an expression of disbelief and pain on his face. He held up his hand like he was trying to block any good will I might send his way. Lunging into the van through the open sliding door, the assailant desperately tried to crawl in as the driver backed up and maneuvered around Stoner's strata car. Left to flounder on the sidewalk, I was bruised and aching.

Jason helped me to my feet just as I saw Stoner hurrying to my aid. "Inspector? Where did you come from?"

"Are you alright?" Jason asked as he looked me over. "Your leg is scraped. We'd better go to the hospital so you can get a tetanus shot. We haven't needed those precautions for years, but since the underlings came up out of the sewers, there may be greater danger of infection."

"I had a tetanus shot when we were in New York months ago," I said as I remembered the barbaric needle. "I don't need another one of those do I?"

"No, it would still be effective," Jason said as he gathered me in his arms. "I'll just clean and dress the wound for you."

"You'll do that back at the Citadel," Stoner demanded. "Get her back to the Cornwall mansion. What were you four thinking?" His face was rock hard. Then he looked at Ivy. "I thought you were supposed to protect her."

"I thought you were," Ivy snapped back.

"Touché," he bowed. "Now—get off the streets. It's too dangerous." Then he shook his head in anger. "Last year, I knew you were here in the city when everyone said you weren't." Then he just waved us off. "Get going. Get out of here."

I steadied my feet and turned to leave. Jason put his arm around my waist and brushed some snow from the folds of my cape.

"Are you people on foot?" Stoner shouted and opened the back door of the strata car. "I cannot believe this," he belched. "Get in the car!" Ivy got in the front; Maisie, Jason and I sat in the back.

I didn't care who saw us as I leaned into Jason's shoulder and he wrapped his arms around me. I felt safe there as a new reality sunk in. "The fun is over, isn't it?"

CHAPTER 11

Evening Meal

Barbara had arranged a marvelous dinner. The first course was Manhattan clam chowder, followed by London broil with fried onion rings, broccoli and mushrooms. A basket of assorted breads graced the table, with pure creamery butter and a ceramic jam pot of orange marmalade and another of honey.

I used the little ladle inside the marmalade pot to slather a generous amount on a yeasty fragrant thick slice of Italian bread. "I cannot believe the flavors and textures of all this wonderful food." I took a bite and inhaled the aroma. "You would be heavily fined or detained for re-education by the nutrition police in the Central Zone, Barbara." I closed my eyes and savored the taste and texture of it all.

Richard passed the colorful pot of honey, with a tiny spoon that stuck out of the sculpted opening. "Be sure to add a dollop of honey on a corner of your bread," he turned to Ivy who sat beside him. "If you eat a little honey from hives in your own county, you won't have allergies to the things that grow in the area."

"That sounds almost decadent." Ivy chuckled as she took the honey and put a little on her bread.

Dessert was an extraordinary espresso crème brûlée. I swooned as I scooped out a spoonful and licked the spoon. "Barbara, this dessert is amazing, but then, anything with coffee in it would be awesome."

Jason laughed, "You may tan even more easily next summer, Christy. The coffee beans may darken your skin from the inside out."

I held my hands out in front of me and checked them carefully. "Do you think so? I've been so pale a little more color would be wonderful."

Maisie was more serious than Jason and I. "It will be time to leave for the rally soon. Will Inspector Stoner pick you up?"

Barbara stopped abruptly. "Inspector Stoner? What does he have to do with your speech tonight?"

"We didn't want you to worry," I explained apologetically.

"Not worry?" she blinked rapidly. Her eyes darted from me to Jason.

Jason chose a calm and quiet tone. "We had a problem when we were out today."

Barbara blotted her mouth on the linen napkin. "I wondered why you came back so soon, Christy," she said slowly as she turned to me. "You said you had fallen and needed Jason to treat the scrape." Her tone sounded like she was hurt. Maybe she thought I had lied to her.

"I did fall," I admitted openly. "I'm sorry I didn't tell the whole story."

Barbara turned to Maisie for answers. "What happened?"

Maisie looked a little restless, like she didn't want to be the one to tell Barbara all of what had happened. "A man tried to abduct Christy as we came out of Trump Tower."

"What?" Barbara and Richard's jaws dropped at the same time.

Jason seemed embarrassed. "I'm afraid the lack of information was my fault. We didn't want to worry either of you." He reached over and took my hand where I had placed it on the table. "It happened, and we all took care of it. I tackled the assailant, knocking him down and accidently taking Christy out along with him. Both Maisie and Ivy pummeled the would-be abductor. When Christy fell, she scraped her leg. Inspector Stoner pulled up to the curb before she was even off the sidewalk. The attacker wore a mask so we couldn't identify him. Stoner brought us back. That's the whole story."

Barbara gasped as she threw her hand to her mouth. "Oh Christy—maybe I'm glad I didn't know. But—you are all home safe." She smiled warmly at Maisie. "Maisie, you're like a daughter to me. If you hadn't come to us from the world of the underlings," she paused as her eyes welled up with tears, "we would still be two middle-aged souls rattling around in this big house."

Maisie blushed. "Barbara, they weren't after me."

"Exactly," Richard added. "They didn't need you at all. They could have just erased you as unnecessary without a second thought." He clasped his strong hands together and lifted them above his head. "I thank God for your safe keeping—all of you."

Ivy cast her eyes down. "I am so sorry. I'm supposed to protect her."

Barbara tapped her finger tips on the table. "There will be no blame, Ivy. But, perhaps we can find a way to keep this from happening again."

"With everyone's cooperation," Ivy began diplomatically, "I do have some suggestions." She cleared her throat. "When we left the Citadel, I walked out to the sidewalk first and looked for anything out of the ordinary."

"Everything in New York is out of the ordinary," Maisie stated.

Ivy smiled but remained professional. "I did check, but you all followed me and entered the sidewalk area beyond the courtyard before I gave an all-clear signal," she said. "In every future instance, I'll need to check each area before any of you enter." To me she added, "Especially you Christy."

I nodded in agreement, embarrassed that I had ignored an obvious safety protocol.

Ivy sipped from her cup and added, "Once the area has been cleared, and only then, do you proceed."

"Agreed," Jason and I said in unison.

"We're lucky," Ivy said with one corner of her mouth turned up, "whether we like him or not, Stoner is good at what he does. He is also here to protect you Christy. But—"

"I know," I admitted as I traced the rim of my water glass with my finger. "I have to take my safety, our safety, more seriously."

"You will," Jason assured me, his voice soft and certain.

I smiled in wonder as I looked around the table. "Until a year ago, people weren't even allowed to talk to a Legacy Citizen on the street. They couldn't so much as touch me. Now, with my grandfather's presidential campaign, there is so much activity around me, it's hard for me to sort out anyone who might want to do me harm. I'm right down there on the ground level." I shook my head and smiled at Jason. "But, you know, the excitement is intoxicating."

Barbara threw her head back and laughed in resignation. "Okay, we get it," she said. "But for tonight's rally, will Ward Stoner pick you two up tonight and drive you there?"

"He will be there to head up security," I said.

"Richard, Maisie, and I are going. We'll take the long-car. It's bullet proof and our driver is a very good bodyguard. You can ride with us." She stopped and added, "I have had to have security for many years—considering who my father is."

I scrapped the last bit of crème brûlée from the dessert bowl and put down the spoon. "Then, it's settled. We'll all go together and together we'll all be safe."

CHAPTER 12

Attacked

Though I'm a Legacy Citizen, I have just as much stage fright as the next person. I know I appear to be relaxed. That's because I know who stands beside me. The Lord calms me and makes it possible for me to talk.

If you remember, before all of this happened, I spent my days in the back stacks of the library reading everything I could find. Some would call me an introvert but that doesn't mean I'm shy. I just get my energy from the thoughts inside myself and drained of energy by interactions with others. Stage fright is another thing. My fear of speaking in front of others is probably due to a half-belief that my opinions are not worthy of all the fuss. I was never the center of attention, except in my own family. Never criticized as a Legacy Citizen, now I wouldn't know how to handle it. If I had received a little criticism when I was young, it would have sharpened my ability to speak in front of others and honed my ability to defend my own positions. It was family love that has made it possible for me to get up in front of others.

Now, I stood in theater wings, hidden by the leg drapes behind the grand stage curtain of New York's old opera house. There hadn't been a performance in so many years those in attendance had never been inside the ornate walls with its colorful trappings. Only the campaign message of Sir Oliver Richly could bring out a crowd large enough to require this kind of space to house his political supporters. While Grand-père wouldn't be there until the next night's rally, I was to give the audience his background and outline the points on which he was running. This was a night of political conversation and enlightenment.

The crowd hummed and buzzed with excitement. When I walked to center-stage the rise in clamor from the assembled-throng startled me and the glare from the spotlight flashed in my eyes. I could see figures surrounding the stage in what would have been the orchestra pit but I couldn't make out who they were. All I saw were dots from the lights. I looked back to the wings for Jason's smile. He nodded and gave me a victory pump of his arm.

"Christy—Christy—Christy—" the crowd chanted in a loud cacophonous rhythm.

Holding up my hand in both greeting and a plea for order, I felt helpless to calm the people. On and on they cheered until my eyes cleared a little and I could see who stood below the foot of the stage. Blue Guardsmen were shoulder to shoulder, alternatingly facing the crowd and the next one facing the stage. *Who and what are they guarding—the speaker—or searching for a possible assassin in the audience?* I shuddered as chills crept down my arms. What could I do?

Closing my eyes, I lifted my arms in prayer and praise. The Lord had blessed me beyond any words of my own to express. How many times had I dodged danger in the last months? With my eyes closed in reverence and my head turned to Heaven, I waited for the words of God to lead me.

Suddenly, a hush fell over the auditorium as one by one some in the room also lifted their arms heavenward. In the standing-room-only area in the back, a wave started as a hum. *Silent Night, Holy Night* they sang, not because it was still the Christmas season, but because it was the only song the people of Capitol City knew and these New Yorkers knew the amazing story of our Gifting Day Eve event of 2112. It calmed the soul.

Ward Stoner, near my feet to my left, put his hand on his weapon and didn't remove it as I stood there. I guessed that he had been convinced of my danger after the abduction attempt that afternoon. I also saw Lieutenant Boone at the base of the stage. She faced the footlights and could see Stoner move for his weapon.

Although she caught my eye and acknowledged me with a small smile, rather than continue watching me, she kept her eye on her boss. Then, I remembered what she had secretly told me on our previous trip to New York when Stoner was out of earshot. "Ward Stoner is not the man you have been seeing. Before his wife died, he was kind and even funny at times. But now, you have become the focus of his anger and resentment. I have seen nothing but good in you and what you are doing." Somehow, I trusted her to keep him at bay, although I could see he had changed. Even though I knew he was there to protect and serve, it was evident he was supportive of Grand-père and the campaign.

"Oh Lord, God," I implored. "Please, come and fill this place with your peace and love."

Crack, crack, crack, Pop! Odd, I not only heard the sound, I felt the pressure of it. In an instant, Jason leaped into action; Ivy jumped out of the wings; Boone charged up onto the stage, followed immediately by the Inspector.

What are they doing? What's going on? They're going to interrupt my speech?

I felt so strange. *Where had my energy gone? Why did I feel so weak? What's wrong with me?* My shoulder felt tender so I automatically reached up to massage the upper right portion of my shoulder and chest.

"What is this?" I whispered breathlessly as my knees buckled under me and blood dripped from my hand. I slipped to the floor as Stoner scooped his arms under me and lowered me to the hardwoods of the stage.

"Off to the right!" I heard Boone yell as feet scrambled and leather pounded.

"Boone, over there!" Stoner ordered as I felt him lift my head and stuff something under my neck.

Jason immediately became both physician and my love. "Grab that cloth from the dais," he ordered a Blue Guardsman. "Put it over her before she goes into shock." More feet shuffling, and I felt the air stir as a man ran past me and into the wings. There was a scream and more frightened voices joined the rumble around me as the sounds began to fade. Through blurred eyes, I saw that Ivy had fallen where she stood in the wings. *Why is she on the stage floor? Why isn't she moving?*

Jason pulled my lower lids from my eyes and looked intently. His eyes showed concern but his hands were steady. "Christy, can you hear me?"

I nodded slowly and touched his hand.

"I'll be right back. I'm not leaving you, Honey. I'll be right over there, checking Ivy." He pointed to Chalky and said, "Quickly, cover her up."

I nodded again and tried to see where he was going. What had happened to Ivy?

As Boone covered me with the cloth she leaned close. "Laying his hands on each one, he healed them."

"What?" I questioned. I knew I heard her, and I knew the words she said, but—how did Chalky know what Jesus of the Bible had said and done?

"What did you say?" Stoner growled. It didn't sound like anger as usual. It sounded like astonishment.

Boone said no more but reached out and took my hand. *What is she doing?* Rather than holding my hand, I could feel her pry it open. Then, she gently moved the trembling fingers of my right hand and placed them into the sticky blood. I could feel her touch my hand to what felt like a gaping hole in my shoulder. The pain I experienced was nearly unbearable.

"What are you doing?" Stoner shouted.

"I'm not hurting her," I heard Boone's voice off in some distant place.

I heard very little more—no buzzing crowd, no words from those around me—but it wasn't silent. There was the deep sound of a man's voice saying, "Stay with me, Christy. Stay with me." I drifted off again, in and out of a white mist.

Then, there was a sound of—something, like the rush of a mighty wind. My face felt warm, like a window had opened and the sun had streamed in. I heard them—the crowd was singing again, "... holy night, all is calm ...." Energy seemed to flow through my arms and I knew—I had been healed.

CHAPTER 13

Another Kind of Healing

Stoner was the one whose wound still festered—in spirit at least. He could feel anger rise within him. Or, was it something else he couldn't identify? He was conflicted by emotions which he didn't understand or even know the feeling-names. One was the familiar anger he always felt, and some other emotion he thought he had not experienced before.

"What happened?" he questioned. Although just shot, Christy's strength was increasing. He looked from Boone to Christy in full detective mode.

"You saw it, Ward," Boone answered in awe as she brushed Christy's hair from her forehead. "I know I saw it," she said. Then as Christy began to stir, she added, "Lay still for a few more minutes. Dr. O'Reilly is over there checking on Ivy. You'll soon be in good hands."

Ward stared in disbelief. "I saw what happened, but still find it hard to believe. What did you just do?"

"I didn't do anything, Ward. I merely guided Christy's hand to the gunshot wound," she explained.

His eyes darted over to his Blue Guardsmen and then back at Boone. She looked up at him with more warmth in her eyes than he had experienced since his wife died. He felt uncomfortable, embarrassed and wanted to look away. But, the responsive feelings it gave him were intoxicating. "Then, how did she improve so fast?"

"It was the Lord who healed her, Ward, not I, and not Christy by herself," Chalky said gently and then stroked Christy's forehead again, brushing back her hair.

Stoner touched Boone's hand as she continued to sooth the wounded brow. Suddenly, Christy stirred a little and turned her head toward Jason as he attended to Ivy.

"Don't worry—rest for now," Boone assured her. "It looks like Ivy is moving. She's sitting up. Your friend Maisie is taking care of her now."

Stoner felt like a distant spectator as he watched Jason hurry over to where Christy lay. The doctor kissed his Lady gently and began to examine her wound. Ward watched as Chalky finally let go of Christy's hand. His lieutenant was so comforting, so loving.

Then, the eyes of Ward's heart opened. "Boone, look at the blood stains on your clothes. It's oozing from your fingers." And then he looked again, "Your hands are trembling."

"Ward, I ...." He saw both fear and wonderment on Chalky's face. Her eyes welled up in tears and spilled over the rims. She began to tremble violently.

Stoner stared at Chalky for a second and then quickly grabbed her to him with strong and massive hands. Wrapping his arms around her, he rocked her back and forth intent on soothing her, warming her—but maybe something else he couldn't admit even to himself. Suddenly, he realized he was looking at her, not with the eyes of her superior, despite his need to hide his own emotions.

Ward Stoner was truly overwhelmed with it all. How could one brief span of time see so many life-changing events?

Someone shot Christy Applewait in front of thousands of spectators and yet healing came through the touch of her own hand.

God sealed her wound and the bleeding stopped. The gunman who shot Christy got away by jumping from the nearest theater box and onto the stage, just like John Wilkes Booth after he shot President Lincoln. All Blue Guard cadets studied that investigation. In the escape of Christy's gunman, he knocked Ivy down. She bumped her head resulting in unconsciousness. But, Stoner had to admit to himself, something that also pleased Christy's Lord, was that on that miraculous night of healing, the searing fire of love had cauterized the hole in his own heart.

CHAPTER 14

2pm - May 2114

It was a new beginning for Jason and me. My body had healed from the gunshot wound and my energy returned. We had been working the small towns and big cities along the New England coast. The crowds had grown larger and more enthusiastic with each event, like the wild flowers in the meadows we passed. As the days sprouted into weeks, blossoms filled the fields and spilled over into the ravines and the banks of the fresh flowing streams. Spring had opened its ample paint buckets and splattered color everywhere.

"Grand-père is already in Caribou," I said as Jason drove along old US 1 north in Maine. "He'll speak tonight at 8 pm. We should get to the hotel in another half hour, rest and clean up, then eat a light supper before the gathering."

"Sean said they built a huge ice hockey arena at the Maine Winter Sports Center years ago," Jason said. "Oliver will speak there."

"It's May. I doubt it will be cold in there?" I thought of a floor of ice in the middle of the room and shivered. "I think I'll take a light jacket."

We drove a few more blocks. "There's the hotel," I pointed to the twenty-story building on the right.

Jason pulled into the drop-off zone and released the door on my side. I stepped out and started into the building when a man in a dark suit approached me.

"Lady Applewait?" he questioned.

I studied his face for a glimmer of familiarity. "Do I know you?"

"We haven't met—but I know your grandfather," he said causally, but his eyes darted back and forth and he clutched at his hands.

Jason got out of the car and came around where the stranger and I stood. "May I help you?"

The man smiled an awkward smile and held out his hand. "You must be Dr. O'Reilly."

"I am," Jason said as I watched him take in the full length of the man. "Again, how can I help you?"

"I'm sorry—is Sir Richly with you two?"

My heart leaped into my throat. "With us?" I suddenly couldn't see or think clearly. I felt rattled. "He got here yesterday."

"He was supposed to," the man said as he continued to look around the front parking lot and entry area.

"Who are you?" Jason questioned, his jaw set and his brow furrowed.

"I'm sorry," the man apologized. "My name is Malcolm Merrick. I work for your grandfather's campaign. Actually, I'm part of his Advance Team. Some of us got here two days ago and began setting up everything for Oliver—but he never showed up."

I felt ill. My mouth was so dry I could barely form words. My lips stuck to my teeth. "He never got here?" I gulped. "Well, Malcolm Merrick, I don't know you at all, and I'm part of his campaign, too."

Merrick looked at me with a worried expression but confident tone. "I know you are Ma'am. I joined the Eastern team a few weeks ago. My specialty is logistics and, I am so sorry—but Sir Richly has not gotten here even though I know he was due yesterday."

I looked up and down the street as if half expecting him to show up. "I don't understand."

"Again—I'm sorry," Merrick apologized. "I don't know what else to say. Oliver is simply not here."

Jason put his arm around me and drew me close. "Let's go inside. Maybe there's a logical answer." Jason opened the car boot, gathered up our bags and handed them to Merrick. "Here, please take these and I'll attend to Lady Applewait."

We hurried inside and looked around the lobby that sparkled with polished marble and brass. Over at the check-in desk the clerk was busy with another customer. My hands trembled. I reached out and steadied myself on the dark marble counter. As I leaned heavily on the broad desk, my knees began to buckle underneath me. Jason scooped me off my feet and carried me to a nearby silk brocade chair.

"Wait here, Honey," he said. "Merrick," he directed the campaign worker, "find Lady Applewait a cup of coffee." Jason kissed my forehead and whispered gently, "Don't leave yet, Christy. Your grandfather will show up at any minute. I'm sure."

I could not stop shaking. "Jason, I am so frightened. What if something has happened to him?" I thought of the danger he could be in. We had our share of close escapes. "I wish Ivy were here," I thought aloud.

Jason smiled and patted my cheek. "I know. It would be wonderful if she were around to help protect you. Something could be brewing with Oliver's absence."

"I talked to Ivy before we left. She said there would be a man here to guide us. Her mother is really ill." I understood and was glad she had chosen family. "I told her I wanted her to attend to her mother. After that attack in New York, she knows the danger. Her shoulder was slashed too as the attacker ran by." I looked over at

Malcolm. "Maybe she was talking about Merrick, but she didn't call him by name."

"Some of Oliver's bodyguards are here,' Merrick said.

"That's good, but I wish Grand-père was here."

"I know, Honey—I know," Jason whispered. I felt his warm breath on my face when he held me close.

Looking up, I smelled the hot coffee Merrick waived under my nose. "I guess it's as good as smelling salts," I said and smiled weakly. As I sipped the hot brew I let the steam warm my face.

Jason looked at Malcolm Merrick up-and-down, taking in the full measure of the man. "Merrick, I'm going to step over to the check-in desk, and I want you to stay here with Lady Applewait. I'll not take my eyes off you. I'm sorry. You've not been vetted according to anything that we're aware of." He kissed my cheek again. "Drink some more of your coffee, Honey. I'll see what I can find out."

Jason stepped to the desk, not more than six feet away from where I sat. He looked near, but I needed his touch. I watched him over the top of my coffee cup and heard every word.

"Has anyone left a message for Christina Applewait, Dr. Jason O'Reilly, or any of Sir Oliver Richly's Advance Team?" he asked.

The clerk blinked his eyes and waved his hands in an empty gesture. "No sir. We are still expecting Sir Richly." He looked over at me and a wave of sympathy crossed his face. "Is something wrong? Can I be of assistance in some way?"

Jason continued to study my face and smiled faintly. To the clerk he added, "Sir Richly is never late—ever."

The man in the black pinstripe suit and white shirt could not have been more sympathetic. His expression was almost pained. "I will let you know as soon as he gets here." He looked over at me and added, "Will you be checking in? Rooms are waiting for you; everything is ready."

"Yes, of course," Jason continued. "Lady Applewait could use some rest."

A young woman in a black jumpsuit placed our bags on a four-wheel cart. I had seen pictures of hotel luggage carriers in old magazines in the library at home. I smiled at all I knew mentally and yet had never seen.

Jason helped me over to the desk so I could place my hand on the palm reader for room 721. He did the same for room 723. I walked to the lift, feeling like I was in a daze. I heard others talking and laughing around me. It was like the buzzing of bees or the clicking of locusts. We rode up to the seventh floor in silence, Jason and I, the hotel worker and Malcolm Merrick. I wondered about the confusing energy I was getting from Merrick. On the one hand I felt like I could trust him, and yet there was an unsettled feeling between us.

Merrick seemed to be aware of it. Halfway up in the lift car he said, "I will help you get settled, and then I'll go back to Campaign Headquarters here in Caribou. I don't think they know anything yet or they would have contacted me. But, I'll see what I can do."

"Thank you, Malcolm," I said. I wanted—no—I needed for him to be an ally. With Grand-père missing, I had to trust those around me. I said no more.

The lift car was small enough, I began to feel claustrophobic. My heart was racing so hard I could feel it pounding in my chest.

The lift doors swished open and everyone paused for a moment. "After you," the hotel worker offered.

We all hurried from the elevator and started in the direction of the 720 room numbers. Jason started to put his hand on the doorknob and then stopped, "You'll have to open your door, Honey."

My hand was trembling as I touched the shiny chrome knob and twisted it in my hand. The hop reached around the open door and flipped on the light switch. The light from the windows on the opposite side of the room let in a deceptively friendly glow. I crossed the room and sank into one of the overstuffed chairs near the desk area.

Merrick walked over to the communication device that sat on the desk. It was an old-fashioned instrument with a funny round dial on the front in keeping with the mid-twentieth century decor of the hotel. He picked up the piece that sat on the top, placed his finger in the hole on the dial marked "zero" and spun it around.

"Yes, operator, please connect me with Sir Oliver Richly's Campaign Headquarters." He paused for a moment and waited. Then he began again. "This is Merrick. Have you heard anything about Sir Richly's whereabouts?" Again he waited for what seemed like a lifetime. Suddenly his shoulders dropped and his countenance fell. "I'm with Lady Applewait right now." He took a small pad and pencil from his jacket pocket and scribbled a few words on a piece of paper. "I'll tell her."

Jason looked at me and then back at Merrick. "Okay, man, what is going on?"

Malcolm Merrick's eyes darted from Jason to me and back again. "Christiana—I cannot spare the words or the impact the message will have." He walked over to a bar area, put ice into a small glass, poured from a water pitcher and came back to me. "Here, My Lady," he offered. "I need for you to drink some of this."

"Why?" I gasped as my stomach knotted, and my hands began to tremble again.

I took the glass and sipped on it mechanically as my eyes fixed on nothing out in front of me. Fear had frozen me rigid. Then, a new determination welled up inside me. I stiffened as a new power filled my body. I could not sit there knowing that Grand-père was missing; I couldn't and wouldn't. The glass thumped forcefully from my hand onto the table beside me as I stood up. "I am not a victim here," I demanded. "Malcolm Merrick, you tell me right now what was said."

"Christiana—a message came in to Campaign Headquarters a few minutes ago." He raked his hand through his hair and shook his head. "The message was strange. It wasn't long, but Ben Summersall said the creep who called it in still managed to say it in a mocking tone in the few words he delivered." Merrick stopped and pumped his fist up and down on the palm of his hand. "And, yes, headquarters said it was from a man."

I couldn't stand it any longer. Now I was getting angry. "And—what did he say?"

Merrick didn't even look at me. He took a deep breath and stared out the window. "The man said, 'You will be enchanted to know—I have taken Oliver Richly—'"

"Taken?" I gasped and grabbed the top of my head, for fear I would explode. "You mean Grand-père has been kidnapped?" How could I believe what he was saying? Helplessness caused my strength to vanish in an instant. With my head buried in my hands, I collapsed into Jason's arms. He helped me to the edge of the bed where I went limp and crumpled onto the bedspread.

"Yes, Ma'am," Merrick said softly, his voice shaking and course. "Oliver Richly has been kidnapped."

"How? Where? He is surrounded by bodyguards." Disbelief flooded my thoughts. It couldn't be possible.

Merrick turned in my direction without meeting my gaze. "I am so sorry, Christiana," he apologized. "I don't have that information." He looked at the floor and then out the window. "The man also said, something like, 'If not you, then the big man. You would have stopped his campaign and now he's just gone.'"

Jason grabbed me and put his arms around me with the force of a warrior-protector. "So the failed kidnapping attempt on you in New York was his first effort in trying to get Oliver out of the race."

"They tried to get you?" It was easy to see the shock on Merrick's face and beaten body posture.

"I didn't want to upset anyone so I had said nothing. Ivy, my bodyguard, was there—she knew. Jason was with me, too. And friends, a couple in New York, knew about it," I told him, reassuring him that I had not kept it a secret. "And—Chief Inspector, Ward Stoner, the head of the Blue Guard knew it, also."

"I see," was all he said.

I wondered what he was thinking. Maybe, he thought of all those people around me and still someone tried to snatch me. But, I wasn't really thinking about me. I whispered, "Now—they've taken Grand-père."

Then Jason and I repeated in one voice, "Enchanted?"

I shook my head. "He said, 'Enchanted?' That's so strange," I added as my mouth went dry again. "How could the heinous act of my grandfather's abduction be enchanting?" Outrage continued to grow within me and became weeds that take over and drown out all healthy living plants.

"Then, the man said," Merrick continued, "'Find him if you can. But, it will take you beyond the election date. You got away, but you still lose.'"

I breathed heavily, my chest was aching. "I'd better call Grand-mère."

CHAPTER 15

Pulling it Together

"Yes, Grand-mère, I'll be careful." My voice cracked on the antique telephone and I was nearly unable to finish my call. "I'm sorry that I didn't call you immediately. But, I was utterly destroyed when I heard about it." Tears welled up in my eyes and rained down my cheeks. "I'm glad the Campaign Headquarters had already called you. I was feeling so guilty. Thinking that I had let you down, I couldn't talk." I looked over at Jason who was napping on the bed and felt my face contort in emotional pain.

Grand-mère's voice was calm but full of emotion. "Oh, my dear, you are my joy. You couldn't possibly let me down. I'm just happy you're all right." I could hear the tears in her voice and it broke my heart.

"Grand-mère—maybe if I had gotten here earlier—"

My grandmother continued. "What could you have done, Christy? Nothing, except, perhaps, get yourself kidnapped with him." She was quiet for a moment and then added, "I will pray for him and I want you to as well. His kidnappers do not know what they have done. They have kidnapped the Constitutional Party's presidential candidate and the Chairman of the Council of Twelve. But, more important than all of that, they kidnapped my Oliver, a man of God, and he will have them converted before this is over." She laughed a little; but her voice choked with tears.

I smiled to myself. "Yes, Grand-mère, I think you're right." I thought for a moment and then checked the clock. "It's getting late," I added. "I'd better go."

"Christy," Grand-mère coaxed, "I need for you to promise me a couple of things."

"Sure, Grand-mère—anything."

"First," she whispered, "you must be very careful. Our family would wither and die if anything happened to you."

"I will be careful. I promise."

She cleared her throat and added, "Please, Christy, do not worry or feel guilty. There was nothing you could have done. If Oliver Richly couldn't have fought them off, you would not have been able to either."

"I'll remember, Grand-mère," I promised. I hung up the phone and crawled up beside Jason on the bed, aching everywhere. I backed up against him, a glowing fireplace on a cold night, and felt comforted by his warmth.

Two o'clock slid into five p.m. like sap dripping from a maple tree. What could we do? We had no more information than we had the three hours previous. I tried to rest but couldn't sleep.

At 5:15 I said, "I've been Grand-père's voice up until now. I guess I'd better go to the Sports Arena. They will expect to see him center stage at 8pm. It's after five now."

Jason curled his arms around me more tightly and spoke from his physician's voice as well as his heart. "You'd better eat something first."

"Eat?" I questioned, a little irritated. "I wouldn't be able to eat anything."

"I understand," he said. "But, Honey, you may collapse from fatigue and worry if you don't support your body with nourishment.

You haven't eaten anything since that cup of coffee. We waited to eat lunch until we had settled into the hotel. That didn't happen."

"Oh Jason, I don't—"

"I know." He paused and then continued. "How about some soup? We could go down to the restaurant—get out of our rooms for a while, and sip soup. They might have New England Clam Chowder."

I perked up a little. We don't have anything like fish soup in the Central Zone. "That sounds interesting. I might be able to keep that down."

Before we went downstairs, I stopped in the bathroom to splash some water on my face while Jason went to his room to freshen up. Shocked by the image I saw reflected in the mirror, I gasped. My eyes sunk in their sockets and the dark circles under them made me look like I had a second pair of tired eyes. I chose to ignore the rude replication of my former happy, carefree self, and instead, ran a comb through my hair and forgot the rest of my appearance.

My luggage still lay on the luggage rack, unpacked. I quickly flipped up the top, pulled out a light sweater, and met Jason in the hall. "I am dreading this," I admitted. "What should I say?"

Jason put his hand on the small of my back and sent caring warmth up my spine. "It's up to you, Honey."

When we got to the lift door, he pushed the button. As we stepped on, he added, "Since Oliver can't be here, you can explain what happened to him or you can give a campaign speech on his behalf. As I said, it's up to you."

• • •

Down in the hotel's first-floor restaurant the mixture of sweet and spicy aromas from the kitchen made me nauseous. Waves of queasiness flooded over me and threatened to pull me under. "Jason, I don't think—"

"I know, Honey. Is there anything that sounds even *okay* to you?"

"A cup of tea would be nice," I thought aloud.

"Would a little honey in it taste good?" Jason asked without pushing me.

Honey struck a sweet spot. "That would be great."

We placed our order with the serving girl. Her name badge had "Tara" printed on it. Jason ordered tea as well. We sat in silence for a moment until Tara returned with a fancy porcelain teapot of hot water and a loose tea diffuser's chain dangling out the side. I smiled at the quaint display. "This looks good. I think it will taste okay too."

"How about some toast?" Jason suggested. "In the old books in the hospital library, people used to eat toast when nothing else might stay down." He looked up at Tara and placed two orders for toasted bread.

"Toast?" I questioned. I, too, had read the wonderful old novels that had survived the book destruction of the previous century. I spent hours in my comfortable brown leather chair in the back room of the library at home, inhaling the fragrance of the novels no longer permitted for mass consumption. I laughed for the first time in hours. "Can you imagine the reaction of the Nutrition Authority if they saw me eating toasted bread with mounds of dripping butter?"

Jason joined in my mental picture with his own offering. "Buttered toast is even better with strawberry jam piled on top."

"Oh, Jason," I said, "what would our lives have been like if we had lived in the country that the heroes and heroines of the great books had lived in—under the original Constitution of Freedom?"

"I don't know, Honey. Maybe that's what you want to focus on when you address the people tonight."

"I'll turn that over in my mind," I said. When Tara returned with our food, the steam rising from the bread filled my nostrils with delight.

CHAPTER 16

Inside the Bubble

Our driver pulled the car up to the side alley door of the Arena. I put my hand on the car door handle but, stopped by someone from the outside, I waited. I tried to peer through the tinted window but the person stood so close, all I could see was a blue shirt and belt buckle. The person was small and I assumed they were female.

"You can get out in a moment, My Lady," our driver said calmly while searching the area that was visible through the windows and mirrors of the long-car.

"What's going on?" I asked as I twisted around to look out of the back window.

"A threat came in to Campaign Headquarters, Ma'am," was all she or he said.

"A threat against me?" I asked.

Jason put his arm around me and held me tight. "It will be okay. I'll stay right beside you."

"Even in center stage?" I asked.

"Of course—I can be on stage, too, if that's what you want," he stated with strength in his voice that made me feel safe. "We can do this however you want to—or not do it at all."

"Jason, I don't know what I would do without you," I admitted.

"Yeah, me too," he said as he kissed my forehead. "I love needing you to complete me."

"Okay, My Lady," the person on the outside announced and slapped a hand twice on the top of the car. When the door opened, I was surprised.

"Ivy," I said and smiled broadly. "I didn't know you were going to be able to make this trip."

"I flew up a few hours ago," Ivy said as she gave me a side hug. "In light of recent events, the campaign insisted."

"Thank you so much for being here." I said as I smiled. "How is your mother?"

"Actually, she is doing better, Christy," Ivy answered. "Thank you for asking."

I looked up and down the narrow alley. With the high side walls of adjacent buildings, it felt like a canyon, nestled in a safe valley. Then I remembered books of the western expansion of our country, and the visual image of marauders firing from mountain tops—or the roofs of the buildings above. It all came rushing in. I cringed as I grabbed Jason's hand and darted from the alley toward the door.

Ivy had her arm around me from the other side and shielded me from any danger as Jason reached for the arena door handle. Once inside, I felt safe, at least less conspicuous.

"Lady Applewait," a man in blue work clothes and matching ball cap said as he approached me.

I felt like a small child as I slipped behind Jason a half-step. This had to stop. I squared my shoulders and lifted my chin.

"Wait, Christy," Ivy said as she put her arm out in front of me. "Who are you?" she asked the man.

"Charles Lewis," he said with a smile and touched the tip of his fingers to his hat.

"Let me see your identification," Ivy order, seeming to be in no mood for friendly conversation.

The man's face turned ashen as he reached for his ID. "I'm sorry," he apologized as he looked from Ivy, to me, to Jason. "I didn't mean to—"

Ivy did not respond but studied the man's card. The small pocket size ID was complete with the required hologram, that when activated, created a holographic image that testified to the man's vital statistics. "Okay, you can move along," she said with a brush of her hand.

"But, Ma'am, I'm an employee here. I need to get Lady Applewait to the force-field bubble and secure her inside." His eyes batted and he appeared suddenly jumpy.

Jason stepped between Charles and me, still in full protective mode. "How much room is inside that bubble?" he asked.

"It can be as large as you need it to be." Then he looked at me, up and down. "She's a tiny little thing isn't she?"

"I'm normal," I corrected him, insulted by any reference to being *tiny*.

Jason was insistent. "I will be at her side, within the bubble."

"Oh, sure," Lewis agreed and started off toward the tunnel that led to the center of the arena floor.

Ivy touched my arm and held me back. "Wait, Christy." She called after Charles Lewis who had already moved quickly. "Stop, Mr. Lewis."

Looking back over his shoulder, he seemed surprised that no one was following him. He stopped where he was and limply turned his palms up.

"We need to have a plan," Ivy insisted, "before Lady Applewait is going out there."

"Oh," Lewis paused and waited for us to catch up to him.

Ivy held her hand up to stop Jason and me, and then walked to the end of the access tunnel. "If the force-field can be expanded to include two people, can it be positioned over here, at the entrance to the arena, to let Christy and Jason walk into the bubble and then cover them while they move to the center?" She finally stopped and waited for the man to answer.

Mr. Lewis looked to the floor and then smiled. "Sure, I can do that."

All three of us exhaled loudly. Cautiously, we moved toward Mr. Lewis who waited at the opening. He stopped us there, and then moved into the arena on his own. With a small, shiny tool, he adjusted a mechanism that sent two laser points onto the floor and a flickering light bubble around it. He motioned for Jason and me to enter.

I experienced no change: no zap, no chill, no sound of any kind as I entered the field. Inside the bubble, it seemed like I was looking through an old glass-bottom boat window at a park my parents took me to as a child, named Life Beyond my Sphere. When Jason reached over and took my hand, I began to feel calm again.

Suddenly, the lights flooded the center of the arena and a voice on the loud speaker announced, "Ladies and gentlemen, please welcome Christiana Applewait, Oliver Richly's granddaughter and exciting spokesperson."

The crowd got to their feet and roared. I felt humbled but not frightened. The bubbled seemed to glow like a holy light was surrounding me.

"Thank you," I called to the crowd. Turning to Jason, I added, "I'd like to introduce you to Dr. Jason O'Reilly, my good friend. A physician, he provides medical advice and assistance to the entire election committee."

Jason squeezed my hand and waved to the people with his free one. He, too, seemed at ease. I was amazed at how quickly both of us had adjusted to being in the center of the light.

"Jason has joined me here to give me strength and a feeling of security." I paused and smiled as best I could.

My stomach churned as bitter acid rose up in my throat, but I knew I had to carry on. "I wasn't sure what to tell all of you." I looked around the room at the sea of shadowy, blurred faces and gathered my thoughts. "My grandfather, Oliver Richly, has been kidnapped, sometime between the late evening hours of yesterday and early this morning. When Dr. O'Reilly and I got here today, we discovered that he did not arrive at the hotel here in Caribou when expected."

There was stone silence. It was like all the air had been sucked up through a small hole in the ceiling and everyone had gone limp, gasping for life.

"I could have told you all about the wonderful things my grandfather stands for—and he does. I could have told you about the importance of returning to our original Constitution—and it is. I could have told you about the Central Zone's adherence to the Length of Days Law and how they kill children, the useless to society and the elderly—and they do. I could have told you how we must stop that un-godly practice—and we do. But, that's not why I am here."

I swallowed hard, trying to hold back tears that had finally seeped through my terrified heart. "I'm here to ask all of you, thousands and thousands of you, to become Oliver's eyes and ears. So far, we haven't heard that he's in physical danger—not yet. We just know he has been taken." More gasps rose up from the midst of the crowd.

"We have received one message from the kidnappers. I'm going to read it to you and—if anyone understands the encrypted message under the words, please call Campaign Headquarters in Capitol City. It reads: 'You will be enchanted to know—I have taken Oliver Richly.'"

"Enchanted?" Some mumbled in the great arena.

"Then, he said, 'Find him if you can. But, it will take you beyond the election date. You lose.'"

Angry outbursts erupted around the room. "Lose?" one man shouted from the left. "Not hardly!"

My own rage seethed inside me. "How dare anyone grab a presidential candidate? That part of the message is clear. The kidnapper intends to disrupt a constitutional election!" I could feel my temper boil under the pot of my new emotions. Before my detoxification, I would have done very little—except where my grandparents were concerned. I wouldn't have had the emotions to care or the energy to do anything about it. The chemicals the government put in our water supply would have robbed me of the ability to raise the anger necessary to motivate me to do something about it.

"Every one of you who are here this day, are drafted into an army for freedom's sake. Talk to friends and family in other zones, track down every lead, listen to every conversation beside you on the PT, and watch for anything unusual or out of place! I will fill in for my grandfather during debates and public appearances, but we must find Oliver Richly before election-day!" My voice had risen to a near scream. The energy and magnitude of our task frightened me. Would I be up to the job I was asking everyone else to do?

Then from the middle of the stands, off to the deep right, I heard one voice. "New Mexico!" he shouted.

"What?" I heard him, but I didn't know what his comment had to do with anything.

"New Mexico," the man repeated. "The Land of Enchantment!"

CHAPTER 17

Looking for Answers

The sidewalks along the edge of the alley outside the arena were still fragrant with fresh rain when we came out. An occasional drop continued to fall, but for the most part, the clouds were beginning to part. It smelled fresh and clean.

"We have to get back to New York, Jason," I said as I yawned. I wandered if my exhaustion was physical or emotional. "I called the Citadel and talked to Barbara Cornwall. The other zone leaders will arrive tomorrow morning."

Ivy checked the shadowy doorways and behind trash dumpsters for anything or anyone who didn't belong there. Safety was always important but now it had become a life and death obsession. There was no place for mistakes. With the door handle in her left hand, she motioned for us to hurry and get into the hotel long-car.

"Get inside quickly," she ordered.

I knew that the power had shifted. I was used to having everyone obey my wishes. Now, it was the safety professionals who ruled the day. I got in and slid across the seat. Once Jason was inside, I said no more but leaned my head on his shoulder. I could tell that the lights and buildings of the city moved past the car windows; I didn't look up. Still, they appeared like flashes of light behind my eyelids.

When we returned to the hotel, we silently got in the elevator lift and rode up. Turning the knob, I opened the door to my hotel room and turned on the light.

"Honey, it's a ten hour drive back to New York City," Jason said and put his arms around me. "You need some rest—and so do I."

"If we leave at 8am, we'll get to the Cornwall's at 6pm." I didn't like that assessment, but I had no other solution at that point."

Jason snapped his fingers together. "I know," he said, smiling, "Barbara and Richard have a helicopter. All above-grounders have one. I'll call them and ask them to send it in the morning. We can freshen up, get a good night's sleep, and then leave."

"What about the car,' I asked, unable to think the situation through clearly.

"Someone from the campaign can drive it back. If you want Ivy to come with us in the chopper, then someone else can drive the car down the coast," he offered. "There is a way to do this."

I sighed and threw my sweater onto one of the chairs. Slipping off my shoes, I curled up on the bed and pulled the corner of the spread over me.

Jason smiled softly and sat on the edge of the bed next to me. Brushing away the hair that had fallen across my face and eyes, he opened his mouth to speak and then stopped. "I'd better let you sleep," he said. As he pulled the covers around me, he kissed my forehead.

"Jason," I said and took his hand. "Please, don't leave."

"Christy—"

"I know. I really do—but—" I couldn't stop tears from welling up. "I can't be alone, not tonight."

Jason caressed my cheek with the back of his fingers. "Christy, I love you. I can't just—"

I understood what he was saying. We had been traveling together for months, but we had rarely been alone. In the night glow of my hotel room, it was so different. It was quiet enough I could hear his breathing and still enough to catch the faint fragrance of his aftershave. If I listened with my heart, I could hear the thump-thump of his pulse as well. I said nothing else.

Jason turned to go to his own room, paused but said nothing. I watched as he went over to the light switch and turned it off. The room was dark except for the light that filtered in through the drapes. He didn't leave. In the darkened room I saw him remove his jacket and tie and lay them across a chair. I could still hear his breathing and the thud of each shoe as it hit the floor. The sheets swished as he raised them and got into bed still partially dressed. We were nested spoons in the silver chest as he wrapped his arms around me and held me close with warm and gentle hands. "Good night, Sweetheart," he whispered.

I felt safe and loved. Where a moment ago I was unable to shake off the trauma, anxiety and panic of Grand-père's abduction, with Jason close, I was able to close my eyes and quickly fall asleep.

• • •

Morning rose like the flowers of spring, with the color of light, and the sweet aroma of coffee which had brewed in the automatic maker. I hadn't moved all night. I awoke just as I had fallen asleep, in the arms of my Jason.

"Can you smell the coffee, Honey?" Jason whispered.

"It smells like ambrosia, the drink of the gods—or so the books in Greek mythology called it," I swooned.

"Does it smell good enough to get up and get some?" he asked as he laughed. "I programmed the coffee maker last night before we went to sleep."

"Almost," I admitted and then rolled over to face him. I snuggled my head in his shoulder and pulled as close as I could get. "Jason, we—"

"I like that. 'We' means a future together." Jason put his hand under my chin and tipped my face to him. Moving his hands with the caress of a lover, he placed his finger tips on my cheeks and kissed me tenderly. "When this is over, and Oliver is the newly elected president, we will think about the future." He looked deeply into my eyes. "Won't we?"

"Yes, Jason, we'll talk—but for now, I can only think about today." I kissed him again, passionately. Suddenly, I stopped. The seriousness of the day's task and our commitment to the cause of restoring our country's freedom were too important for talk of "us". God had trusted us to see His power in the plan and not abandon our promise to it.

"Where's the coffee?" I laughed and jumped out of bed.

CHAPTER 18

A Gathering

The helipad landing on the roof of the Citadel in New York was as thrilling this time as it had been in the past. Jason and I had first been on Cornwall's roof months ago when Barbara and Richard had permitted a few of the underlings to bask in the sunlight of a glorious day, away from the belly of the city underground. We had ridden to the top on the home elevator. Today, entering the familiar lift, we whished down to the entry.

Harold, the Cornwall's every-man, met us in the grand hall. The rose marble floors shone in the crystal chandelier light. "It's good to see you again, Christy." To Jason, he nodded, "Doctor." Turning, he motioned for us to follow him. "They have all gathered in the sitting room."

As we walked, Jason's hand at my back was the knot on the mooring line that secured me to safety. "Why am I so afraid of everything?" I felt like I had changed so much, even I didn't recognize myself. "I was so brave, so independent, just months ago."

He pulled me back before we entered the sitting room. "Christy, your life has changed a lot in the last few months. Gunmen managed to take shots at you twice. You have a gunshot scar in your shoulder.

Someone even tried to snatch you off the street, and now, with the kidnapping of your grandfather, your world is no longer safe."

"How am I supposed to feel strong and safe, when I know I'm not?" I asked in a hushed but anxious tone.

"We live in a dangerous world, Honey. We always have. But before, in our drugged state, we didn't know we were supposed to fear everything."

"Gracie knew she wasn't safe," I said as I remembered the young woman I found on the bathroom floor of the medical center in Capitol City. "No one said anything, complained or spoke the truth. We lived in the age of silence, Jason. Now, reality is hitting us hard."

Jason drew me close at the entrance to the sitting room and whispered, "Would you rather live your life with buried thoughts, drugged emotions and unspoken love, or risk the dangers of really living?"

"I choose life, Jason," I announced and knew I was sure of my choice.

"Come in you two," Barbara called from her chair by the fire. Richard stood beside her, his arm resting on the marble mantle, the same beautiful rose color as the entry floor.

Inside, Kasamar and Raymar Goring sat on the sofa. The Spires couple, Martin and Rebecca, enjoyed the two wing back chairs near the windows. Edward Musselman sat between his wife, Maud, and Rachel Claudette around the game table with its fine leather top.

"I can't believe it," I gasped when I saw all of the lovelies Jason and I had met and depended on for our lives, just months before. "I get to see all of you, at one time, in one room."

I went around the room and hugged each dear friend, catching up on the immediate past. But, the activity for that day was not fellowship. "I don't know who is aware of the events of the last twenty-four hours."

Each one looked to the other. It seemed by their facial expressions, and the few words of condolences they offered, that most of those gathered there knew that Grand-père was missing; but, I had to say the words again.

"Yesterday, when Jason and I got to our hotel in Caribou, Maine, we discovered that Grand-père hadn't gotten there yet as he was supposed to. Later, we received a call that he had been kidnapped."

Some nodded in acknowledgement while others gasped in shock after hearing the terrible words spoken out loud.

"How could it happen?" Martin asked in anger. "Where were his bodyguards?"

"Malcolm Merrick, a member of his Advance Team, said he hadn't even arrived in Caribou." I looked around at each one. "The team in Maine could not have protected him since Grand-père hadn't gotten there. There was no flight logged into any airport. Right now, we don't know where security broke down."

Richard ran his hand through his hair and slapped the back of his neck. "Are there any clues at all?" He shook his head and set his jaw hard. "There has to be something."

I knew Richard was right—but, the fact was, there was nothing. Nothing I could think of.

Jason's eyes snapped to attention. "Wait, Christy—remember? The note said, 'You will be enchanted to know—I have taken Oliver Richly.'"

"Enchanted?" Richard barked, his eyes narrowed and his mouth set in a scowl.

"That's what I said," I admitted. "Then someone at the rally last evening yelled out from the side seats, 'New Mexico—it's the Land of Enchantment.'"

"New Mexico?" Rachel protested. "What is this, a treasure hunt? You have to be able to read the clues to find the buried treasure?"

"It feels like it," I admitted.

"New Mexico?" Barbara asked. "New Mexico," she shrieked in one gasp. "My father has investments in New Mexico—hotels, ranches, all kinds of stuff."

"Alister Bedlum is behind this?" I couldn't believe it. "I thought he was going to try to be a positive force. Not the most hated man in the world."

"That's what he promised," Barbara said as she twisted her hair. "He said, if he could talk with Mother, he would repent and become a better person."

"Did Mrs. Bedlum agree to talk to him?" Jason asked as he controlled his anger but not his body language. His fists were white knuckled and the veins in his neck bulged. "With the way Sondra had to drastically change her life, it's hard to believe she might even consider it."

Barbara squared her shoulders and smiled a wry smile. "She told me to tell him that he'd have to prove himself. If he would set up some sort of foundation to distribute part of his wealth to those in need, and prove to her that he has done it and has started giving it away, she would talk with him."

"And?" Raymar asked.

Barbara's eyes flashed with strength and assertion. "He hasn't set up a thing. Mother would know, because the foundation was to be in Mother's name and she would have to sign papers to put it in place." Tears welled up in her eyes. "Not a single paper has been drawn up."

"Barbara, I am so sorry," I said as my heart boke for her disappointment. I thought about my own father, his integrity and honesty. I could not imagine how I would feel if my father were Alister Bedlum.

"Don't be sorry, Christy," she said as her voice grew stronger. "I'm not. I have dismissed him. He's a monster, not my father." Then her eyes grew sad and tired. "I remember once, when I was very small, my daddy and momma took me to the tree lighting program at Rockefeller Center. We were happy, a family." Tears rolled down her cheeks and she wiped them away with her fingertips. Richard handed her a handkerchief. "Thanks," she said and kissed his hand.

"Then, that next year," she continued, "his business took off with the use of dishonest and gangster-like activities and my world crumbled. I knew then that Daddy had died that year and the Alister Bedlum the world knows was born."

"So—Bedlum has a New Mexico connection?" Jason asked. "Then, we need to contact Campaign Headquarters out there and see what clues may have been dropped."

"Barbara," I held my breath, "your chopper?"

"The little city helicopter won't make it that far, Christy," Barbara quickly added. "The flash-rail!" she clipped with enthusiasm. "You can board here is New York at Grand Central Station and disembark in El Paso, Texas. A car can be waiting for you at the station-terminal."

Everyone was silent for a minute. "How does that sound?" I asked.

"You're still packed," Kasamar reminded me.

"We might be rushing off thousands of miles away, with very few cues," I said, anxious to find Grand-père but terrified of wasting time and what that could mean to my grandfather.

"The trip will take about eight hours," Richard said. "Part of the tracks runs underground and some lines are far above the roads. Both of you will have your 281 Palm Devices with you for research and messaging." I could see his mind work as he paced back and forth, his hands motioning in the air.

"As an attorney, I have built many criminal cases," Richard added with enthusiasm. "We will build a case against Bedlum here in New York while you find Oliver." He beat his fist on the satin finished mantle. "Every step you take, every person you talk to, every clue you find can and will be used against that monster."

"You can do it, Christy," Maisie assured me. "You are my hero."

"Hero?" I blurted out loud. "My grandfather is the hero," I said as I looked at each person there. "Those of you from the other zones, stay in close contact with your campaign workers. Reassure them that Grand-père will be back soon and encourage them to spread my grandfather's message to everyone they meet, in small groups and large gatherings. We will find him—before it's too late. And, he will win."

CHAPTER 19

Flash-train to Texas

We ran along the boarding platform to the last car from the front, the exclusive private coach Barbara had arranged for us, and hurried up the steps. My pulse was pounding as I fell into the seat. Panting, I gasped with relief, "We made it."

"Are you all right, Baby?" Jason asked as he plopped into his seat and laughed.

I couldn't catch my breath enough to answer. I tried not to laugh since laughing seemed like a series of exhales and I thought I had none in me. Then I smiled. Even though someone kidnapped Grand-père, Jason and I had enough hope within us to laugh at the events of the day.

I grabbed my chest and willed myself to breathe slower. That would slow my pulse and let me catch my breath. "I talked to Grand-mère before we left the Cornwall's Citadel."

"How is she holding up?" Jason asked as he adjusted the pillow at the back of his head.

As I began to gather my thoughts and look around, I quickly saw that our rail coach was a penthouse luxury experience. The seats were sleek, with hard poly-infused sawdust frames, bright red deeply tufted seats and reclining backs with pillows. Raised, they sat at a broad table for work and dining.

I sighed as I thought about my dear grandmother and the years she and Grand-père had spent together. "She prays constantly and is leaving Grand-père's life in God's hands."

"And your parents?" he asked.

I closed my eyes and saw my family. "Mother and Daddy are spending their nights with Grand-mère. I think she's the one comforting Mother. But, I'm relieved they're all right and that they are together."

Barbara had arranged the private flash-rail car for us so we could rest, research and study in quiet. It was mid-morning when we came up for air and pulled our chairs up to the table. A rail steward came in with a tray.

"I hope that's coffee," I swooned when I saw the steaming decanter.

"Yes, Ma'am," he said and smiled. "I also have a plate of cinnamon rolls. Enjoy."

"Thank you," Jason said and reached for the plate with both hands. The steward poured two cups of hot coffee and excused himself to the door.

"There is a button on the arm of each chair. Just push it if you need something. Lunch will be served at 12:30." He bowed and backed out of the car.

I looked at my palm device and waved it back and forth. "How do we begin?"

"Okay," he started to process as he opened his own device. "The only clue we have is New Mexico. Well, two. Bedlum has a connection with the state and owns ranches, hotels, and other properties."

Just then, a hologram of Barbara Cornwall rose up from my device. "I'm on my secure Cooper-line," she began breathlessly, "so no one can cyber-hack into our conversation. This is very dangerous, Christy. Bedlum is a very dangerous demon."

"I know he is, Barbara," I agreed. "My own grandfather has been kidnapped, and I was shot. I know how dangerous he is."

"I asked my mother about a New Mexico connection," Barbara started.

"Of course," I threw my hand to my chest and gasped. "I hadn't even thought about asking her."

"Mother said that Bedlum owns a hotel in Las Cruces, New Mexico. He was investigating the possibility of buying more properties in the area before he got reconnected with the mob."

"Reconnected?"

"Remember Christy," Barbara whispered, "my father, his father and his father's father were each the head of a crime family. They were mafia kingpins—godfathers."

"I remember your mother, Sondra, telling Jason and I."

"That note that was given to Bedlum at the opera when you were first here, had the combination to his safe written on it." She paused. "I have to trust that this information is safe," she said with a deep sigh. "When Mother left the mansion, where she had lived with Bedlum for years, she took the scrapbooks and ledgers from the safe that covered the first years of their marriage and that also merged into his la Cosa Nostra era. That's really why Bedlum is looking for her—not because he cares about her."

"Oh, Barbara—I am so sorry."

"Mother is safe for now. I'm not concerned unless Bedlum finds out she's here. Then—I don't know." She was silent for a moment.

I could see from her shimmering holographic image that she was thinking. "Barbara—what?"

"Those scrapbooks—pictures and ledger entries," she said slowly as she rubbed her forehead with her hand. "Mother, Richard and I will pour over those books as quickly as possible for any clues about Bedlum's holdings and interests in New Mexico so we can get back to you as soon as possible." She took a deep breath. "I called to say that you could research the mafia and any connection they may have had to the Southwest, based upon old books and documents you could find on your palm devise."

"Old books and manuscripts?" I immediately thought of Marge Cummings, the curator of the historic documents at the main library in Capitol City.

"I know most books were burned or destroyed during the devastation of the last epoch." Barbara was a reader and she well knew of the loss to mankind of all the books published before the mass destruction. "And, I don't think there are any electronic data bases of previous books and manuscripts."

I looked over at Jason who was busting with excitement. He grabbed my arm and held on. "Barbara, yes," I reported, "there are not only data bases, there are books: the classics, novels, TV videos and copies of the original Constitution, Bill of Rights—everything, in the old back stacks and warehouses of our library in Capitol City. I can call the curator and ask her to do some research as well. She is part of the *1787-Constitutionalists* Campaign team." I reached over and hugged Jason, my life-line to reality.

"Great, Christy! I'll talk to Mother and we'll get busy on scrapbooks and other papers. You contact the curator. You and I will talk again before you get to El Paso."

"Barbara—you have brought some hope to Grand-père's disappearance." I choked up and had to pause before going on. "Grand-père will be found. He will win the election; we will overturn the Length of Days Law. God bless you."

CHAPTER 20

Research

"Marge?" I spoke into my 281 Palm Device.

"Hi, Christy. You look tired. Are you all right?"

"Marge—something has happened." It was hard for me to form the words. "Grand-père has been kidnapped. I need your help."

Marge said nothing for a second. "Sir Richly? How is that possible?"

"We don't have the details yet. And, we have just a few clues." I was sure Marge could find something regardless of how small. "Marge, we need for you to do some research in the back rooms and in the old files."

"Of course," Marge offered. "Anything."

Waiting for her to calm down and focus, I counted to ten in my head. "We need whatever you can find about the old mob, the mafia, la Cosa Nostra and any connection they may have at all with the state of New Mexico."

"Wow, how esoteric. The mafia?" Marge seemed to stumble through the request as if saying it over and over would bring clarity.

"Right—and look for any mafia dons with the name—Bedlum," I asked and held my breath, waiting for her to melt down again.

"Bedlum? Like in—Alister Bedlum?" Marge sounded like the concept was incredulous. "How—"

"It's a long story and we have very little time to spare," I apologized. "I'll catch you up later. Alister Bedlum is Barbara Cornwall's father. Enough said."

"More than enough," she agreed as her image shimmered in front of me. "I'll let you know what I find."

As Marge's hologram dissolved, I closed my device. "I should call Grand-mère." I felt tired and defeated. I stole a glance out the window at the flying scenery. "But, I don't know what to say to her," I admitted.

Jason reached over and patted my knee. "We don't have any new information, Honey. It would be hard to call and report nothing."

"I know—but I still feel guilty."

"Christie, I think you could use a nap. Your voice is weak. Your body is slumped. You're not yourself. I know that Oliver—"

"It's that—and more." I stopped, unable to find the words to express feelings I also couldn't identify. "I feel like everyone is expecting me to find an answer to everything, and I can't even find my own grandfather."

"Honey, if any of us have made you feel responsible for all the solutions, I am sorry."

"You, Jason? I didn't say you—"

"I know you didn't. I guess I'm really the one who thinks you can do everything," Jason admitted. "You healed the man who was out of his mind with drug intoxication. And again, when Jewels felt abandoned and without hope, you used words of encouragement that really made a difference." He took my hand and whispered. "I'm sorry if I made you feel overwhelmed."

I smiled at him and began to stack up all the events of the last year. "It wasn't just me, Jason," I admitted. "It was so many of us. And, it started when the whole town gathered to sing, *Silent Night*, on Christmas Day Eve, at a time when no one heard the name of Jesus. In order to not make a few people uncomfortable, millions lived their lives in silence."

• • •

We continued researching for hours using our 281 palm devices. With all the books confiscated and burned years ago, it was hard to know where to begin. It isn't like there was a list of books somewhere, until—

"Eureka!" Jason shouted.

"What did you find?"

"Here—listen—I found it on something called the dark web. Authorities thought they had shut it down years ago, but the websites that were located there just dug in deeper," Jason said as he sat up straight and waved his 281 back and forth.

"The dark web sounds sinister," I said with a shudder.

"Some of it was." Jason stood up and walked back and forth. "But, it was also a way to post something anonymously. Like, reporting a crime but not wanting anyone to know who called the Blue Shirts. Or, reporting an industrial or governmental mismanagement and keeping the whistle-blower's name a secret."

I said nothing but waited for the information he had uncovered. I knew I was becoming very impatient and it was best to stay silent.

"Christie, someone, or many someones, put massive amounts of information about the mafia on the dark web." Jason concluded.

Just then, my 281 device flashed and Marge shimmered forth. "Christie, Jason, I found something!"

"So did Jason," I said eagerly. "Tell me first what you found."

143

"Okay," she began. "Back in the middle of the last century, before the great collapse and before speaking up was banned, there was a story posted about Bedlum's grandfather, Mafia Boss Charles Bedlum, or Lucky Charlie as he was called by the press. He slipped through authorities' fingers a lot."

"That sounds exactly right, Marge." I was so excited, I thought I would hyperventilate. "Is there any connection to New Mexico?"

"Yes," she said with anticipation. "Lucky Charlie bought an old ranch in the foothills of the Organ Mountains near Las Cruses, New Mexico. He liked the legend that Pat Garrett's mother stayed at the ranch when she came to the area. Sherriff Pat Garrett captured Billy the Kid, so Charlie thought he had one-upped Garrett by owning the ranch or something like that."

"Oh, Marge, thank you so much! I'll stay in touch." And, with that Marge dissolved.

I stood up, reached out and hugged Jason as we jumped and danced around the room. As he swirled with me around the rail-car, the steward came back in with a huge silver tray.

"Lunch, Ma'am—Sir," he said as he placed the tray on the table. He removed a silver domed lid from the platter with smaller dishes arranged on it: savory slices of roast beef, small red potatoes dripping in butter and sweet smelling tender carrots. An assortment of desserts waited on another plate: dark rich chocolate tortes and white cakes with raspberry filling.

"Thank you," I gasped. "It all looks wonderful."

The Steward turned to leave and then added, "If you need anything else, just ring for me."

Grabbing the steward's elbow, Jason asked. "We will be getting off at El Paso, Texas. A car is waiting for us. Then we'll drive into New Mexico." He paused and seemed to choose his words carefully. "We heard of an old legend that says Pat Garrett's mother stayed at a ranch near Las Cruces. Have you heard of that story or where the ranch would be located?"

"Yes, I know that story." He smiled and relaxed his professional posture a little. "Follow the War Road out of El Paso and you'll come to the entrance to Dripping Springs Ranch. It's beautiful up there. They turned it into a National Park but in recent years it's become a little overgrown. But, you'll find it."

"Fantastic!" I shrieked. "We have food and a destination! Perfect!"

CHAPTER 21

Stoner in the Southwest

Ward Stoner could not believe the events of the last few days. His trusted Blue Guardsman, Daniel Washington, had followed him to New Mexico. Why? The man knew the Chief Inspector's rules of conduct. And, number one on the list was, *follow all rules*, written and spoken. Stoner had told him to stay back in Capitol City and watch the Richly Campaign Office. Oliver Richly was missing, and it didn't matter how distasteful Stoner found the new "Freedom March" of the *1787-Constitutionalists,* it was his job to keep the peace and protect the people, in whatever fashion or method he deemed necessary.

Yet, when he and the lieutenant got off the airplane, Ward had seen Washington dash past him and Boone, and slither behind a colonnade in the terminal. Certainly the man didn't think no one had seen him. That would be childish. Did he think, "If I cover my eyes, the world goes away?" But, enough of that.

With his dash-bag firmly in his hand, Stoner darted toward the door. He never even glanced over his shoulder to see if Boone was behind him. He assumed she would be there. He always assumed.

In front of the terminal, a car waited from the El Paso, Texas Police Headquarters. Quickly whisked into the vehicle, Boone and

Stoner barely saw the passing buildings on their way to meet the police chief.

They came to a stop in front of the two story flat roofed, tan adobe style building of police headquarters. Nearly running, they darted from the car, hustled through the doors and made their way with fixed gaze to Chief Montoya's office.

"Please, take a seat, Chief Inspector Stoner," Montoya offered with a smile.

"We have no time for pleasantries," Stoner barked without the slightest trace of a smile. "You would not know yet. It's important that the upcoming presidential election is not compromised." He paused making sure the chief heard the seriousness of his message, not just the words. "Oliver Richly has been kidnapped."

"What?" Montoya gasped as he rose from his desk chair.

"It's done, Sir." Stoner said with a crisp clip of his heals. "We must move on. We heard that his kidnappers brought him into New Mexico. This stop at your office is just a formality. Since we flew into your airport, we stopped here to let you know we're in your area." He turned to Boone. "Let's go."

Montoya rushed from behind his desk with a unique car door key in his hand: a finger-simulator lightning etched into an aqua-plastic card. "Take any car from our fleet, Sir." He handed over the sim. "This master finger print simulator will open and start any vehicle in storage."

"Thank you, Chief," Stoner snapped, in his assumptive manner. With that and a handshake, he and Boone left the office and went into the police garage. They selected a SPV within minutes, slipped the simulator near the lock, opened the door and got in. The vehicle responded to the fingerprint sim with a hum and they quickly pulled onto the road.

"That was nice of the Chief, don't you think?" Boone asked.

"What else could he do? Of course he handed over a car. The man who might be the next president has been kidnapped and may be near El Paso." Ward said no more.

Stoner followed the old I-10 highway out of El Paso toward the Las Cruces, New Mexico area, heading north. An underground inter-zonal informant told him about some unusual activity at the old Dripping Springs Ranch, in the foothills of the Organ Mountains that rose like the majestic peaks of a mighty pipe organ. The rising of the immense full moon behind Organ Mountains lit the sky like a blazing wild fire.

"Ward, it is breathtaking," Chalky whispered as she gazed with amazement at the brilliant red sky above the mountain ridge.

Stoner said nothing at first. He had been driving the small police vehicle, or SPV. He felt like he was in an alone-place, at peace with the gathering night around him. He had nearly forgotten that his lieutenant was in the seat beside him. He found that odd. It had been harder and harder to forget or ignore Boone in recent weeks. He could feel her near him, even before she spoke. He found it distracting and enjoyable at the same time. But, Ward Stoner was rarely distracted.

"Yes," he admitted as he gazed skyward. "Beautiful, I guess." But, his mind was not on the magnificent sky or the majesty of the mountains. It was on the uppity legacy brat, his name for Christiana Applewait, and her insistence on disregarding the rules.

"Ward," Chalky began diplomatically, "the prohibition against travel between zones was lifted. What has she done?"

"I told her that I would find her grandfather. She should stay in Capitol City. But did she? No!" he seethed as he gripped the steering wheel.

Chalky looked out of the side window at the passing desert sand, creosote bushes, yucca plants, and desert grasses. "Which one makes you angrier," she asked in a controlled voice, "Washington or Applewait?"

"That's another one. What does he think he's doing?" Stoner snorted, like a challenged bull moose.

"I received a message on the flight out here," she said boldly. "Daniel has accepted a large assignment from President Alexander."

"What?" Stoner shrieked. "You're just now telling me?"

"Ward, I was waiting for the right time."

"The right time?" Stoner's neck veins bulged.

Boone set her chin and jaw firmly. "You have been more difficult since Sir Richly was kidnapped than at any other time in recent years."

Ward's knuckles turned white on the steering wheel. "Washington has agreed to another job while on my watch?" He pounded the wheel with his fist and paused. "Now, what's this grand and fearful assignment?"

"Alexander refuses to consider failure at the election, Ward. And, while the Blue Guard has been a staunch defender of everything about the new government—Alexander no longer trusts the Guard. Call it paranoia. Call it mistrust of the developing interest in spirituality as re-introduced by Christiana Applewait."

"Oh, you cannot be serious!" he thundered.

Boone reached over and patted his hand, causing him to flinch. "Ward, whatever the reason, someone told me that Alexander has hired Washington to take you out, since you are the head of the Blue Guard."

Ward Stoner drove on in silence. Darkness would have been a blessing. It would have hid the rage that was building within him. "How dare he!" Stoner hissed.

"The road up to Dripping Springs is off to the right, past the University," Chalky directed. "Why is the University still here if there are no books?"

"My sources tell me doctors, teachers, and other professionals are taught my rote memory since there are no books," he paused. "Isn't that stupid?"

"Christy Applewait told me about a community of people called, the Keepers. They—"

"Never mind that, Boone," Stoner barked and said no more. He turned east on University Avenue and followed it until it turned into Dripping Springs Road.

The scenery hadn't changed much according to those who had given directions in El Paso. The great upheaval of the previous century had halted progress everywhere. What did not lie within the great cities, deteriorated alone in the dry deserts and windswept prairies in many zones. There were no buildings along the road that could cast light from their windows or open doors, creating shadows and contrast. Stoner and Boone's only blessing was the brilliance of the moon that lit the path.

As they neared Dripping Springs Ranch, both of them stiffened. Old adobe buildings lay in rubble with gaping holes where windows and doors had been. Weathered earthen bricks cluttered the area. Most structures didn't have all four walls or roof. Overgrown hiking trails, once enjoyed by walkers willing to trudge the walkway from the La Cueva rock outcropping to the rugged spires of the mountain peaks, were barely visible.

"I don't like this, Ward," Chalky spoke. It sounded like she wasn't breathing.

"Don't be silly. If Richly is imprisoned out here, they wouldn't have blazing lights to give away their position."

Chalky's eyes darted from rocks to ruins, like an animal that sees no escape. "The Park Service used to keep this area up, but money hasn't been allocated for park upkeep for decades." She rigidly clutched the door handle. "Ward—who gave you the tip to come out here?"

"It came through a third party," he said with measured speech. Nearing the structure with the most promise of habitation— it had walls and a roof—he slowed the SPV and turned off the lights.

"Ward," Chalky whispered as she searched the area around them from inside the car, "I don't think we should get out. There's no one around. And, if there is—I'm not sure who is hunting who."

Stoner opened the vehicle door with disgust. "Harrumph," was the only sound he made, and an occasional snap of a dry plant underfoot. With only lunar light, he approached the building that appeared to be the most intact and pulled out his sidearm.

Boone was slower to emerge from the impenetrability and safety of the SPV. She unfastened the clip that held her firing arm securely inside its holster. Then, she stopped in place.

Stoner heard nothing. But—he could feel a presence in the thicket at the corner of the crumbling building. Turning with a snap, he aimed his weapon.

"No! Ward!" a familiar voice snapped. "It's me, Boone."

Stoner lowered his weapon and searched the long shadows cast by the bright moonlight. "What are you doing? You nearly got yourself killed."

"Ward," she rushed toward him. "You know that Washington followed you here. I told you—you are his target! This feels like an ambush!" she whispered hoarsely.

"A what?" he bellowed like a bull elephant protecting his territory.

"Let's get inside something. It's—" Instantly, the blast from a 980 short-distance firearm drowned out her voice.

With the crack from the weapon, Ward Stoner hit the ground like the falling of a giant timber, strong, full of life and now face-down in the dust and the sand of the desert.

Stoner saw Boone crouch low and whip around, with her 980 in her hand. He could smell no tell-tail sign of smoke like from an antique weapon. Then the sound of running crunched and rattled down the path and disappeared. He watched through blurry eyes as Boone holstered her weapon when the whirl of a motor started up in the distance. Ward felt her kneel beside him as she snapped on the light mounted like a broach to her upper, left shoulder. In the flash of the light, he saw little but felt her hands run along his back. His shirt felt warm and sticky.

"Ward?" she whispered, her voice sounded desperate as he felt her roll him toward her. The light from her shoulder flashed on the dirt as it fell from his face. He saw her eyes fix on the upper left quarter of his body. "Oh Ward," she gasped.

"Miriam?" he whispered, his eyes blurry with pain.

"No, Ward," Boone sighed. "It's Chalky. Miriam died—a few years ago." He heard her choke on the words that separated her from the ghost of his dead wife and then she swallowed hard. Tears drip down her face and gather in pools where she caught them on the back of her hand.

He gripped his chest and thought of his son Christopher. The boy had already lost his mother. He could not lose his father as well. Not tonight. Grabbing Boone's hand, he brought it to his lips.

"You have followed the words of the healer, Christiana Applewait." He gasped for breath as he lay with his head in Boone's lap. "Heal me," he pleaded.

"Ward!" Her hands trembled and her voice cracked. "I can't. I'm not—"

"You are, Chalky," he said as he clutched at her more desperately. "I have seen the love in your eyes."

"But, I—" Tears choked her words. She wiped them with the tail of her shirt.

"Now, Chalky, now!" he insisted, his voice growing weak and thready.

Boone bowed her head and prayed to the God of other people, those she had chased to the great waters of the west. The moon light that lit the evening seemed to focus a beam on her hands, on Ward's gapping, bleeding wound. Suddenly, she thrust her hands, her left palm pressing on top of the right, into the opening in the shoulder of the man she had admired, feared, loathed, and lately— loved. Stoner knew that but could not admit it to himself or to her.

He could hear the thumping of his pulse in his ears. At first he feared, with each beat, his life-blood was pumping out of his body. Truthfully, if he could have thought clearly, he would have known it was, but he preferred to think of it differently. Through the growing delirium of his pain, every thump, thump reminded him of the people's march, a year ago on December 25, when Christmas returned to Capitol City on Gifting Day Eve. He let go of the agony that tortured his body and saw himself walking with the faithful, singing songs of love and joy. No one knew the words that glorious evening since singing had been silenced. But, there was a knowing, and a sharing of musical phrases, one beat behind the next. That's where Ward Stoner mentally crawled while Chalky forced life back into his body.

The compression beneath her blood-soaked hands slowed the escape of his blood, beat by beat. When Ward gasped, filling his lungs to capacity, Chalky eased up, her face shining in wonder and amazement. "Praise the Lord," she sang with a joyful sound on her lips.

"How did you do that?" Stoner asked, aware that he was in the arms of his lieutenant.

"I didn't Ward. I followed a—an instinct, a knowing I didn't hear or understand. It just came to my heart that I should place my hands in your wound and stop the bleeding. Just like with Christy." Chalky shook her head in seeming disbelief although she had seen the glory of it. "Amazing, yet I believe it came from God."

Ward Stoner searched his soul for another answer. The name of God and his son, Jesus, banned so long ago, still came to mind when needed. How could that be? How could anyone know the name of a friend they had never met? But, he could not deny the fact. Touched by the King of a kingdom he never knew existed—he had been healed.

CHAPTER 22

The Organ Mountains

The night moon still hung in the star-peppered sky, a garden lantern in a bejeweled tree. Jason and I followed the War Road out of El Paso and into New Mexico.

"There it is," Jason pointed. "The sign says, Dripping Springs Road that way."

Jason turned our rented vehicle toward the Organ Mountains. Since individually owned cars in the Central Zone did not exist, except for medical and police personnel like Jason and Stoner, it was exciting to ride in a really fancy vehicle anyone could buy in the southwest.

"This is beautiful," I admired as I ran my fingers over the ebony leather covered dashboard. "Look," I pointed at the headlights of an on-coming car, "so many people have their own transportation here. Just like in the Western Zone."

"It sure is dark out here," he said as we both searched the sides of the narrow road along the path out to the ranch. "Watch for anything, a clue, a warning that might tell us something about where they've taken Oliver."

"I'm looking," I whispered, almost afraid to speak, "but—I see nothing."

"I know, Honey," he said. "But, it feels better to look for something, anything."

"What is that up ahead?" The lights at the foot of the mountains looked like a cluster of emergency vehicles, with red and blue lights spinning around, flash—flash.

As we neared, there were so many lights, they were blinding. "Do you think they found Grand-père?"

"We'll see," Jason said as he slowed and prepared to talk through the window speaker.

"What are you doing way out here at night?" A southwest version of a Blue Guardsman clipped, his brow deeply knitted.

Jason shielded his eyes from the man's bright lapel light. "What's going on?"

The guardsman put his hand on his weapon. "Sir, I asked you a question. First give me your name and then answer me. What are you doing out here?"

"Certainly," Jason began slowly. "My name is Dr. Jason O'Reilly and this is Lady Christina Applewait. We're looking for her grandfather, Sir Oliver Richly."

"Out here—in the dark?"

"Sir," my words came hesitantly. Could I trust him? "My grandfather has been kidnapped." I watched as the man's expression turned from stern-man-in-control to a person of true concern. "We received a clue that led us out here."

"I'm sorry to hear that Ma'am, but this area is deserted."

The lights of the emergency responders flashed in my eyes. "What are all the lights and storm troopers about?"

"An important Inspector of the Blue Guard was shot. We received an emergency beacon signal from the SPV he drove out of El Paso."

"Inspector Stoner?" I gasped. Flooded with feelings that tore at me left and right, fear finally won. Ward Stoner was nothing if he wasn't a staunch fighter for what he believed was right. Lately, he had been on my grandfather's side—and mine. Had we lost a valuable alley?

"Yes, Ma'am," the Stormtrooper acknowledged.

Jason gripped the steering wheel and cleared his throat. "Have they caught the shooter?"

"No, Sir. He apparently got away."

"I'm a physician," Jason offered. "Does the Inspector need my help?"

"Go on through, Doctor," The trooper said as he waved us past.

The dirt road, lit by moon glow in spite of the nighttime hour, left a cloud of dust in our wake. "I wonder if Chalky Boone is with him." I thought of the time she tried to "explain" Ward Stoner to me, saying that he is actually a nice guy. "I think she really likes him."

As we neared the source of all the lights and activity another trooper held up the palm of his hand. "This is a crime scene. You'll have to turn around."

"I'm a physician," Jason offered again.

"Good," the guard said. "First Attenders are here but no doctor."

Jason pulled off the trail and stopped. He opened the door, jumped out and headed over to those gathered around a man on the ground. Getting out of the car, I looked down to make sure my feet were on stable ground and noticed some sparkly stuff under my shoes. "What's all this?" I questioned, although not to any one in particular, just a question I spoke aloud.

One of the many troopers gathering clues in the area, smiled and said, "That's crystalized jalapeño granules. A store here in the area is marketing the powder as a night-hour substance to identify a homeowner's property lines. The fire in the peppers mixed with other chemicals causes the product to glow after heating all day in the New Mexico sun. It's made in Old Mesilla, a very, very old historical village around here."

"That's nice," I whispered. "Few people in the Central Zone own property." I didn't wait for a response and turned to walk over to where Jason was in attendance.

"My Lady," Lieutenant Boone called out as I approached her.

"Lieutenant—"

"Call me Chalky," she asked.

"It's Christy, Chalky. How is he?"

"Better—he was shot, Christy."

I gasped at the thought of the stern warrior, shot down in the dirt of the road. "By who?"

"We think Daniel Washington was the shooter," she said, her breath short and choppy. She seemed overcome by events that brought down her friend. "He got away, but he can't hide. He'll want to go home sometime."

Boone and I walked closer to Jason and his patient. "It looks like the bleeding has stopped," we heard Jason say. "The bullet will have to be removed."

"I understand," Stoner said—his voice not as clipped as usual. "But Chalky stopped the bleeding."

Jason's eyes widened, "Lieutenant Boone?"

"Yes—" Stoner paused. "Doctor," he whispered, "I need to tell you—my lieutenant believes in the things your Lady believes in. And—I guess I must too—because I asked Boone to heal me like Christiana would if she were here."

Standing in the background, close but yet not, my heart seemed to stop beating and still pounded harder. Had I heard him correctly? Did he say, he believes?

Jason stopped and felt the pulse in Stoner's wrist. "What did Boone do?"

"I told her I knew she could do it," Stoner began. "Then she placed her hand in my wound and the bleeding stopped." He grabbed Jason's wrist and leaned toward him. "I could feel the life in my body return." He grabbed Jason's arm, hard. "Doctor, I know I could."

I watched as one of the First Attenders tapped Jason on the shoulder. "Doc, we're ready to transport the patient."

"Stoner," Jason corrected him. "His name is Ward Stoner." Jason stood up and motioned for me to come closer.

The attendants placed a lift board on the ground beside Stoner and transferred him onto it. Reaching out, I took Stoner's hand in mine. I could feel energy transfer from my body to his and my knees felt weak.

Stoner smiled. "Thank you."

As they moved him onto the patient transport, Chalky reached out and threw her arms around me. "Christy, I am so glad you brought Dr. O'Reilly to us."

I looked into her eyes. "We were following the same lead you were on," I explained.

"Be careful," she warned. "Daniel Washington, that animal, is on the loose."

"We'll watch for him, thanks, because, we can't leave. We came here following a connection we found with the mob of many years ago, and Dripping Springs Ranch. Sheriff Pat Garrett's mother would stay there when she came to visit."

A First Attender standing nearby chuckled a little. "If you want more Sheriff Garrett flavor, he put Billy the Kid in jail here in Doña Ana County."

"Where?" I questioned, excited about a possible new lead.

"Old Mesilla, Ma'am."

CHAPTER 23

Old Mesilla

The adobe village of Old Mesilla lay just off the highway that ran southwest out of Las Cruces. The road would continue past the old pecan groves and on toward La Mesa and the Texas border if you didn't turn off into Mesilla. The world of Las Cruces in 2114 was fast and sleek with only patches of real estate saved for the past, but the color and flavor of the southwest splashed over everything. Old Mesilla was one of those preserved treasured jewels of yesteryear.

Once we turned off Route 28, I felt transported from the present, twenty-second century, back to when the Butterfield Stagecoach stopped at La Posta where the Corn Exchange Hotel and restaurant provided an oasis for tired salesmen and visitors as they climbed out of the coach and rested or stayed for a while. I could imagine cowboys I had read about riding in on dusty horses to refresh themselves at the cantina and enjoy the beautiful terracotta Mexican-American culture. Flat roofed adobe buildings with rough dressed viga logs projecting through the roof to the outside were still the architecture design after hundreds of years.

"Jason," I whispered in reverence to the years of history the village represented, "is it possible that Grand-père could be hidden in one of these small buildings without people in neighboring stores and homes knowing about it?"

"I don't know, Honey," Jason said, his voice full of amazement peppered lightly with doubt. "But, we have to check it out." He pulled into a parking space in the lot behind La Posta Restaurant where we sat in the car for a moment.

"We have to have some sort of plan," I said, knowing we had followed the sparkle-lead with nothing more than the name of a small village to go on.

We got out and walked along the sidewalk in front of the stores where the aroma of scented candle and strings of hanging red peppers mixed into a delicate southwestern perfume. The old Saint Albino church anchored the plaza at the opposite end and the stores flanked the square.

"Jason, look," I said as I pointed. "Some of those crystalized jalapeño granules are scattered there on the edge of the brick and concrete walk. They must have been swept off the walkway."

"That's right, Christy," Jason said as he studied the particles under his feet. "Good eye. I would never have seen them."

"Where did they—?" I drifted off as I traced the path the granules had taken.

"There's some more," he added as we inched along.

The last store where there was any trace of sprinkles boasted a window full of gleaming silver and turquoise squash-blossom necklaces. "I read," I smiled to myself at how many times I prefaced a statement with "I read...."

"What, Honey? You read what?"

I pointed to the beautiful jewelry. "The upside down crescent is what the Navajo called the 'Naja.' It's said to protect the horse that has it on its bridal as well as the rider who wears one. First mentioned in the Bible in the book of Judges, the symbol found its way from the Middle East, through Spain and to the early native peoples in the new world."

"That's amazing," he said as we both stood and admired the display.

"Why would the crystals lead us to a jewelry store?" I wondered aloud.

"The trooper said some shop owner here in the village makes the crystalized jalapeño granules. Why not this store?" Jason studied the store front and reached for the door latch.

Inside, the store hummed with customers searching for a Charles Russell print of a fearless cowboy gripping the reigns of a bucking horse; the gleaming nuggets of Navajo jewelry and the fine crafted needlepoint bracelets of the Zuni tribe; or the woven Native American rugs and blankets draped over wooden sawhorses.

"May I help you?" a woman behind the counter asked.

"We're looking for someone," I began.

"You're Lady Applewait, aren't you?" she whispered, diverting her question from listening ears.

"Yes," I mouthed with a nod of my head. I touched the woman's hand and she came from behind the counter. I leaned my head in her direction and whispered, "We're looking for my grandfather."

"Sir Richly?" she questioned. "Why would he be in New Mexico? Our telecommunications messages have stated that he's in Maine. You're a long way from the Down East coast."

I looked at Jason and knew what I had to say. "My grandfather has been kidnapped. We had a lead he may be in Old Mesilla."

"Here, in my store?" she gasped, her faced turned ashen. "Are we in danger here?"

"I wish I could say you weren't," I said slowly.

Jason quickly added, "We just don't know, Ma'am. And, my name is Dr. Jason O'Reilly."

"I'm Faith Rodriguez," she offered with her hand to her chest as in a pledge of honesty.

"Does your name have any significance?" I asked her, hoping there was real faith behind her name.

"My family and I are Christians. My ancestors have been for hundreds of years."

"I was hoping you would say that. We are people of the Word as well, Faith," I told her. "I wish I could tell you that none of you are in danger, but the truth is, we have no idea who is involved, how many there are, and how dangerous they may be."

Faith took a deep breath and asked, "What can I do?"

"Are these the only rooms you have here? Where do you make and package the crystal product?" I was confused. How could they have another business out of this space?

Jason looked around as well. "Do you have a basement?"

"My husband, Manny, invented the **crystalized** jalapeño granules and makes them in a garage-factory near our home. As he has orders, he brings them in here for bookkeeping, tracking, packaging, and shipping since my staff handles those services all the time."

"So you have no basement?" Jason asked again.

"We don't mean to pry, Faith," I reassured her.

Faith smiled and patted my **shoulder. "I know you're not prying. You're worried and I understand."**

"No basement?" I chimed in.

"No—and yes," she began, her brow furrowed. "We were approached by the owners of the adjacent store. They wanted to rent our basement. Since we weren't using it, Manny said, 'Yes.' That was a few years ago. How long has your grandfather been missing?"

"Just a couple of days," I told her and turned to Jason. "How can a space rented years ago, have anything to do with all of this?"

"I don't know, Christy," Jason admitted his own bewilderment. "But remember, this is a mob connection we're following, not political."

"What's a mob?" Faith asked with a wide-eyed, innocent expression.

"Never mind that," Jason brushed off. "I shouldn't have brought it up."

"I'm sorry," I interrupted. "What is the store that rented your basement?"

Faith's eyes welled with tears. "It's has had many names over the years but has always been known as the store with the Billy the Kid connection."

I closed my eyes and shuddered. "Lucky Charlie's favorite outlaw."

CHAPTER 24

The Basement

The store that consistently boasted a relationship with Billy the Kid, sat of the southeast corner of the Plaza. It was the jail and courthouse in 1881, where the Kid, tried and sentenced to hang in the wild west of the eighteen-hundreds, actually walked.

"Jason, look," I said as we entered the old building made of adobe-mud bricks. "The windows are set into eighteen inch thick walls. The lower level would be completely sound proof and isolated from the rooms above."

"This place was the capitol building when Mesilla was the capitol of the Arizona Territory," Jason offered. "A book in the hospital library told of men hammering out aspects of the Gadsden Purchase here."

"Yes, Sir," a man said as he approached Jason and me. "I heard you two talking about the Kid. After his sentencing they took him to the courthouse in Lincoln where he escaped. Doña Ana's sheriff, Pat Garrett, later tracked him down and shot him."

"Pat Garrett?" My head swirled as I tried to take in all that had happened. I studied the man for just a second. I had no time not to trust him. "You have a basement—right?"

"A basement?" he asked. "Look around. We have enough space; we don't need a basement."

"It looks wonderful," I soothed the clerk, not wanting to arouse his anger or suspicion.

The man brightened a bit but remained tense, his jaw clenched. "The display of hunting knives in front of you was made by a local man," he offered as he opened the case without taking his gaze from mine.

I tried to take his mind off our question about the basement for a moment. "This one is beautiful," I said.

"The handle is made of petrified bone with embedded accents of opalized wood." He ran his fingers over the hilt as if caressing a baby. "Every one of these superb blades is unique. No two are alike."

Jason joined in the admiration with a twinge of honest appreciation. "They are all magnificent."

Temporarily caught off task by the shinning swords and exquisite cutlery, I quickly refocused. "Do you store the additional inventory in the basement?"

The man looked at me, hard; his eyes seemed to bore a hole in mine. "The basement is not open to the public," he growled, his expression growing dark and flat.

Jason stepped in the gap between me and the man, like a wedge protecting me from the dangerous world. "We don't want any trouble. We just want to look around."

"Look around? The boss would kill me."

"Boss? You don't own this store?" I asked.

He looked around the room, like one searching for a hidden informant. "This whole place was purchased years ago by an organization out of New York, Charlie somebody is the CEO."

"Was the—CEO's name, Charles? He died years ago." I corrected and thought of Bedlum and his seeming legitimate and philanthropic group. "There's a new leader—or Don."

"Don?" the clerk said with a question on his face. "His name is Don?"

"Something like that." I stopped and thought of Barbara Cornwall. "We talked to his daughter just a few days ago, and she gave us permission to go into the basement to look for something that's missing."

"There's a staircase that goes down off the back workroom and another one that enters through a bunker or shed in the back of the building." The man seemed to shudder. "I never know who—or if anyone is down there."

"Thank you," I said as I finally exhaled. "Which way?"

The man made a small, silent gesture in the direction of an exit into a back hallway. Jason and I approached cautiously, slowly turned the door knob and looked down the stairs.

"The light is on," I whispered.

"The light seems to be on all of the time," the clerk said quietly behind us.

I jumped. I had anticipated something unexpected from the basement below us, not from the man behind us.

He put his index finger to his lips and motioned for us to continue on downstairs—silently. With hand gestures, he indicated he would remain on the retail floor.

The old, narrow wooden steps were uneven and steep, each tread a little different in height than the other. I felt unbalanced as I made my way down the sixteen rungs to the hard, polished earthen floor. We stopped and listened. The very thick walls were good insulators for heat, cold and sound. We heard nothing. Jason pointed left then right and shrugged.

I had no idea which way to go. I knew it could be dangerous in either direction. To the right, there was an alcove that led into a dark windowless room.

"The bunker," Jason mouthed and pointed to the left. He motioned for me to get behind him as we slowly moved on.

The lower level was a maze of rooms that stretched out under several of the stores above. It smelled dry and dusty down there, not at all like a musty old basement of the Midwest. New Mexico's semi-arid desert left no moisture for mold.

It was eerily silent down in the hand carved caverns of the underworld. The pounded dirt of the floor made for silent steps as we moved back deeper into the cellar. Rickety wooden shelves lined the walls scattered with dust-covered boxes and cans.

I stopped. Did I hear someone behind us? Who? How? There was no one to the right of us after we had descended the steps. We waited for a few seconds but heard no more. There was still no sound from the left.

I listened hard. I couldn't hear anything that sounded like Grand-père. Was he alright? Until a year ago, I had lived in a safe world. Down here under the desert floor, all sense of safety was finally shattered.

As we inched through the dust, our pace didn't match my rapidly pounding heart. I felt as terrified as I did the first time I walked through the gapping cavern of Howard Mountain and witnessed the atrocities there. How could any place so silent, scream at me so loudly from the dark corners?

Creeping slowly, the muscles in my legs began to ache. I was tense, with every inch of my body readied for fighting or fleeing. Suddenly, Jason raised his hand and signaled for us to stop.

When my anxiety settled a little and my heart stopped pounding in my ears, I was able to hear distant muffled voices.

"How long are we supposed to hold this guy?" A deep gruff voice asked.

"Let's just kill him," another voice snapped. "He cannot turn up before the election and that's still a long time from now."

I threw my hand to my mouth to muffle the screams of fear that wanted to escape. With only my grandfather in mind, I suddenly felt a fierce determination grip me and I stepped forward taking the lead. I could feel the presence of people not too much farther ahead.

Jason touched my arm and motioned for us to step into the shadows under a stairwell that led down from yet another store. There was a rustling behind us that stopped almost as abruptly as we did.

I knew we had no weapons with us. That hadn't really occurred to me before I was there to find Grand-père. I had anticipated calling authorities if we found him, not staging a heroic rescue. As I strained to see around the dimly lit space, it occurred to me, we were as trapped as Grand-père.

"Hey, Old Man," one of the men taunted. "In a minute, we'll find out what to do with you."

At that moment, a dark figure blocked the light from the window that was high in the room, near the ceiling. I nearly gaged on my own surprise. It was Daniel Washington.

"There you are, finally," the first man bellowed when Washington charged around the corner. "What're we supposed to do with this guy?"

"He really looks important, doesn't he?" Washington jeered. "Caged like a mad dog and drugged out of his mind."

I gasped. They drugged Grand-père?

"What's that?" The second man asked.

"Nothing," Washington barked. "You've been down here so long; the rats are talking to ya."

"No," the man protested. "It ain't nothin'. It's somethin'."

No one said anything more. Jason and I waited.

I felt movement—behind me—around me—where? The silence was deafening.

"Well look what I found," Washington hissed as he grabbed my wrist and dragged me out from under the stairs. He held a Henry long rifle, barrel pointing down, in his left hand.

Jason grabbed the animal's arm and pulled, trying to free me from his grip. Washington swiped Jason with the back of his hand

and sent him smashing against the wall. He slid down the adobe surface and landed unconscious on the floor.

"Jason—no!" I screamed as Washington pulled me into the next room where Grand-père lay slumped on the floor.

"*Screech!*" What was that? A nonhuman sound filled the space down there, so many feet below the surface. An animal in strange clothing leaped between me and Washington, its eyes full of rage. He slammed my captor to the floor and leaped, his feet forming wide arches that spanned all the area around him.

"Raymar!" I shouted in amazement and relief.

The former hollow one crouched low; he was a mountain lion readying for attack. As Raymar held them at bay, Ivy Trudeau rushed in with her weapons drawn. Washington raised the rifle into firing position while the other two captors jerked their pistols from their belts. Ivy shot Washington in the knee before he could get a round off and delivered well-placed bullets to the other two evil ones in their shoulder and thigh. They dropped to the floor in astonishment.

"Where—" the mad dog, former Blue Guardsman began in fear and amazement. "Mr. B. said there would be no interference. He said no one would think of New Mexico."

The ugly little one with the shoulder wound, glared at Washington's humiliation and began to smirk. "So smart, no one will find him down here." He doubled up the other fist and lunged in my direction.

Raymar pounced on the man in one leap, a great cat with sharp and powerful reflexes. He tore at the man's bloody arm and opened his mouth as if to devour what remained of the loathsome one.

"No, Raymar!" I screamed, unable to face what he was about to do.

Instantly, Raymar stopped, looked at me and smiled. Ivy covered us with her firearm as Jason came to. I rushed to his side and threw my arms around him.

"Jason, I was so worried," I gasped.

"I'll be alright. I'll probably have a headache but—" he stopped as he looked over at my grandfather. "Let me check on Oliver."

"Grand-père," I called to him as I hurried over, knelt on the floor and eased his head onto my knees. "Grand-père," I repeated.

He rolled his eyes slightly and a faint smile crossed his lips. "Christy, I—"

"Shh, shh," I urged for fear his words would use breath he didn't have to spare. "I don't want you to talk, Grand-père—please."

"Your grandmother—"

"I'll call Grand-mère—I promise—just as soon as I get back up on top again." Hugging him close to me, I tried hard not to cry and frighten him more than the whole experience already traumatized him. But, since I found him, I didn't want to let go, not even to call my grandmother.

Grand-père started to speak and then nodded weakly in agreement.

Jason felt my grandfather's pulse and lifted his eyelids to check his pupils. "They said he was drugged. His pulse is weak but seems to be rhythmic." He looked around at our situation, then at the mud brick walls of the rooms under the stores of Old Mesilla.

His eyes were sympathetic but insistent. "Christy, hurry back up to the store above and get help—police and an ambulance for Oliver."

"Ambulance?" I whispered and cast a darting glance at my grandfather. I couldn't pull myself away from him, even to call for the help he needed. I stood up and started to leave, then looked back. How could I leave them there?

"Tell them we need a transport for three gunshot wounded perpetrators too, Christy," Ivy added. "And hurry, Washington will probably lose his knee."

"Oliver will be all right, Honey," Jason assured me. "Your grandfather needs your help. I'll be here with him while you run upstairs for a few minutes. Just remember, it's really a miracle that we found him. That was the hard part."

I hurried back through the shadows of the cellar to the stairs and started up. It seemed darker and more sinister now than it had before. Then, I smiled to myself. I was beginning to feel again, to think more clearly and not out of fear, or as a response to danger. All the numbness was beginning to wear away. It was true. "Praise the Lord—Jason was right," I said aloud. "He has been found."

CHAPTER 25

Late June

Grand-père's room at Memorial Medical Center in Las Cruces was bright. Warm, bold splashes of color replaced the all-white décor of previous years.

I slipped into his room hoping not to awaken him. Ivy and Raymar were with me. When Grand-père's eyes opened to slits, I spoke to cheer him on. "You look better," I whispered close to his ear.

"Hi Sweetie," he began. A faint smile crossed his lips. "I may look better, but I feel crumpled, like an old piece of paper."

"I could lie just to make you feel better," I laughed. "But, an old piece of wadded up paper pretty much describes you."

Grand-père took my hand, "I talked to your grandmother already. She'll be here soon. Barbara Cornwall is flying her out."

"We could have no better friends than the Cornwalls," I agreed.

"We have so many good people around us, including you two," Grand-père said to Ivy and Raymar.

"Thank you, Sir," Raymar said as he offered his hand. "It is a privilege to serve you."

"You have already served me for years, Raymar. Your poetry and writings lift my spirits every time I read your works—Robert Gross," he said as he placed his hand on top of their handshake.

"Again, thank you Sir," Raymar said blushing a little. "It is strange for people to know who I am. As a hollow one, they didn't even see me unless I threatened to attack them."

My grandfather's eyes grew large. "I know I was drugged, but seem to remember a wolf-man flying through my dungeon cell."

"That was me," he admitted. "But, I wouldn't really have devoured anyone. I just wanted them to think so."

"Even in my dazed state, that's what I was hoping," Grand-père's eyes twinkled. Then he turned to me. "Speaking of loyal friends, where is your doctor?"

I looked toward the door. "Jason is talking to *your* doctor."

"Is he going to spring me out of this place?"

"You're not in prison, Grand-père," I assured him.

"Funny, it feels like it," he said with a wry smile.

At that moment, the door popped open. "Are you still lying around here in bed, Oliver?" Grand-mère asked as she breezed in.

"Praise the Lord, the cavalry has arrived," he pulled the edge of the bedding back, sat up and started to put his feet over the edge of the mattress.

"Hold on there, Oliver," Jason warned as he came in the room behind my grandmother. "The results of all of the tests aren't in yet. There's still the Cranial-Graph feedback, to determine if Oliver's hit on the head, which resulted in his unconsciousness, will leave any lasting damage."

"When will that report be in? I have a campaign to get back to." Oliver Richly was a man of determination and acceptance of the role he played in history. Nothing would stop him for long.

The door opened again and a woman in a light blue, bamboo fabric business suit waked in. "Doctor, I have the results. Do you want to meet me in my office?"

Grand-père pulled himself up again and planted his feet flat on the floor. "Absolutely not," he demanded. "It's my head. I want to hear the outcome before you two physicians have a chance to spin it, making me out to be some invalid or something."

"Oliver, now get back into bed," Grand-mère ordered.

Grand-père glared. "I want to say, 'No, I will not,' Connie." He added in mocked surrender. "But, I know you'll win anyway."

Grand-mère gave him a love pat on his knee. "Oh stop and pull the covers up." We all assumed he would do as she asked.

"Sir Richly," Dr. Gayle Raddin began.

"Oliver," he insisted.

"Oliver, I just thought you'd want some privacy," the doctor began. "That's why I suggested my office."

"Privacy from my wife and granddaughter? Why?" he growled. "And, this fine woman is my granddaughter's bodyguard. The gentleman here," he pointed at Raymar, "can be the bodyguard to the world." Everyone laughed.

"It's your choice," she concluded, not seeming to hear all he said. She finally opened the patient record tablet in her hand. "The results indicate a small area of swelling which we can control with a skin-wicking application of Vascular Repair. We can teach you to treat any headaches with icy water and fist flexion therapy."

"No lasting damage?" I asked to make sure I had heard her correctly.

"None," she said and smiled a little, like her face had lost its elasticity. "You may want to take the flash train back home rather than fly. The pressure on your head will be less." Closing her tablet she added, "If you have any questions, I'll be available. I'd like you to stay the night and get plenty of rest."

Grand-père waved her off. "I'd like to check out right after lunch. They say the food is good here."

"I can sign off on that—if you agree to call me this evening and again tomorrow afternoon." She sort of smiled again. "That's for my own peace of mind. I won't have to explain how I let the next President of the United States out of the hospital too soon, and he collapsed at one of his speaking events."

Jason put his hand on my shoulder and gave me a reassuring squeeze. Then to Dr. Raddin he added, "Thank you, Doctor. Remember, I'll be traveling with Oliver."

Ivy patted her sidearm in a habit of assured authority. "Dr. O'Reilly will be there for Oliver's medical needs, and I will be there as well." She grinned a little. "Raymar will be there to cover our backs."

"And, I'll be there, too," I said as I looked at my grandparents with love and pride. I am so thankful that I still have them. If Silas Drummond hadn't broken the silence, they would have entered the never-ending-sleep at the end of December 2112 and never awakened. If we hadn't had friends like the Cornwalls, Jason and I would never have reached Grand-père in time. I could see the Lord's hand at work at every turn.

CHAPTER 26

Down the Hall

Five colorful rooms down the hall, Ward Stoner also lay on his hospital bed, itching for release. A young doctor with dark hair and large glasses came in. He was tall, with down-turned lips that made him appear to wear a perpetual frown.

"Hey, Doc, when do I get out of here?" Stoner barked as usual.

"Mr. Stoner—"

"That's Chief Inspector young man."

Doctor Martinez's expression didn't change. "There are no inspectors in here, just doctors and patients."

Instantly, Stoner came up on his elbow and glared into the physician's eyes. "Mister, wherever I am, there are only Inspectors and suspects."

"I'm under suspicion for what?" the doctor managed to raise one eyebrow.

"For being arrogant," Stoner snapped back. "Now, discharge me, or I'll walk out on my own recognizance."

The doctor rolled his eyes. "You're not posting bail, Sir."

"No, but you will be if I don't get out of here soon." The veins in his forehead bulged and his eyes grew large.

"Well, well what's all the yelling about," Chalky Boone called out as she breezed into the room.

"I am not yelling," Stoner bellowed.

"Then protest at a lower decibel, please," she said as she smiled. Turning to the doctor she added, "Could I please talk to the Inspector—alone?"

"My time—"

Stoner looked at him beneath hooded eyes. "Your time is no more important than my time, Doctor."

Dr. Martinez only stared for a moment and then added, "I have to see a patient across the hall. I can be back in five minutes."

"And charge them for a visit, I'm sure," Stoner sneered.

Dr. Martinez only smiled in his unique, starched way.

Stoner didn't look at his lieutenant, but he directed his question in a mellow tone. "What are you doing here?"

"Nice of you to ask," she said and smiled. "I'm here to check up on you and see how long the doctor thinks it will be before you can get out of here."

"If you can get that information, you're a better man than I."

Chalky's cheeks flared. "In case you haven't noticed, I'm not a man."

"Oh, I noticed," Ward said as he allowed his fingertips to touch Chalky's hand. A warm silence, like an August breeze, filled the room.

She placed her hand on top of his. "Ward, really, how are you feeling?"

"Did you change the subject for a reason?" He said and actually smiled—something he rarely did unless his son Christopher was around.

Flustered, she babbled as she smiled. Embarrassed, she turned away. "No, no—of course not. I just—"

"I know—I haven't been very warm and friendly, let alone—"

"Warm and friendly?" she said as she whirled back to face him, although she seemed unable to look into his eyes. "No—no one could accuse you of being friendly. But—Ward," she groped for words that didn't seem to flow freely. "I don't know what I'm allowed to say." Her hands were shaking and tears gathering in the corners of her eyes.

"Allowed to say? Chalky, you've never needed permission to say what you're thinking." Ward reached for her hand again.

"About work, yeah, but—Ward—never about anything personal." She permitted him to take her hand in his and not pull away.

"Can we change that rule?" he asked, still mellow even when the doctor came back in the room. "Ah, the great healer." He actually smiled.

Dr. Martinez stopped in full stride. "Well, it sounds like you're feeling better."

"I am," Stoner stated as politely as he could. "So, when can I expect to get out of here?"

"I will sign you out now," he said as he pulled a pen from his lab jacket pocket. "The wound is healing nicely and your blood count is good. If you take it easy," he stopped and looked hard at the Inspector, "and I do mean easy, light desk work only, you should be okay. Check in with your doctor at home."

"Yes, Sir," Ward said and saluted. "Boone," he barked in his usual way. "Make flight arrangements for us. We're going home."

CHAPTER 27

Escape

My grandfather was still a little weak, but with Grand-mère's help and coaching, we were able to arrive at the flash-train station twenty minutes before departure.

Grand-père's eyes brightened when he saw Jason and I prepare to board with them. "You two are going to take the train with us?"

"Oliver, I told your physician I would travel with you. So—here we are. We hired more bodyguards. They'll travel in the next car. Ivy and Raymar will be with us."

I tried to joke and treat all that had happened with some humor. "You certainly didn't think I would let you two go by train with Jason while I flew home, did you?" I said, but inside I knew the danger Grand-père had been in, that we all had been in. "This is a family trip back to the Central Zone. I even brought some cards—if you want to play."

"Maybe, Sweetheart," Grand-mère patted my hand after I helped her up the train steps.

I noticed Raymar's usual constant hyper-vigilance. This time it made me feel safe. Ivy scanned the front and back of the car, apparently checking each exit.

As we walked through the passenger car I studied each face and wondered if any of those on board were a further danger to Grand-père. I had to be vigilant and not worry at the same time. How was I going to do that?

The porter directed us to a private car much the same as the one Jason and I took to El Paso. "Here we are, Sir Richly," he said as he opened the door and carried in a pitcher of water which he placed on a side bar. "The glasses are there for your use," he pointed to the gleaming glass shelves behind the bar.

"Thank you," Grand-père said and reached in his pocket to tip the man.

"No, Sir," the porter said as he put up his hand to decline the gratuity. "I don't have extra money to contribute to your election campaign, but I can help by serving you at my pleasure."

I saw Grand-père look at the porter's name plate. "Thank you, Ronald." He patted the man's shoulder. "I really appreciate it."

Ronald smiled broadly. "It is the least I can do for freedom's sake."

"It sounds like the most you can do," I suggested. "And, we do appreciate it."

We settled into the comfortably sleek, poly-infused sawdust framed chairs, the same as in the south-bound car a few days past. Ivy sat off to the side. She seemed to be with us and on guard at the same time. Raymar was silent and sat at the bar. We were all quiet, almost like we were afraid to speak for fear the peaceful moment would go away. At least, that was my experience.

"What is our next event?" Grand-père asked. "I've been a little tied up."

"Oh, Oliver," Grand-mère moaned. "That was awful."

"Sorry about that," Grand-père said as he grinned, seeming to return gradually to his former jovial self.

I glanced at my 281 Palm device. "You've missed several rallies, but that couldn't be helped." I felt my head begin to pound from the stress of the last days. I rubbed my forehead and closed my eyes.

"Headache?" Jason asked. "Go over to the sink at the bar and run your hands under the cold water like Dr. Raddin suggested. Then come back over here, sit by me and close your eyes for a while."

"That sounds like a great idea," Grand-mère agreed. "We should all rest and start again in a little while."

Ivy crossed her arms and settled in with a healthy measure of alertness. "I'll keep my eyes open for all of you," she offered.

I did as instructed. Raymar ran the water for me until it was icy cold. He put his fingers under the stream and nodded in his silent way. Putting my hands under the frigid water, I held them there until I could no longer take the cold. When I pulled them back, my fingernails were purple.

"My head does feel a little better," I admitted and let Raymar dry my hands with a towel made warm in a special small heater mounted on the wall. When I went back over to where we were all sitting, I snuggled up in the chair beside Jason. Leaning back, I let my feet lift off the floor as I cozied into a tranquil space in my head.

A few hundred miles passed in a streak. I kept my eyes closed, hoping I wouldn't disturb anyone else if I stirred.

Suddenly, our whole world was shattered. Tossed out of my chair, legs and arms flew around me by the percussion created by a large impact. We were on the floor but the floor wasn't where it belonged. We were more on the side or wall than down. I heard the moans of my loved ones around me and smelled the distinct odor of sweet hot metal. The ssss of hissing steam came rushing into my awareness.

"Out!" I shouted with the small amount of voice and breath I could rouse. "Get out! Smoke!"

"Christy?" Jason whispered with a faint raspy voice. "What happened?"

"I don't know," I said as I tried to clear my head. "But, it sounds like something is still escaping. It smells like gunpowder or dynamite, as my books described it. There's also something leaking. Maybe gas but I can't smell it."

"I know," Jason said as he tried to standup in the tilted train car. "The odor of gunpowder is overpowering. I learned to identify it in medical school. We'd better get out of here just in case something blows."

Ivy shook her head and pawed at the air for something to grab hold of. Finding the edge of a chair, she pulled herself up and quickly checked for her firearm.

"My grandparents?" I gasped, realizing that I hadn't heard their voices.

Then, I heard Grand-mère's voice first. "We're here, Christy." She was silent for a second. "Oliver, are you all right?"

"Yes, Connie," he groaned. "This sure has been a challenging trip."

"Okay," Jason said urgently, "let's get out of here, but be careful. Where you step may not be where it's safe to place your foot. We seem to be tipped over."

I struggled to my feet and worried about my dear ones. How were we going to get them safely out with everything on its side?

"Grand-père, can you stand?" He was not only my beloved grandfather he was the candidate for president in the *1787-Constitutionalists* party. I was overwhelmed.

Grand-mère's voice was both loving and insistent. "Oliver, you must stand so you can help me get up."

"Coming dear," he agreed as he struggled to his feet.

The hissing sound had increased. I looked at Jason and Ivy. They both nodded. Raymar tilted his head like an animal stretching his senses beyond their range.

"Let's move out of the train—" Jason began and seemed to be searching for words. "They will have to get this car, and maybe many cars, back on the track. We might be able to help others who are struggling, so, let's hurry."

I looped my arm around both grandparents as they wrestled with upturned chairs and broken glass. Jason shepherded all three of us as we groped our way toward any outside opening we could find. Ivy went ahead of us with her firearm ready. Raymar, as usual, fell in behind, protecting all of us from anyone or anything that might approach us from the rear. The door at the side-end of the car would have opened out to the entry but it was now on the bottom of the upturned railcar. Our next hope for escape was a window. I wondered if we could push one of the tempered panes out. We had to do something. I could hear shouting coming from other cars.

"Listen," Grand-père said as he stopped and listened.

"Screaming," Grand-mère agreed.

"No," he insisted. "I heard gun fire."

Ivy didn't look back but added, "I heard it too, Oliver," she said. "Let's just keep looking for a way out."

"Here, Ivy," Jason shouted. "I think we can break this window out." Immediately, he pulled himself upside down by the decorative bars that flanked the window and began to kick at the shatterproof glass. When it popped out, he stuck his head up through the opening.

Crack!

"Jason, no," I screamed. "Get down!" When I heard the sound of the same round that had pierced the window of Campaign Headquarters I began to panic.

Ivy grabbed his pant legs and pulled him down. "You're struck," she said calmly while her eyes scanned the opening created by the kicked out window.

I felt sick. Blood was dripping down Jason's forehead and soaking into his shirt.

"Christy," Ivy spoke firmly. "See if there is any water still in the sink pipes and a clean towel. Then she grabbed my arm, "Christy—he'll be okay if the wound is cleaned right away."

Jason patted my arm. "She's right, Honey. Get a couple of clean, wet towels and one to pat the wound dry."

"I'll help you," Raymar volunteered.

"What happened out there?" Grand-père demanded. "What in the world is going on—again?"

"Someone doesn't want you to be the new president," Ivy stated flatly.

I was trembling but had to help clean Jason's wound as he asked. The bar was lying on the end of the car. "I hope I can drain out some water," I said aloud and then wished I had been silent. I had to stay strong for everyone, or at least appear strong. I was so afraid, I didn't know if I could convince myself. We were all in serious jeopardy. If we didn't know who was firing at us, how could we stay safe?

With a towel bunched up under the faucet, Raymar turned the faucet handle. I held my breath. A stream of cool water flowed out and soaked the cloth so much I had to gather another clean towel beneath it.

Ivy blotted the towel on Jason's head with the rest of the cleansing water, in obvious haste. Finally, Raymar gathered up the wet cloths and tossed them in the corner.

"Okay," Ivy announced with a firm booming voice. "We need another quick plan."

Grand-père climbed over the chairs and fallen table. "We had just passed over a bridge just before the dynamite and crash." He looked back and forth along the side of the car but there was no way to see out. "It just might be—." He hurried into the lavatory at what had been the back of the car and forced the folding door open. "Yes!" he shouted. "All of you come here quickly."

We all crowded into the small bathroom, just large enough for a stool and corner positioned sink. We all looked up.

"Don't look up," he insisted. "Look down!"

Beneath our feet, the scene from the overturned window, the one that would have been on the north side of the car, was now of the tracks and the river below. "We're still over the bridge. I knew it. Force that window open, if you can Raymar."

Raymar squeezed into the tiny room and studied it quickly. "I think it will just open, since there's no pressure from below holding it closed." He quickly slid the sash to the side. The aroma of gun-powder, mingled with the peaceful sound of river birds, drifted into the car.

"Quick—down and out," Ivy threw up an arm to block our path. "You'll have to drop into the water. Can anyone not swim?"

"We have all been swimming all of our lives," Grand-mère reported. "How about you Jason? Raymar?"

"Sure, I can swim," Jason agreed. Raymar, the quiet one, nodded in agreement.

Oliver looked at my grandmother and then at me. "Jason, you'll have to jump in first, then Connie, and then you, Christy, so you can both help your grandmother if necessary. Then Ivy, because she has the gun—then I'll jump."

"It all sounds good except the last part," Ivy said. "Oliver you go before me, just in case someone storms into this car."

"No—"

"Yes," Ivy insisted firmly. Her tone indicated no compromise.

"Go Jason, fast," Ivy pushed. "Christy—Ma'am," she called out as the next jumper stepped up.

Raymar, then Grand-père followed in a matter of seconds. Ivy dropped in last. The water was warm, but we all splashed wildly, probably from the shock of jumping and hitting the water from high over the river.

"Swim!" Ivy ordered. "To the opposite shore," she redirected.

"Oliver," Jason said as he swam beside my grandfather. "I'll swim with you, and Christy will swim with Connie. Raymar and Ivy will pull back-up detail."

We splashed and swam and made our way to the shore. It wasn't far, but after the crash our energy had drained from our bodies. As least, mine had. I hoped no one had seen us escape. If they had seen us jump in, they could be waiting for us when we waded out of the water.

As we neared the opposite edge, we came up in the shadows under the bridge. Panting and panicked, we looked at each other for any stress and obvious reassurance.

Jason went over to Grand-père, lifted his wrist and took his pulse. "I think we're pretty good, considering all." Shaking his head and smiling, he added, "Oliver, you are amazing."

"And, to think," Grand-mère chimed in, "they wanted to do us in over a year ago. They said we were too old to live."

"How about you, Connie?" Jason asked as he reached over to check her pulse as well. Then he reported, "You two are unbelievable."

"Maybe we should be safe and call Dr. Raddin and report in," Grand-mère suggested. "I know you're okay Oliver, but I'd feel better if we told her about all of this."

"No," Ivy snapped. "We don't know who else knew that the presidential candidate was on the flash-train, but we do know Dr. Raddin knew it. She's the one who suggested it."

"Ivy," I gasped, "you don't suspect the physician of anything do you? How could she have caused a train wreck?"

"I don't like to think about it either, Christy," Jason stated. "But, our main concern is for our safety. We're soaked. We'll have to find dry clothes as soon as possible."

"We can't all go into the stores," Ivy stated emphatically. "Oliver, I am sure your poster is all over town. It pops up on mass communication screens every fifteen minutes. But, no one will recognize me. The village is right over there, past the bridge." She turned in the direction of town. "I'll go buy all of us some clothes. You might have to wear wet shoes. If I bought six pairs of shoes, it would be too obvious that we just walked out of the river."

"Okay," I agreed. But, inside I was scared, for myself and for my loved ones. If I couldn't trust Dr. Raddin, I doubted my ability to know who to trust.

Ivy looked around the side of the bridge abutment again. "It looks like the building on the left side of the street, just over the bridge, is empty. Make your way there, one or two at a time. I'll bring the clothes there."

"All right," both of my grandparents responded in unison.

When Ivy left, I suddenly felt cold, vulnerable. Maybe my helplessness was because she had taken the sidearm that protected us all with her. I had seen pictures of guns in the books I had read, but had never seen one in person. Could the very idea of a firearm make me feel safe?

Jason took my hand and massaged the soft spot between my thumb and index finger. I felt some warmth return and began to feel safe again. Holding my hand tightly, he stretched up tall and looked past the bridge. "It looks safe—but then, we thought the train would be safe too."

Grand-père squared his shoulders and reached out for Grand-mère's hand. "Connie, hold your head up high. Walk with dignity and not like your drawers are soaked."

We all laughed as they started up the little hill to the pavement. I counted to twenty. Jason kissed me and, with my hand still in his, we walked up the little embankment to the street above. There was much more traffic on the road in that little village than in Capitol City, where few people owned their own cars. We cautiously darted across the street, walked casually along the sidewalk, then slipped in through the worn, faded door that Grand-père had left ajar.

Inside, the large, empty room was dark. I hate dim, dark places and have a need to shine light on it all. A few paces more and we stepped into a room with a wall of large windows. The sun was shining brightly in there, creating a greenhouse effect. My grandparents were standing in the brightest sunrays, hugging and rubbing warmth into each other's backs with gentle strokes, like kittens warming themselves in the sun. It was almost like scenes from years past, so familiar to me, of Grand-père protecting Grand-mère and she nurturing him.

Soon, Raymar slipped in the door. He said nothing but began the restless and stealthy prowl he always exercised in new spaces.

Raymar was the same as always. I wondered if life in general would ever be the same as before for him or for any of us. But then, maybe the same is not what was best either. I didn't want to go back to a life without feelings. And, Raymar would not have wanted to go back into the hills and forests and live as a hollow man, with anger as his only emotion. To feel, to love, to be free to make our own choices requires a lot in return. The past was free from concern, by being free from fully living. I was learning that true freedom costs a very high price.

CHAPTER 28

Worn-In

It seemed like hours, but it really wasn't. Ivy came into our little hothouse with bags of clothing within a half-hour.

"There was a re-sale shop up the street so I got our things there." She stopped with a sheepish expression on her face. "I am so sorry to give you used clothing, but I thought there would be fewer questions at the Worn-In Shop," she apologized.

"Not worn-out—worn-in," Grand-mère mused. "I like that," she added and reached out her hand. "I'll be very happy to wear them."

"You've given so many clothes to the needy," I reminded her. "Now you get to be the one on the receiving end."

"I couldn't be more blessed," Grand-mère said as she smiled. She took the clothes and stepped into the next room.

"Thank you, Ivy." I too was thankful for dry clothes and joined my grandmother in our private changing room of pealing walls and the stench of rat dropping.

"Isn't the boudoir lovely?" my gracious grandmother said as she waved her arms around like a model displaying her products.

I changed quickly, zipped up my pants and smoothed my hair with my fingers. "That's the best I can do."

"You look lovely as always, dear."

"You're just saying that because we're related and any comeliness may be inherited," I teased.

"You're right on that, Christy," Grand-père agreed as we came out of our "fancy" changing room.

Jason and Raymar looked dry at a minimum. On the other hand, "interesting" may better describe their appearance. Their clothing was so miss-matched I wondered if their strange attire would soon give us away.

"I'm not saying you two look bad, but Jason if you and Raymar would switch shirts you would look less like escaped prison inmates who had just stole clothes off a clothes line," I offered as a strong suggestion.

"A clothes line?" Ivy questioned.

"We still hang our clothes to dry on a rope stretched between two trees out in the mountains," Raymar said quietly. "Hence—a clothes line."

Ivy smiled briefly at all of us. "Clothes line is it?" Then her expression fell as she addressed the serious issue at hand. "We'll have to keep moving—fast. They must have discovered by now that Oliver escaped."

I sighed and resigned myself to the situation we were in. "Actually, for one minute, I had forgotten about all of that."

"A nice vacation from the mess of our new reality," Jason sighed as he put his arm around my waist and squeezed.

"While I was out," Ivy began as she pulled hats out of another sack, "I contacted Barbara Cornwall. She was the only one I could think of with the financial means to help us out of this—and someone we can trust."

"And?" I asked. I hadn't thought about how we were stuck in the empty building. The walls had seemed like a solution. Now they were part of the problem. Once we would go outside, we would be at risk of capture again.

"Obviously, she can't send an airplane from New York in time to get us out of this one."

"Therefore?" I asked again.

Ivy looked around at each of us "She has business connections here in New Mexico. A helicopter can land on the roof of this building in twenty minutes."

Jason's eyes snapped to attention and studied Ivy hard. "She has a business relationship with people down here?"

Ivy nodded. "Yes, that's right."

"I imagine she has business contacts all over the country," Grand-père added.

Suddenly, I knew what Jason was getting at. "The head of the New York mafia, Alister Bedlum and his ancestors have done business in New Mexico for nearly two centuries. The mob seemed to like the idea of rubbing shoulders with the ghost of Billy the Kid. It somehow gave them power by association. Ivy, the mafia bosses? That's Barbara's family."

"But Christy," Grand-mère protested. "You said that Barbara is a true patriot. She wants to blot out the mistakes and mayhem caused by her father and all the Bedlum fathers in the past."

"I know—I know." None of it made any sense to me either.

"Christy," Jason reminded me, "that has been Barbara's problem all of her life—living down the sins of her father. Her mother has to be in hiding from him."

"You're right," I agreed.

"Christy," Grand-père came over and put his arms around me. "There comes a time when we could run out of friends if we begin to trust no one."

Raymar had been silent, but he too had sat around the table at the Citadel in New York City. He had an animal's sense of danger and the intuition to identify a friend. "Barbara Cornwall is a good woman," he stated decidedly.

I heard the quiet whir of a six-blade helicopter overhead and realized that Jason, Grand-père and Raymar Goring were all correct. "Okay, we take the flight home. I'll trust again."

Ivy snapped her fingers. "Listen up. I don't know how much time we have, but I'll just say—very little. While you all changed out of those wet clothes, I poked around for another way out. It appears that this building had been an old furniture factory. There are huge freight elevators in the center of the building. The elevators operated on electricity. There are also smaller lifts that operate manually, like old dumb-waiter systems, used to move small amounts of goods and material from one floor to another."

I felt a surge of hope creep up from the center of my being. "Dumb waiters don't need electricity or other means of energy?"

"Just muscle," Ivy said. "We can manually pull the ropes and lift each other to the roof." She clapped her hands together. "Now, let's get at it."

We quickly fell in line behind her and followed as she led us to the center of the building. She lifted a three by four foot door in the wall and stepped aside. "We'll have to have the women go first because we'll need the men's upper-body strength below to lift the men last."

"What about the last man?" I asked. "Who will get him out?"

"Oliver and I can pull Jason out last from above," Ivy said as she motioned for Grand-mère to crawl up into the little lift.

"No," Raymar countered, "I will go last. I can shinny up the rope on my own if I have to. I do it all the time back home."

"Thank you, Raymar," Ivy said as she patted him on his back. Turning to my grandmother she said, "I guess I'm most worried about you, Connie."

My grandmother looked at me and winked. At seventy-five years old, she and Grand-père still danced together, walked several miles daily and ran up and down their stairs at home many times a day. Preparing to crawl into the lift, she stepped on Jason's knee as he knelt on the other, grabbed hold of the inner top of the lift and pulled herself up and into the small space of the dumb waiter. She crawled around on her knees, turned and sat down on the floor of the lift with a big smile on her face.

"Fantastic!" I yelled and gave her a big thumbs-up. "You showed us how to do it Grand-mère."

One by one we slipped into the little cubby and rose to the roof. Lastly, Raymar grabbed the rope, and hand-over-hand he lifted himself to the tar paper covered flat area above. A large copter waited on top with the blades till spinning. We crouched, hurried to the open door and quickly boarded. Before we could lift off, the sound of bullet fire shattered the sky.

"Close the door!" the piolet shouted.

Ivy slammed it close. It was easier to hear without the sound of the motors from outside. "The sides and glass are bullet proof," she assured us.

Ting, ting—two more rounds glanced off the hull. I held my breath as we lifted off and rose into the sky, first a few feet, then, the copter became God's might hand, snatching us up to Heaven. I exhaled.

CHAPTER 29

Still late June 2114

The helicopter was flying high, far above any ability for gun fire to pierce the cabin. I felt relieved for the moment. The sky was a color of blue rarely seen on the ground where a canopy of clouds blocked the beauty overhead. I couldn't help wonder what else would happen before Election Day.

November 3, 2114 was a little over four months away when our great country would vote for a new president. We had been living under a quasi-right-of-succession to the presidency, not under constitutional law, just a ruling-class decision of what they thought was best for the "little people." People we talked to were excited about the election, but I wondered how much they really knew about any of it, the election process or even their own rights as citizens.

"I am way out of the stream of things," Grand-père admitted. "I have no idea what our next political event is."

"The dates are a little tentative," I told him. "You were missing and we had no idea when—or if you would be found," I answered cautiously and studied his face. "You do know the danger you were in don't you?"

Grand-père scratched his head. "Yes—in retrospect I do. Drugged when they grabbed me, I remained under the influence of chemicals the entire time. Now, hearing all you have told me, I see I was in a lot of danger."

"Oh, Oliver," Grand-mère whispered as she linked her arm in his, "you could have died."

"But, I didn't Connie," he said as he patted her hand.

Raymar sat in hyper-aware silence then asked, "Did you see their faces when they first took you?"

My grandfather's face grew taut and an unfamiliar scowl crossed his face. "No—none." His brow furrowed, "But—dots. I saw three dots on a man's hand, between his thumb and forefinger. It looked like they were punctured into the skin with ink."

"Tattoos," I gasped when my words tumbled out of my mouth.

"Tattoos?" Ivy asked. "What are tattoos?"

Raymar rolled up the sleeve of his T-shirt. An angel, drawn in blue and white ink with outstretched wings, descended from his shoulder to about four inches above his elbow. "This brand on my arm distinguishes the hollow people who want good for our people and those who just want to destroy everything in their path."

"Raymar," I said as I lightly touched the drawing, "I had no idea."

Jason studied the ink carefully. "Does anyone ever get infection from the punctures?" Rubbing his fingers over the emblem he added, "It looks like tiny puncture wounds."

"They are Dr. O'Reilly," Raymar said with a slight smile. "Yes, you didn't ask, but, yes—they do hurt as the needles go in, but we don't get infected. Infection is prevented with the reintroduction of the old medication, mercurochrome."

"Mercurochrome?" Jason asked in surprise? "Where could you have possibly gotten mercurochrome? The government banned it over a century ago. The mercury can be deadly."

Raymar smiled again. "There is an old hospital, buried now in the bramble and overgrowth near the foot of the mountains I lived in. In the old pharmacy, I found medication, bandages, and splints—all of the things my people have needed."

"But Raymar, some of those medications would have expired," Jason's eyes were wide. He appeared startled.

Raymar pulled his shirt sleeve back into place. "It was our belief that expired medication was better than none at all."

Jason shook his head. "Not always."

Raymar sat back and closed his eyes. "Then, the spirit that hovered over the valley beneath us and whistled in the caves we sought shelter in, surely must have been with us."

"So—" Grand-mère drew out slowly, "the three tattooed dots represented something to the evil ones who captured you. Some sort of club or fraternity."

I didn't like the sound or idea of a fraternity, as if the gangsters who kidnapped my grandfather were just young men interested in an education and a good time. But, there was something I could do.

"I'll contact Marge Cummings at the library and see if she can find out something for us." I checked Holly for the time in Capitol City. "Marge will be there. Maybe we'll have an answer by the time we get home." I pulled my 281 Palm Device from my pocket. "I hope the river water didn't damage it," I said holding it up to the light. Instantly, I brought Marge's hologram into the helicopter's cabin.

"Hi everyone," Marge shouted out with enthusiasm. "I hadn't heard back from you Christy, but the news has already broken that Sir Richly was rescued."

"The news?" Grand-père shouted. "They knew about my abduction?"

"Yes and no," Marge began. "They found out that you had been missing, at the same time they learned you had been rescued."

"Oh, good," Grand-père said with a deep sigh. "People may have doubted the strength of my campaign if they had heard that I was only taken."

Jason nodded in agreement. "And, if they found out there was no trace to your whereabouts."

I shuddered at the thought. "The story now comes from a position of strength. Even though you were taken, you're coming out as a superhero that broke free from your captors and captured them in the process."

"Wow," Grand-mère grinned, "I've been living with Superman and didn't even know it." She grinned sheepishly. "Well, maybe I suspected it when I would occasionally hear the telephone booth door fly open."

All of us who had access to books, films and graphic novels laughed; Marge joined in on the stress-relieving fun. I felt a moment of relaxation. "Ivy, I'll loan you my stash of comic books."

"Comic books?" Ivy asked.

Raymar smiled. "You'd be surprised at what we found in the old hospital."

"No, I wouldn't," Jason joined in. "I have an old wing of a hospital too, with a well shelved library."

"Marge," I got serious again, "I need some research."

"I would be honored to help," she agreed.

"Marge, Oliver here," Grand-père chimed in. "I saw three marks on one of my captors. Raymar Goring here tells us it's a tattoo and has a special meaning."

"Robert Gross is there with you?" she asked with the enthusiasm of a reader encountering her favorite author.

"Yes, Ma'am," Raymar laughed. "I'm here, too." Then, he quickly rerouted the conversation back to the need for research. "Marge, we need some information on a very small but unique tattoo."

"Yes, my friend," Grand-père leaned forward and rested his forearms on his knees. "The tattoo consisted of three equally spaced dots, in triangular formation, inked into the soft spot between his thumb and index finger."

"Okay, I'll get right on it," she agreed. "Anything else? I am here to serve you."

"Thanks, Marge," I added. "Get back to us when you know something."

"Agreed." Her hologram dissolved leaving the cabin dim again.

We were all quiet except for the silent hum of deep thoughts that screamed in my ears. The energy level was mounting as strained energy erupted.

"I'm going to be grandma to all of you now," Grand-mère spoke softly. "I know we are all wound up, but like old watches our mainsprings will snap if we don't unwind a little." She smoothed her hair and leaned over on my grandfather's shoulder. "Let's try to rest. There will be plenty to do when we get home."

"Once we pull into Capitol City and gather again around our table in Oakwood, we'll have to hit the ground running," Grand-père added.

Each person settled into their own comfortable spot. I leaned back into the seat and curled myself into the cozy security of Jason's shoulder. I felt at home there and in a foreign land at the same time. How long had it been since Jason and I had been able to snuggle up together? It didn't matter that I understood the reasons for our growing distance. We had both been through so much and we went through it all, right out in the middle of the action, with no privacy.

He wrapped his arms around me and pulled me close. I felt safe for the moment but—there was something so different. His skin still smelled like expensive men's cologne but now, mixed with river water and the stale odor of used clothing, it was different. In his arms, he felt like a familiar stranger. Had we left our relationship wilt from lack of time just for us? Would we be able to nurture what had started to grow, or was it too late? Maybe the roots had not run deep enough to stand strong during the hard times. As I pressed deeper into Jason's arm, I wondered and worried before I finally gave up and fell asleep.

CHAPTER 30

Doubt

It was so good to be back home. And yet, home was different, smaller than I had remembered. Jason and I had been from one coast to the other and states and their zones in between. Now, we were enjoying the warm July day, with the sky so blue it took my breath away. Summer flowers bloomed everywhere in the town square and around the parameter of the gazebo. How could I put my finger on the difference, when it had no name and resisted description? It just was. Ever since Grand-père's kidnapping; my being the target of a gunman; our train wreck; and our escape by jumping into the river, my safe and same world was shattered.

Jason had picked me up at the Indian River Apartments and we rode the few miles to Oakwood, to my grandparents' home, mostly in silence.

"What's wrong, Honey?" Jason asked as he pulled up in front of Grand-père's house with its wonderful large porch. "You've been so quiet."

How could I tell him how I really felt? "I don't know," was all I could say. I was telling the truth. I didn't know myself what was wrong, or if anything was. Things had changed. Jason seemed distant, or I was the one who was distant from him. I didn't know that either.

"Do I need to worry? Is there something wrong—with *us?*" he asked as he took my hand.

"Us? Are we an 'us?' We haven't talked about you and me for a long time, Jason." I didn't physically pull away but felt withdrawn within myself.

Jason released my hand and looked out of the window. "I guess I assumed—" his voice sounded heavy and hurt like it came from a place inside him I hadn't heard before.

"Christy!" Grand-mère called from the wide front porch. "Hurry, we're about to begin." She waved her large white apron at us. "Your grandfather just took steaks off the grill."

"Steak? Wow! I think Rachel Claudette must have inspired your menu," I said as Jason and I got out and walked up to the house.

My conversation with Jason stopped. But, deep inside, I had so many questions—so many things I needed to sort out. My internal conversation had only gotten started. But, it would have to wait.

Grand-mère shepherded us up the steps and into the house with a wave of that apron. "There's a lovely salad and cookies for dessert."

"Sounds wonderful, Connie," Jason said as we walked through the entry and living room.

The chairs around the table in my grandparents' dining room were full of friends and family. Ivy and Raymar sat beside my parents, then Jason and I. Sean McDermott. Carl and Silvia Brunner and their son Michael were opposite us, with my grandparents at the head and foot of the table. Everyone seemed to be in their place. However, one chair was empty beside Michael.

"Ah, the last one," Grand-mère announced as she jumped up when the doorbell rang.

"Who else?" I asked. As I turned, I saw a stooped and shuffling Silas Drummond drag into the dining room. His eyes were dull and sharply etched lines dug into his face.

"Silas!" I was shocked and could not hide it. "Are you well?"

"Yes, Christy, yes, I'm fine," he answered slipping into the empty chair across from me.

When Grand-père announced that he would offer prayer, Jason reached for me. His hand felt warm in mine. When everyone else had their head bowed, I watched Jason. He finally opened one eye and winked. As Grand-père said, "Amen," Jason squeezed my fingers gently. I felt my cheeks grow warm and rosy. I wondered if anyone else noticed. What was going on with me?

"Oliver," Silvia's eyes sparkled with wonder, "these steaks look great. I know the food police don't patrol in Oakwood, so we're all safe. We haven't had steak at our house in months. Carl is on a chicken binge."

Raymar didn't look up from his plate, but cut his meat, placed a forkful is his mouth and closed his eyes in a swoon. "It is very good, Sir." He sliced slowly into the meat again and watched the juices run onto his plate. "We are used to eating berries and fruit in the forest and mountains, and what rabbits we can catch."

"Even Robert Gross?" I asked without thinking.

"Yes," he answered as he looked up, "Robert Gross has been locked in the body of the hollow one, Raymar Goring, all of his life."

I wished I hadn't spoken so quickly. "I'm sorry Raymar. I don't know what's wrong with me lately."

Smiling at me, he waved his hand before cutting into his steak again. "There's nothing wrong, Christy. You have honored me over and over." He stuck his fork into the meat and popped the piece in his mouth.

Silas cut his meat but then pushed the bites around on his plate and sighed. His arms rested on the edge of the table and his fork seemed heavy in his hand.

"We can begin our meeting while we eat," Grand-père started.

"Oh, Oliver," Grand-mère interrupted, "we have all been through so much. Can't we just have a nice meal?"

The corners of Grand-père's mouth turned up slightly. "Well, okay. We'll begin in—" he checked his timepiece, "thirty minutes." He looked at Grand-mère as he glanced up from his plate. "Is that enough rest, Connie?"

"Actually, no," she stated firmly. "But, I'll take what I can get." Then she laughed a little and we all joined in. Grand-mère had a way of taking a rough situation and smoothing out the wrinkles.

• • •

Jason and I helped by clearing the dishes as Grand-mère refilled the coffee cups. There was no more stalling. We had to get back to the work at hand, electing a new president. Strangely, I didn't have the same fire for the election as I had before Grand-père's kidnapping. It all seemed mechanical, like I was just going through the motions.

Judge Brunner began the meeting. "It goes without saying that we are all happy that Oliver is back, safe and unharmed." He looked around at all of us. "The report said that all of you were in danger. Even Inspector Stoner was shot trying to find you and in pursuit of those who kidnapped you, Oliver."

"We haven't had any news about him," I stepped in. "How is he doing?"

Carl rolled his eyes. "The acting Blue Guard leader told me that the Inspector is back in Capitol City. He'll rest a few days and then return to the office."

"A few days?" I gasped. "How will he be able to return to work in a few days if he was shot?"

"Well Christy," the judge said looking straight at me. "Stoner is alive partly because of you."

"Because of me?" I blurted out loud. "I thought he was shot because of me."

"Lieutenant Boone said she heard of your healings and experienced your touch when you stopped the hemorrhaging in your own shoulder," Carl began. "So, when Stoner was shot, she prayed and then put her fingers in his wound and stopped the bleeding, as she believed you had done. So the Inspector didn't have to recover from blood loss, just the wound."

I was stunned. "What a blessing," I whispered. But, deep inside it was almost more information than I could take in. Good and bad bits and pieces piled on my shoulders until I felt weighted down under it all. Jason reached over and took my hand again.

"As for the election—" Carl pulled a leather bound notebook from under some other papers on the table and opened it. "We just rolled into July the other day. There are four months left until the election."

"Rallies, debates, town hall meetings, and a lot of ground work shaking hands, meeting people and answering questions," I sighed. "Will you have enough energy for it all Grand-père?"

Jason leaned on the table. "We'll have to plan a lot of rest into the schedule." He smiled at my grandfather. "If you will follow medical advice, you should do okay. Rest, then talk, then rest again. No one should even be aware of your down time. Politicians for generations have had to pace themselves."

I wondered aloud, "The people know he was kidnapped and that we had to escape from the wreckage of the train. What has been their reaction?"

"We're not sure about all of that," Carl responded with a frown. "We know the mass media had gotten hold of the story, but after first posting it, the information outlets went black. That may mean that someone has blocked more information from getting out. On the other hand, if we pose the question to the people at town hall meetings, we've already told them what happened. Will Oliver sound stronger if we don't say much about it? It's tricky."

Sean pulled some newspapers from his large brief case. "Oliver, if you notice these last four or five papers, I haven't expanded the details about the recent events in your lives beyond the initial public notification. I assure you, no one has gotten to me. I simply thought the information about your kidnapping would have suggested a weakness in your campaign and perhaps endangered your lives even more. The public had a right to know the event happened. I will not be a part of making Oliver look weak, however."

"And, their escape would indicate strength," Carl added. "So you made sure that was reported. Good."

"I say we go with the truth," I suggested. "If we get ahead of the story with complete details, we can present it all from a position of strength."

As we told Sean the entire story, he jotted down many notes about the kidnapping and escape. "This is amazing, Oliver," he said. Then he added, "I'll get it all in the next issue if that is your desire."

"Go with it," my grandfather stated with a pound of his fist on the table.

Grand-mère twisted her napkin between her fingers. "How do we make sure the visual media won't get their version of the story out first and twist it another way?"

Sean looked up and shrugged. "How would they possibly know that I'm going to run the story? And, how and where would they get the details?"

Bam, bam, bam—someone banged on the front door. I jumped and my skin crawled. Confused by the reaction of those around the table, I saw that they were amused.

"Stoner," they all laughed out loud.

Neither startled nor amused, Silas's lack of reaction shocked me. His expression was so flat, I couldn't stop watching him.

Grand-mère jumped up and hurried to the door, but Stoner had already walked in. I heard my grandmother's usual gracious welcome. "Inspector, it's good to see you are able to get out and about."

"And why not?" he bellowed.

She smiled sweetly and led him into the dining room. "Well, with having been shot and all."

His eyes scanned those present at the table. "Oh yes, that."

Jason stood up and brought over another chair that sat beside the antique buffet hutch. "Here you are Inspector. Have a seat."

"I do not need to sit down," Stoner growled.

Grand-mère placed a cup on the table in front of him and started filling it. "You'll be more comfortable while you drink your coffee if you'll sit."

Stoner rolled his eyes. "Yes, Ma'am."

No one said a word but in my mind I thought, *Grand-mère can charm anyone.*

Jason actually reached out and patted Stoner's shoulder. "We're all glad you're healing, Inspector."

Stoner stared into his cup for a second, then mumbled, "Thank you."

Grand-père cleared his throat. "To what do we owe this visit?"

"Sorry," Stoner blustered as he placed his cup on the saucer. "You weren't kidnapped in my zone, but you're a citizen here. Is there anything my department can do to help keep you safe? I know you have your own body guards." His voice sounded mellow.

"I would welcome anything you can do," Grand-mère said sweetly. She ran her hand across her hair and smoothed some stray wisps.

Stoner lifted his cup in an informal salute to his new general, "I will double my people on campaign duty." His gaze drifted down and he added, "Lieutenant Boone and I will work very closely with your people to keep you safe, Sir Richly."

"Oliver, Inspector. Call me Oliver."

"I'm not sure I can do that Sir. But please—call me Ward."

"I'm not sure I can do that, Inspector," Grand-père said as he smiled.

"Tell me this," Ward said as he placed his cup firmly in the saucer with veiled anger. "Did any of you recognize any of the kidnappers?"

Did Stoner actually not know? I couldn't believe his question. "I thought you knew, Inspector. Daniel Washington led the men who kidnapped my grandfather. But, he was not the brains behind this whole thing."

Stoner jerked his gaze in my direction. "The brains?"

I felt my face grow hot again. "That's an expression used in old mystery books."

"I suppose they used to talk like that," the inspector blustered. "You're saying there is still someone above Washington."

"Yes," I stated. "But, we don't have any idea for sure who that is."

"For sure?" Stoner's eyes leveled on me hard. "Do you have a guess?"

At that moment, my Palm Device glowed and Marge appeared in the midst of us. "Hi, Christy, I have the information you asked for."

"What information?" Stoner snapped as he leaned in the direction of Marge's glow.

Jason touched Stoner's shoulder again. "Let her talk at her pace, Inspector."

Stoner sat back and gave in to Jason's request. "Of course."

I was so excited I felt my stomach quiver and my heart pound. However, I'll have to admit, I would have preferred to get the information in private. I didn't know what Marge was going to say and I guess I feared it might involve the Cornwalls. "It's okay Marge. Inspector Stoner has joined us at our campaign meeting. Please, just give us what you have found."

"It's very interesting," she began. "The three dot tattoo on the hand was known in Turkey as Görmem, Duymam, Söylemem. It means, 'I hear nothing; I see nothing; I tell nothing.' In that country, the tattoo meant that the person took an oath to a given society. The one who is tattooed is willing to sacrifice his or herself for the sake of the society. It's like a la Cosa Nostra tattoo–the mafia."

A unified gasp rose up around the table at the sound of the old gangster group–the mob. Silas gagged and grew pale. But, Jason and I knew something else. It meant for sure that Alister Bedlum was behind it all.

CHAPTER 31

The Lie

I awakened the next morning, yawned and stretched. The July sun sparkled high on the horizon. I knew I must have overslept. Jumping out of bed, I hit the shower, then dried off and quickly dressed. Shakespeare wrapped her furry body around my legs, in and out as I walked over to the window and looked out on the morning. My palm device hummed on the table. When I answered the page, Mother's holo appeared.

"Are you watching the news?" The pitch of her voice rose and sounded urgent.

"No," I stammered. "I just got up. Why?"

Her voice shook with worry. "Quickly, turn it on."

The huge screen danced alive but what appeared could have marked us all for death. "The details of Oliver Richly's kidnapping have been kept secret up until now," the news reader said. A large picture of my grandfather, weak, beaten and lying in his hospital bed, flashed across the screen. "Perhaps his campaign is worried that his age will prevent him from completing his presidential race. Contests of speed aren't for old men."

"What?" I shrieked.

"Now, for the latest in the progress of the Public Transit station at Mulberry and Main Streets. The PT Board has asked resident to walk the mile to the next station at—"

"PT stations?" I yelled at the screen. "Mother," I turned to the hologram, "where is the redeeming follow up, how the train was sabotaged and how we all escaped using our own intellect and strength?"

"They ran this story about fifteen minutes ago and there was not a single word about the escape there either," she said through gritted teeth.

"It's not only the story," I barked. "Where could they possibly have gotten that picture?"

She shook her head. "I have no idea, but the image would worry me if I didn't know better."

"Mother," I turned and pointed at the screen that was still devoting more time to the PT story than the kidnapping of the head of the Council of Elders and a candidate for president. "That's it. You and I do know better and—I think the people do too. They've wised up to the lies and tricks perpetrated on them by an elite controlling media. I think they'll believe Sean's story over the mass communication fable."

Mother's excitement was obvious. She nearly jumped up and down. "When will Sean's exclusive report hit the streets? Will there be enough papers for everyone to get one?"

I laughed when I thought about Sean's operation. "Sean started his newspaper distribution by hand-carrying copies of his paper right out in the open on the PT. Then, truckers would pick up stacks and stacks of them at the zone borders and transport them further into the forbidden areas. No one suspected him of producing and distributing contraband alternative news. Newspapers finally met their demise a century ago in order to silence an alternative voice to the state visual mass media."

"And—?"

"And, yes there will be plenty of newspapers for everyone. But—no trucks this time. Sean worked out a digital copy to send to underground printers in the major cities. The papers will be in millions of citizens' hands an hour after he pushes the send button."

"Everyone?"

"It will also appear on people's Palm Device—instantly."

Mother's face brightened. "When will he push the button?"

I checked Holly. "About forty-five minutes ago. The papers will be in everyone's hands in a matter of minutes. And, it should be on your device—now."

We both pushed the split-screen button on our devices. A hologram of Sean burst forth on my device in duo with Mother's image. "I'm going to have a full living room of virtual-people soon," I said and laughed.

"I'm Sean McDermott," Sean's holo began, "columnist, editor and publisher of The Free Voice Newspaper. Our feature story today is about the recent kidnapping of presidential candidate, Oliver Richly. Drugged and dragged to where he was held in the cellars under adobe buildings in New Mexico, he was rescued by Christiana Applewait, Dr. Jason O'Reilly, Ivy Trudeau and Raymar Goring."

A selected picture of my grandfather, smiling and well, with all of us gathered around him, appeared on the device screen. Sean's holo shimmered again. "After a day or two in a hospital, he and those with him took a flash train to travel back to the Central Zone. However, terrorists attacked, derailed the cars, overturned the train and injured many in the forward coaches."

An inserted photo of the wreck appeared next on the device, with smoke billowing up and twisted metal poking their tentacles toward the sky. "Oliver Richly organized those with him and found a way to escape the wreckage. They all jumped into the cold river below the bridge on which the last cars still remained and swim for the shore. It was Oliver Richly's strength and leadership that saved the entire group."

Sean had placed a photo of a strong although wet image of Grand-père, smiling, tanned from the New Mexico sun with his wet sleeve draped around my laughing grandmother's shoulder. "It takes strength, intelligence and maturity to solve the very real problems in our country. Oliver Richly is our man for that job."

"Mother," I sang out. "Sean did it!"

"Wait! Wait, Christy," Mother hushed. "There's more."

"I have with me," Sean continued, "Inspector Ward Stoner of the Blue Guard."

I looked at Mother's hologram and we both opened our mouths in surprise at the same time. "Stoner?" we mouthed in unison.

Ward Stoner's hologram appeared before us. I winced at the thought of the Inspector standing in my living room before I had my morning coffee. "Perhaps I should put on a fresh pot for our little party."

"My friends," Stoner began. I covered my mouth so my laughter wouldn't drown out his words. The thought of him having friends was too humorous for words.

"I am Inspector Ward Stoner, the head of the Blue Guard. I want to reassure everyone of Oliver Richly's safety. He has a private group of body guards around him now and I have doubled the number of Blue Guard normally assigned to protect a politician." He looked down and gathered himself, an action I had never seen before.

"Oliver Richly is a man of honor, a quality of esteem I have never seen before. He is a brave, honest, brilliant and masterful leader." Stoner gazed with steely eyes. "Know this, I will catch those who kidnapped Oliver, then tried to kill him a second time by wrecking the train that endangered all those on board, whoever they are. If you are the terrorists, know that you will not slip out of my grasp. I will follow you to the ocean's edge." With that, Stoner's hologram dissolved and Sean spoke again.

"Thank you Inspector. A full story of Oliver Richly's capture, rescue, and escape again is the feature article in my newspaper, The

Free Voice. You can find a copy in stores around your town. Pick up the current issue." Then, Sean's hologram was gone too.

At that moment, I heard a knocking from the hall. "Gotta run, Mother. Someone's at the door."

"Love you, Christy," Mother sang out before her hologram dissolved and left the room darker than it was.

Hurrying to the door, I caught sight of my image in the mirror at the entry. "Oh my," I gasped as I ran my fingers through my hair, pinched my cheeks for color and pressed my lips together firmly, raising the pink a little. Any harder and I would have drawn blood.

With the door knob in my hand, I slowed down and opened the door cautiously, remembering all the warnings about acting smart and staying safe. "Jason," I said with relief. "I'm glad you're a friend, not a foe."

"I hope I'm more than a friend," he said and pulled me to him once we both closed the door. "Did you check the security feed Ivy had installed before you opened the door?"

"I did," I lied. How could I admit that I had forgotten the surveillance camera so soon?

"You did not," he teased.

"You're right," I admitted and buried my head in his chest. "I forgot." I grabbed him by his shirt and pulled him over to the couch. "I'll make some coffee."

"No need," he said as he offered a tall cup of coffee from the Demitasse Coffee Shop.

"Jason," I gasped, "from my favorite place in the world."

"I know. I remember." He placed our cups on the table in front of the couch, took my hand and pulled me next to him. "I think you're right, Christy, about not having enough time together. We have had almost no time alone since all this began. We had only begun our relationship when we were thrown into the chaos around us." He wrapped his arms around me and snuggled close.

"Thank you for understanding, Jason."

"Now, I won't keep you from your coffee any longer," he said. As he handed me my cup of the steaming brew he added, "What have you been doing this morning? You look great."

"Oh you are a good guy," I said and laughed. "I have been watching Sean's Palm-cast."

"Sean?"

"Here, let me show you." I reached across Jason for my Palm Device from the side table, went back into the archives and brought up Sean's hologram again. Sitting on the couch, sipping our coffee, we entertained our guests in hologram form. The morning felt comfortable.

When the hologram evaporated, I leaned back into the crook of Jason's arm. "I was only detoxed for a few weeks when our running began, first to the west coast, the Midwest Zone and then the east. I hadn't even learned the names of the feelings that the chemicals had robbed from all of us. At least, as a privileged citizen, Jason, you were able to prescribe the detox pills for me when I turned twenty-four. I truly don't know how I feel because I had only begun to feel just before we lost all of our privacy."

"Well," he drew out, "there is like, dislike, and then there's love." He chuckled a little. "I've been detoxed longer than you."

"Oh, so I'm with an old man."

"Old—no. Older—yes." He kissed me on the nose. "Now, let me educate you, young one."

"Grasshopper?" I laughed as I remembered an old movie Marge and I had seen in the library.

"Grasshopper? If you like that. In the love category: there's the love of family-familial love; the love of friends-platonic love; the love of God-Agápe love, and the love between a man and a woman-a mix of eros, familial, and unconditional love."

"And, what are we?" I teased.

"Well, I'm no god and you're not my sister."

"Are you my best friend or—what?"

Jason leaned down and kissed me, tenderly, passionately. "I want it all, Christy."

I said no more. The words and feelings were all too new, too unpracticed, too raw. I caressed his cheek and my mind was at rest in our new understanding with the naming of our relationship. I guess I had believed it wasn't a relationship if I couldn't identify it by its name.

I won't say Jason and I had enough time to bond together, but we had a little. I was thankful for that but wondered if it was enough.

CHAPTER 32

The Last Week in October

In the next weeks, we were all *toes along the starting line of the fast lane.* I wondered if I would be able to catch my breath and run a good race.

We had meetings stacked upon more meetings. It helped to divide up the work among all of us. Even quiet Silas Drummond agreed to meet people in coffee shops and diners, shake citizens' hands and answer questions about my grandfather's position on many issues. I did worry about him. He looked sick and weary each time I saw him, but he denied ill health.

Everyone made sure Grand-père rested frequently. No one was more diligent at policing his sleep, diet and exercise than Grand-mère. As the months stretched past, the pace picked up.

It was early in October when Grand-père had a major speech at the restored McCormick Place along Lake Shore Drive in Chicago. It was a Friday evening event. My grandparents had gone to the city the day before the event to meet people and acclimate to the city's wind and change in weather in the colder climate. Jason and I stayed at the same hotel, arriving at the Blackstone, about a mile and a half from the event center, early on Friday.

The hotel was on South Michigan Avenue. It felt good to be among the tall buildings. I remembered how much I liked New York City when we were there.

Jason, Ivy and I went to the check-in desk and waited our turn. The desk clerk was busy. Her expensive silk jacket and the flower in her button hole identified the finer care the hotel put into each detail. As we waited, I leaned a little on Jason. He planted his feet firmly on the plush carpet to allow for the pressure of my arm to drape across his shoulder. I looked up as he smiled softly and put his arm around me.

When we got to the head of the line the clerk covered her mouth, "Oh, no. Lady Applewait, I am so sorry you had to wait."

A little embarrassed by the favoritism she was displaying, I responded, "That's fine. I can stand in line just like everyone else."

"But, the hotel security team will have my job when they find out."

"Then, let's not tell them," I whispered.

"Yes, Ma'am. Thank you."

Ivy's brow furrowed but she spoke softly. "Please, move them out of the lobby quickly."

"Of course, Ma'am," the clerk responded politely as she looked down at her booking list and glanced up. "I have you down for three rooms on a secondary, secure hallway," she looked from Jason to me.

"Yes, three rooms," I agreed. "I believe they were booked as adjoining."

"Yes," she agreed, consulting her booking notes again. She looked around as if checking to see if others were close enough to hear and explained, "There is the public hallway for that floor, which opens by palm ID to a smaller, private hallway that connects the three rooms, plus Sir Richly's rooms. None of you will have to walk out into the public space to move between the rooms."

"Perfect. We all have a lot of work to do," Jason explained.

"Yes, Sir," the clerk agreed and pointed to the palm scanner on the desk. "Please, check in."

We each placed our hand on the scanner and stepped back while vetted bellhops gathered up our luggage. Following them to the lift we soon arrived on the executive floor with the hallway the clerk described. I opened the door with my room number on the outside and walked into the second hallway with multiple doors, just down from my grandparents' suite.

I opened the door and was pleased with the relaxing setting. There were massive windows overlooking a park and Lake Michigan in the distance. As I unpacked the few things I brought for the evening's program, I heard a tapping on my door. Reaching for the knob, I then remembered the safety precautions. A light touch to the keypad to the right of the door allowed an image to come into view on the small screen above the coded numbers. Touching the O, a picture of the empty outer hall appeared. The "I" key brought up Jason standing in the inner hall just outside my door.

He was not going to catch me unprotected so I called through the door, "I see you Mister." On the other side of the door, I saw and heard Jason laugh.

I flung the door open and Jason gathered me in his arms like a movie clip I had seen in the library of banned romantic films. Feelings fluttered through me and emotions rushed in that had been drugged out of existence all of my life.

Laughing, I threw my head back. "Maybe it's been good that we have had no time alone together."

He nuzzled his head in my neck and then said breathlessly, "I am positive of it, Baby."

The buzzer on the door interrupted us as usual. The "I" key brought Ivy's image to the screen. When I opened the door she dashed in and began pacing back and forth.

"I didn't like the choice of hotels from the beginning," she began as if she were in mid-thought. "We should have been booked into the hotel adjacent to the event center," she said as she bounced from one side of the large room to the other. "We could have gone to lunch in the hotel and later walked over to the arena/center in the underground passes."

"Ivy, stop." Her pacing was making me nervous. "Sit down and tell me the latest news. Something is bothering you."

"We have received some intel," she said as she sat on the edge of one of the chairs at a round table near the window. "There are at least three assassins in the building with their cross hairs fixed on your grandparents—and on you too, Christy."

"Ivy, we can have someone bring our lunch to the room. We won't have to go out."

"And getting to the program this evening?" she asked.

"I asked Marge to research this old building," I admitted as I sat with Ivy and gazed out on Grant Park below and the cold water of Lake Michigan out beyond.

"And?"

I leaned in toward her as if there were "bugs," as my old mystery novels would call them, secretly stashed in the light fixtures. "There is a tunnel under this building."

"Yes, of course," Ivy agreed.

"No, no," I shook my head. "Yes, there's the tunnel everyone knows about. Then, about thirty years ago, a very powerful man, a recluse really, secretly had another tunnel dug under the original one. Access to that second one is through the walk-in freezer in the kitchen. A car backs in through a grove of trees in Grant Park and coasts down a long ramp to the tunnel below."

"Are you sure?" Ivy gasped.

Jason sat with us and added. "Of course. Marge is able to find almost anything."

"Okay. We'll eat in our rooms and then use the sub-tunnel to get to the arena." Ivy slapped her hands across her knees indicating a decision was made.

Grand-père and Grand-mère joined us for lunch; we ate at the table in my room. The hotel brought up a platter of shrimp, cheese, small pieces of fruit, and little sandwiches made with ham, pepperoni, salami, and pizza sauce. No one was still hungry after the leisure time we took over our feast.

Lunch and an afternoon of planning did interrupt the time that Jason and I had together. I had to recognize that we weren't in Chicago on vacation. Grand-père would give the most important speech of his life and the lives of every citizen in our country that evening. Jason and I were there to help him polish it. Ivy was there for all of us.

I changed into black wool slacks and a festive top of spun gold and silver threads over a tight shirt of silk. The creation moved with ease like a shimmy dress I'd seen in an old movie depicting clothes of the 1920's.

"Wow," Jason gulped when he came into my room before we left. "You make my eyes water, Honey." He started to put his arms around me. "Maybe I'd better not. I might bend the shirt or get stabbed by precious threads, I don't know which."

"Thank you, Sir. I'll take that as a compliment," I said as I feigned a small curtsy.

Ivy came in the door behind Jason and immediately growled, "That door was not latched. I'm serious about assassins in the building people."

"All right everybody," Stoner said as he followed Ivy into my room. "Here's the way we're going to do it." He swaggered over to the large windows and peered out. "Boone, take a look at this," he ordered.

Chalky walked immediately to the floor-to-ceiling windows that faced the park. "Down there," she pointed.

"What?" I asked. I had no idea what they were looking at except the beautiful crimson and gold leaves that I had sat and watched, filling the color-loving part of my brain.

"The two men on the park bench below," she pointed.

"So—two men. There are people all over the park on a wonderful fall day like this." What was she talking about?

Stoner was firm but somehow kinder than before. "Christy, those men are carrying long duffle bags. The three could have come from the gym down the street or the bags could conceal rifles."

I didn't know what to say and mumbled. "I didn't notice them."

The inspector actually placed his hand on my shoulder in comfort. "I know you didn't, Christy. That's what I'm trying to teach you." He turned to the park below. "You have lived a privileged life. That's good for you but bad for your safety. Even the people around you, who weren't allowed to approach you or touch your garment, were so drugged they didn't notice anything around them either. That was the government's plan. You and Dr. O'Reilly have been through a lot in the last year, but you haven't learned. You still trust people. You have come to a point in your life when, if you don't watch the actions of everyone around you, your life and the lives of your loved ones could be in mortal danger."

I felt my heart sink and my hope waver. "I don't want to live a life of doubt and mistrust."

"Then you might not live a life at all," Stoner stated with firm resolve. He turned to Chalky and snapped his heals. "It's time to go. Boone, I'll take the lead and you and Trudeau take the rear." He threw out his arms to shepherd each of us out of the room on his time and by his plan.

Another moment of precious time with Jason burst, a lovely soap bubble—that hits the wall and breaks.

• • •

All of us crowded into one elevator car. Dividing our party would not have been safe. Ivy pushed the button for the ground floor. Stoner faced the front, his hand on his sidearm.

As we rode down, someone pushed the call button on the fourth floor. Ivy over-road the elevator call and we passed by.

"I went down and walked through the kitchen while you all changed for the event" she announced. "I didn't go near the freezer. I couldn't give away the escape route."

"So, we don't know if the access is even in the freezer," Grand-père said.

Ivy was facing the lift door and didn't turn around. "No, we don't, Sir."

"It will be there," Stoner stated decidedly. "I trust Christy's research."

"Marge's research," I corrected.

Grand-père did not hesitate. "Then, assuming it's there, we will have quite an adventure."

When the door opened on the main floor, Grand-père's security staff met us before we stepped off. The men, many of them over six feet six inches tall, surrounded our party like a picket fence. We walked in rhythmic dance, always with Grand-père at the center of the march.

I could barely see past the bodyguards so I had no idea if anyone was stalking us. Suddenly, I heard the crack pop of gun fire. The guards, with many angel wings, swooped low and hovered over us, pushing us all down to the floor.

"Stay down," Stoner ordered when I started to lift my head. Suddenly, more shots rang out.

I heard my heart beating so loudly, I thought I would lift off the ground. My breathing was short and labored. I worried about Grand-mère but I couldn't see her. With one eye fixed past a dark blue suit that was laying heavily over me, I saw the bloody body of two people on the marble floor to the left of us. Just as quickly, a suited arm jerked me not-so-gently off the floor and whisked me down the hall. I tried to look around to see if Jason and my grandparents were following but all I saw was navy blue. I did hear Stoner's voice barking orders.

After what seemed like too many steps, I could smell the aroma of fine gourmet cooking and knew we were either in or near the kitchen. Frazzled and mussed, I soon stumbled into the walk-in freezer.

Strangely, I wondered if my clothes were torn or damaged and if my hair was still in place. I was embarrassed by my egocentric obsession and glad no one could read my thoughts. We were in a gun battle and I wondered if I had remembered to bring a comb. My life had become so used to danger that nothing seemed dangerous.

"Christy," Grand-mère called out from inside a gathering of guards. "Your granddaddy is with me."

"I'm here Grand-mère," I sighed deeply in relief. "Jason? Where are you?" There was no sound in return.

"Christy?" Finally he asked as he entered the freezer.

"Okay, we are all here," Stoner announced. "Ivy called for the cars to pick us up in the sub-tunnel. How do we get there Christy?"

As the giant guards stepped back, I moved through the crowded walk-in freezer to the back. "Here it is." I ran my fingers along the wall, momentarily forgetting my manicure. "Behind this wall-size poster of the various cuts of meat—it should—"

My hand felt for anything that seemed different, until I finally touched a tiny spring lever. When it snapped, a fourth of the poster sprang open revealing the handle to a heavy door. I jerked it down and a large portion of the wall opened like a normal door. Inside, wide grey terrazzo steps descended to the right and flowed to the tunnel below. With a guard's hand under each arm, my feet barely touched the ground as I slipped and slid down the old steps. The only thing that kept me from falling was the heavy coating of dust, dirt and mouse droppings on the unused treads.

The descent was a blur as they hustled us along. Once we got to the first tunnel, we found another elevator in the corner of the space off to the right and entered it silently. I pushed a button simply marked with a dot inside a circle and the car went down again. We all turned toward each other and smiled.

"Thank goodness it still works," Grand-père said.

"I'll bet it hasn't been serviced in twenty or more years," Ivy winced.

When the door slid open, the rush was on again. Guided, pushed and jostled toward waiting long-cars, I grabbed Jason's shirt to make sure we would end up in the same limousine.

"Thank God you're all right," he said as we slid onto the leather seat and he threw his arms around me.

Suddenly, I started shaking uncontrollably like someone chilled to the bone. But, I wasn't cold. Feeling completely out of control, I started to cry.

Jason rubbed my back gently and hummed "Silent Night" softly in my ear. It wasn't Christmas or Gifting Season, but it was the song we loved. I slowly began to calm down but felt so very tired. My arms were nearly too heavy to lift.

"Less than a month to the election," Jason reminded me quietly. "Then all of this will be over."

"Will we all make it until then?" I asked and laughed wearily but truly saw no humor in any of it. The question was real, and I knew it.

CHAPTER 33

The Event

The roar of the crowd at the event center was deafening. Energy seemed to hang from the catwalk. A band was actually playing a rousing song. I wondered where they found a group of people who could still play instruments in the Central Zone. Then, I thought of Dahlia Zoobamba's beautiful playing on the grand piano in the sitting room of the Indian River Apartments. Music seemed to be buried in people's hearts even though banned decades ago.

A stage was set up at one end of the arena. I could see that it was within a force-field security bubble. The Jumbotron, hung from the ceiling, showed multiple images of the audience as it panned around, in and out of the roving spotlights. It was hard for me to take my eyes off the giant screen. Perhaps I expected to see a slithering assassin taking aim in some corner of the arena and trapped in the image on the Tron.

Chants of, "Oliver—Oliver—Oliver" filled the place. My eyes scanned the entire area of ten thousand people. All seemed smiling, full of energy and happy, but then, so much of the scene was a blur.

When I heard, "Christy—Christy—Christy," my blood froze. I wondered how long I could stand in the center of an adrenalin flood and not completely burn out.

Ivy studied the lay of the arena, turned and talked to Grand-mère and me. "Nothing has changed from the early setup. I checked it over this afternoon." She pointed at the area to the right and said, "Oliver and Christy will come out of entrance A1A, just as the athletes do when they enter the arena for the True Warrior vs Avatar Games. Your only vulnerable spot will be where the low ceiling of the entry hall meets the open secure area of the arena. While the security bubble extends from the stage to the hall, there is no overlap at the entrance. Space yourselves wide apart so you're not a waiting target. Hurry through the void," she instructed. "Any questions?"

My mind was a dichotomy of emptiness and flashing ideas all spilling over one another as they crowded in for attention. "No," I whispered.

Looking up at Grand-père, I nodded. Grand-mère and Jason kissed us for luck as we started toward the arena and out of the shadows of the hallway. Grand-père stepped back to position me so I would enter the bubble first, since I should arrive on stage before him. I would say a few words of thanks and then introduce him.

Looking at the bubble, I could see the wavy haze that demarked the entrance and the gap where there was no protection. Then I did the very thing I wasn't supposed to do. I stopped.

"Move!" Ivy yelled.

Behind me, Grand-père nearly stumbled over my heels. I jumped which threw me into the gap between safety and danger. Inspector Stoner grabbed me in a great bear hug and lifted me past the unsafe zone.

Crack, pop, pop! Shots rang out from the stands in the section above us. I heard a projectile glance off the floor Doris the spot I just stepped out of and chip the concrete. A small piece of flooring hit the back of my leg and nicked the wool of my pants. Several bullets struck Stoner's protective vest. I felt the impact through his arms. *Thud, thud, thud,* the bullets jolted us there in the gap. Stoner slumped in stride. I wondered how weakened he was from the previous attack in New Mexico that had only begun to heal. Other shots struck the force-field which sent off ten-foot high rockets of flash, sparks and fire like an erupting fountain of flames.

"Go!" Stoner demanded and shoved me into the safety of the force-field.

Looking back, I saw the inspector grab his chest, his face drawn and pinched. "Are you okay?" I shouted.

"Yes, yes, go!" He bellowed with the wave of his hand toward the center of the stage.

Some of the people didn't understand what had happened and cheered on what seemed like a brilliant entrance for their new leader. Others screamed in fear and started to stampede out of the arena. Retaliating fire pinpointed with laser accuracy the source of the shots and nearly shoved the bullets right up the barrel of the assassins' firearms. An announcer came on the microphone.

"Calm, please everyone. The authorities have taken out the terrorists. Everyone is fine. Let me assure you, you're safe." The noise of the crowd lowered to a mumble from person to person.

"Now, let's give a hand to Christiana Applewait!" He roared into a hand-held mic.

I thought for a moment I might vomit. My hands trembled and my knees barely held me up. I looked back at Jason who still stood on the edge of the hall reaching out for me with fear written on his face. Finally, he straightened his back, smiled and blew a reassuring kiss.

A microphone hung from the catwalk on a cable so thin it was nearly invisible. Now was my time. Now was my hour. I closed my eyes in prayer, a prayer for strength, courage and the words that would inspire the thousands there.

"Ladies and gentlemen," I began and wondered if I sounded like the ringmaster in an old circus. I heard my own internal voice remind me, *It's not about you Christy. It's not even about Grand-père. It's about our beautiful, blessed country and the wonderful people who have only begun to awaken from their deep, dark sleep.*

I continued with new energy. "On behalf of Oliver Richly and the entire *1787-Constitutional Party* I thank you all for coming tonight. You are the last great hope of our nation."

The crowd roared with enthusiasm and fidelity for our cause. They stood and stomped their feet, waving their arms and whooping in joy. It sounded like thunder on distant hills.

Their response filled me with a power I had never experienced before. "Now is the time to listen with open ears and an open mind. Now is the time for each of us to learn of our blessings, our privilege, our obligation and our responsibility. Now is the time to have the courage to stand and be counted." Again the people shouted and cheered.

I looked out and into the bright lights focused on me as the granddaughter and warm-up act for Grand-père's speech. "You may not know this man yet, like I do. Oliver Richly is a man of honesty, steadfastness and honor. His dedication to our country and our people is based on his knowledge and love of the country we used to be, when the Constitution of 1787 was ratified and was the law of the land, and who we can become again."

Then I paused and added, "Now is the time for us to awaken in a new land of hope and opportunity—and the time for me to introduce my grandfather—Oliver Richly."

Grand-père stepped into the center of the stage as the spotlight glowed on him like the sun from a near-by galaxy. The arena went wild. He bowed from the waist, a true servant of the people, and dipped his head in respect to all those gathered there. Finally, he raised his hands to the people in a plea for quiet and held his eyes on them until they all grew calm and still. It was like each one had moved to the edge of their seat and waited in anticipation. Grand-père opened his mouth.

He cleared his throat and placed his hand across his heart. "We gather here to make a decision, a decision about our future, the future of our children and our children's children. The good news is, what we decide today and what we do next week will affect every man, woman and child in our country and those people who used to depend on us around the world." A hushed silence washed over the arena.

He continued. "Let me be very clear, there is no argument between the freedom we as a people would enjoy under a return to the original constitution and the alternative of spending the rest of our lives under a cloud of drugs and dying on the government's schedule. I am here to proclaim freedom for the prisoner in this government's prison of life. There is only one way to guarantee life and a life worth living, and you can have it in one week—vote."

I studied the faces of the people I could see in the first rows. Some were in tears but all were in rapture of the man and his words.

Grand-père raised one hand in affirmation. "I know there's a risk in showing up and being counted at the polling place. But, more danger exists if you don't vote and we fail in our efforts to return the country to the people.

"There is a risk in following a course toward a restoration of freedom. We saw it played out a few minutes ago when assassins tried to take us down right here in the arena. But, history has taught us that this great nation and the freedom she promised and provided decades ago, is the one great hope of the world. That hope is nearing total extinction. It flickers in a window left open by those who went before us. Are we going to be the generation that lazily blows it out?"

"No!" The people yelled.

Grand-père held up his hand again. "The greatest risk and danger lies in turning our backs on freedom and giving in to the fear that the new constitutionalist spread like a cancer, eating at our resolve and killing our dreams. The current government's policy is total control and it gives us no choice but to escape the bonds they try to hold on us."

"Oliver, Oliver, Oliver!" voices rang out.

As soon as the noise level lowered, Grand-père went on. "We must fight to the death or surrender. If we do continue to yield to their ideas of government, we give our children no hope of freedom.

"Nathan Alexander has told you that we are weak and afraid. He has told you that we have no right to live beyond the days they decide—those wiser and better than we number our Length of Days. I tell you that is a lie!" He shouted. "Alexander believes it because he has heard some of us say, 'Take care of me. I cannot do it on my own.' My friends, you cannot do it at ALL under the new constitution. The ruling elite have decided your education, your work, the strength of your relationships and your ability to love. They have robbed you of the joy of Christmas and the name of your Creator. They even have the date of your demise written in their book of death.

"We are not weak: not morally or spiritually. We speak out of the wisdom and faith of the Word. In Proverbs it is written, 'My son, do not forget my law, but let your heart keep my commands, for length of days and long life and peace they will add to you.' How can we know the law if the book has been banned? We don't even know the commandments of God any more.

"Those voices of surrender do not speak for me, and they don't speak for you. Your current leaders tell you that fighting isn't your job. They say, 'Sit back, watch the flickering screen that dominates your home, play your games and let those above you tell you when to put yourself into action.'

"My friends, there are things worth fighting for. Freedom is first on the list. Your God has been hidden from you; the music of your life has been silenced; the joy and meaning of Christmas have been cauterized out of your celebrations; the history of your own country has been stolen from you, along with her stories of honor and valor."

He raised his voice in a call to action. "You can decide what is best for you and your family. You can say to the government, there is a price to be paid, and I am willing to stand and pay it. We must have the courage to trace our finger in the sand and say there is a line over which the government cannot cross. President Reagan, a president you have never even heard of said, 'We have a rendezvous with destiny.' He was right. We either step boldly and courageously into the light of freedom's beacon or we will live forever in absolute darkness."

"No," someone yelled in the otherwise silent room.

Grand-père shook a triumphant fist in the air. "Next week is Election Day. On that day, we have an appointment with the future. Do we have the courage to face it boldly, or will we let fear grip us and turn out the light of hope? My friends turn out next week and—vote!"

CHAPTER 34

November 3, 2114

Election Day

I was excited to vote, but didn't want to go to the polls by myself. Not that I would be alone. With Ivy, the Blue Guard and many of the party's security people surrounding me, I hadn't been alone in a long time. My parents' single family home was not in Oakwood where my grandparents lived, nor near the Indian River Apartments. Since Election Day fell on Saturday this year, Daddy didn't have to go to work as the Director of the Schools in Capitol City, and Mother, the Chief of Staff to the Center Chair of the Council of Elders, was also home. So, they voted at 6 a.m. when the polls opened and then came over to my apartment to accompany me to my precinct.

The Campaign Committee would have provided a long-car to take me to vote, but I didn't want flash and pomp to further draw attention to myself. Daddy's car had two seats so that wouldn't work. We would have taken the Public Transit; I rode it every day before my world turned upside down. However, if Grand-père's bodyguards heard about it, their height and size would have derailed the train when they all boarded at the same time with us.

Ivy had the solution. She pulled up in front of my apartment building at 7 a.m. in her small four- passenger boot-car, the few personal vehicles that had storage. She stashed her weapons in the lockable boot. All four of us were able to fit into her car, which solved my need for a measure of anonymity.

• • •

November 3 was a beautiful fall day. Mums of many colors in brightly painted terracotta pots flanked the walkway in front of the polling place where I would cast my vote. Jason's apartment was in another district so he would meet us at the airport after I voted.

That wasn't all that lined the sidewalk and the perimeter of the polling building. Huge men in tan paramilitary shirts and pants with black berets worn low across one side of their brow stood elbow to elbow. The door was the only part of the building that wasn't blocked.

Mother and Daddy walked beside me with their arms linked in mine while Ivy went a few steps ahead, her hand on her weapon. We all said nothing to the tan-shirts, but I'll admit I felt intimidated. Ivy pulled her Palm device from her pocket and pushed one button. Ward Stoner appeared in a haze.

"What's going on?" He bellowed when he saw the background of tan.

Ivy panned the screen so Stoner's holo could see all of the men. "It doesn't look like they're stopping anyone from voting, but voters feel intimidated," she said. "At least Christy does. I can tell."

"Miss Applewait?" Stoner blasted as he talked into the space. "Christy, are you all right? Some of my men are less than a mile way. I'll have them there immediately."

"Yes, Inspector, I'm okay," I answered with my head held high and my chin out. "People better than these have tried a whole lot harder to harass me. But, I'll admit, I don't want them here. They do make me feel uncomfortable. And—many of our citizens are not as experienced in dealing with bullies."

242

The sickening sound of a trio of Blue Guard sirens whined in the morning air and tires screeched at the curb. Four large men jumped out of each car and the dozen Blue Shirts descended on the sea of tan.

"Break it up and move on," one of the men in blue ordered as he approached the wall of men. I could see it was Tayton Braxton. As in the old behavior pattern of the infamous Blue Guard, he took his prodding stick from his belt and smashed it over the first black beret he came to.

"Hey!" other paramilitary troopers yelled and started in Tayton's direction.

What they hadn't noticed was that the other eleven Blue Shirts had raised their fully automatic handguns at the same time Tayton pulled out the stick. The Blue Shirts stood in a circle, elbow to elbow, facing those who were there to crowd-out voters. The black handguns perched like vultures in the men's hands.

"We are a kinder, gentler Blue Guard," Tayton hissed. "But— where's the fun in that?" He took aim at the slouched crown of the man's beret. "The cute dip that little hat makes creates a perfect target." He smiled, baring his teeth as the red laser light from many firearms marked the kill-spot on the man's head.

"Whoa," the man in the beret pleaded with his palms raised. "We didn't do anything but stand here. We were hired to be a presence—that's all."

"By who?" I heard Tayton ask.

"A friend of Alexander's. No one gave the name," he whimpered as the prodding stick poked him in the belly.

"Out of here—now," Tayton ordered. "Take off those silly uniforms and stay home. The Blue Guard presence is four-fold today, so none of you are going to be able to slip by us. If I catch you out again, you will suffer a fate you don't want to know about."

"Yes, Sir," the man answered and waved off the rest of his group. "Get out of here. Go home."

Tayton turned to Ivy. "We'll stick around to make sure the last one is gone, but then we'll go. If we stay, we'll become the intimidators."

"Fine, clear these hired bullies out and then go. It's early. It shouldn't change the turn out," Ivy responded.

Tayton touched his guard cap at me in a salute and turned away. He was never one of the former guardsmen who beat up on citizens and terrorized children. He was no tyrant, and I knew it. Tayton based his approach on the fact that the tan shirted hired-bullies wouldn't know him.

• • •

I went inside. The polling station was in an old abandoned church and it was amazing. Since speaking the name of God had been banned under the new constitution adopted one hundred years ago, few people knew the reason for the building or the meaning of the emblems and stained glass pictures. I owned one of the few remaining Bibles that had not been burned years in the past. Grand-père had given it to me and told me to hide it in plain sight on one of my bookshelves. No one would have heard of a Holy book called a Bible, so it was unlikely anyone would discover it and identify it as something precious.

"Look at these beautiful pictures made of glass," Mother whispered in awe.

"They tell a story," I said. Pointing to a picture of a man in a long garment with a flock of sheep around him, I said, "That depicts the truth that Jesus is the Good Shepherd."

"You know a lot about Jesus," Mother said with a wisp of a smile.

I studied her carefully and wasn't sure what to say. "Some, yes—but I thought you did too."

"I found a black book in Daddy's library one day," she said with her finger to her lips. "I started reading it and couldn't put it down. The last fourth of the book told about Jesus. But, it didn't have any pictures."

"I know. That's the Bible I have," I said and smiled. "But there were many picture books in the library, of churches and some with pictures of old masters that were representations of Bible stories," I said as I looked past the art and to the voting booths.

"Sign in with your thumb and index finger," Daddy reminded me. "Then—vote."

As I stepped into the voting area, I thought I would burst with pride. Grand-père's name was the second on the list of two candidates. The only other item was the citizens' referendum to over-turn the Length of Days Law. I tapped the screen for Oliver Richly for president and a "yes" for the referendum. I left the booth and didn't look back.

After I finished voting, it was time to hurry to the airport. Barbara Cornwall would have a large helicopter waiting for us, one large enough to hold my grandparents and parents, Jason and I, Ward Stoner and Chalky, Silas Drummond, Sean McDermott, the Brunners with Michael Brunner and his daughter—Vonny, Dahlia Zoobomba, Ivy Trudeau and Tayton Braxton. We would wait out the vote in New York.

CHAPTER 35

The Grand Ballroom

We flew over the beautiful Blue Ridge Mountains on our way east. The flight path had to do as much with security measures as anything. It wasn't on a direct path to New York. We were tacking into the east.

The morning sun danced off the copter windows and sent prismatic rainbows across the cabin. It was impossible to see the ground below. The sun shimmered through the tops of the trees, causing the canape to sparkle with morning dew, a wedding veil, kissed with diamonds. I wondered if the people on the mountain peaks and in the hollers knew about the election and the events of recent months. I knew they were bright, well educated people, but I also knew that the mass communications had exerted considerable effort into keeping the citizens uninformed about the election and my grandfather's heroic escape. I closed my eyes and reviewed the events of the week.

It was just after twelve-noon when we got to New York. Barbara had arranged for a sleek chauffeured bus to pick us up. Suddenly, I felt so tired I couldn't believe it. My head keep nodding so I rested comfortably on Jason's shoulder. I drifted in and out and picked up bits and pieces of conversation and the sounds of the city beyond the windows.

"Why did you choose New York to wait out the vote, Sir?" Stoner asked Grand-père from across the side aisle and behind Jason and I as we road through the streets of the city.

"Maybe you'll have a chance to see the underworld of the city," Grand-père said. "Christy and Jason can tell you all about it," he explained. "We'll check in for a minute at the Grande Hotel a few blocks from the Citadel. I'll want to meet and thank all the volunteers. Most of this bus load will stay there. Rooms have been reserved. Then some of us will go back to the Citadel."

"I was in New York before," Stoner smirked. "I saw a few entrances to the subway. But, why this city?" Stoner asked again.

Grand-père nodded across the aisle in my direction. "Christy told us the underlings lived in the old subway tunnels and sewers of the city for decades. They made connections that no one knew about through cellars under many buildings into the world above them. They were told they would be killed if they surfaced." He paused and looked out the window. "If there is a problem, any danger, more terrorists, and we can't travel above ground between the Citadel and the hotel—we can easily get there underground."

"Interesting idea," Stoner mused.

"But," Silas interrupted over the back of the seat. "How do you know that the tunnels haven't been filled in?"

I heard the question, even through my drowsy fog, and turned in Stoner's direction. "There are hundreds and hundreds of miles of subway tunnels under the city, Silas. More than a century ago, there was reclamation of valuable land for construction of important homes. Streets were reconfigured which also changed some old sewer lines. A forgotten manhole comes right up through the basement of the Citadel."

I watched Stoner's face as it seemed to brighten with possibilities and then added, "If we have to, we can walk from the hotel to the Citadel underground and come up in the Cornwall's basement."

Grand-père smiled with satisfaction and closed his eyes. "And that, Inspector, is why we chose New York. With everything that has happened, we need to stay a few steps ahead of those who would do us in."

I watched Stoner close his eyes in contemplation. Instantly, they popped back open as he frowned. "I'm not sure who is ahead in this race to the Inauguration."

I settled back and rested my head on Jason's shoulder again. There was no sleep however. I couldn't shake my worry over the Inspector's last statement. Who was getting ahead of us?

• • •

A large crowd of volunteers and supporters were already waiting in the Grand Ballroom of the hotel when we walked in. Grand-père was prepared to walk in ahead of the rest of us. Ivy, Inspector Stoner, and his entire party of bodyguards stopped him.

"Sir," Stoner said firmly as he placed his hand on Grand-père's chest. "You are not taking the lead going into that room. There are too many unknowns: people as well as the layout of the room."

The Inspector motioned for five of Grand-père's bodyguards to enter the room and fan out. Their reconnaissance would be vital to Grand-père's safety and the safety of all of us. They went in and moved to every corner, checking packages, people, and every possibility.

When they had totally swept the room, Tayton reported, "The room is clean."

"Copy that, Mr. Braxton," Stoner responded. "When Sir Richly is finished here, you will accompany the family to the Citadel."

With everything clear, Grand-père held his head high and charged into the ballroom with a burst of energy I attributed to his brief nap on the bus. Grand-mère followed and stood a few steps behind him on the small stage.

"My friends," he began, "I had to stop by. In years past, a candidate often didn't come to the gathering place until it was time to either thank them for their supporters in spite of their loss—or thank their supporters for making their win possible."

The crowd cheered and clapped, shouting, "Oliver, Oliver, Oliver."

"Thank you," Grand-père repeated over and over with his hands raised to silence the people. "You are the reason for my running for president, you and your children and your children's children."

Again those assembled cheered warmly, enthusiastically.

"Connie and I want to thank you all." Grand-père began again as he stepped back, put his arm around Grand-mère's waist and drew her into the spotlight. "We cannot begin to express our gratitude for your time, your sacrifices and your belief in our message of hope for a bright and free future."

"Thank you President Richly!" Someone called out.

Grand-père bowed and smiled. "Thanks to you, my friend." Grand-père called back. "Because of your dedication, there will be food and coffee and punch here in the hall all day. Any of you who want to drop by and cheer each other on are welcome to enjoy whatever is here. After you have eaten and rested, we would appreciate it if you would go out and encourage all you see—to vote! It is a rare privilege, one that people haven't enjoyed in their lifetime," he rang out. "Thank you all—and we'll see you later."

After the cheering and applause, Grand-père excused himself. Once off stage, he surprised everyone by sweeping Grand-mère off her feet. He swung her around, her feet two feet off the ground as both of them laughed and filled the room with joy. This is the man and woman the government saw no need for any more, even though he was the Center Chair of the Council of Elders and as full of energy as any man I know. Their Length of Days was up at the end of December 2112 when they turned seventy-five. Now, at the age of seventy-seven, he was running for the office of president. And, God-willing, it would be so by the end of the day.

CHAPTER 36

The Promise

The Citadel sat back from the street behind a protective drive, decorative foliage and artistic statues. In many ways, I was glad to be back. Barbara and Richard were wonderful friends. The city, in spite of the evil we had found under the streets, was magical. Most of all, today was the day the election results would come in. A lovely lunch was waiting for us when we came downstairs from freshening up.

"Maisie," I greeted her with a laugh, "it's so good to see you again."

"Christy," she shouted with glee. "It's great to see you, too. We have a special surprise for lunch."

"Sounds wonderful," I said as I gave her a hug. "Tell me about it."

"Come on into the dining room," Maisy coaxed. "Everyone is here."

"I'm sorry," I said and blushed as I walked in. "I hope you haven't waited for me."

"We just got here too," Grand-mère assured me and patted the seat between her and Jason. "Come—sit."

As I walked behind him, I ran my hands over Jason's shoulders. He reached back and touched me gently.

The table, spread with sliced duck breast and Wagyu beef with assorted sweet and specialty breads and salads, was beautiful. For dessert, there was a lemon tart with blueberries and whipped cream. Coffee, ice-chilled water and several juices were on the side board.

Richard gave thanks for food, friends and the faithfulness of the Lord. After the Amen, he said, "Oliver and Connie, we cannot tell you the privilege it is to have you in our home. I guess we can thank the sewer system of New York for that."

"Richard," Barbara scolded. "Not at the table." Then she looked at each of us. "You do know it was a little joke—right?"

"I did," I agreed, hoping to deflect some of the teasing from the others.

"Yes," Oliver smiled at Richard. "I recognized right away that it was a very little joke."

"Ouch," Richard said as he winced. "I deserve that."

We laughed and enjoyed our meal time together around the table, but we all knew we wanted to get to the media reports of the election turn out. Silas excused himself to go to his room upstairs for a short nap. His shoulders slumped and, as I watched him, his feet shuffled so much I was afraid he wouldn't be able to take the next step up the stairs. The rest of the group retired to the sitting room. I joined them once I saw Silas safely disappear upstairs.

Barbara reached for the tray that Maisie brought into the room and placed it on the library table. "I know we just ate, but there will be refreshments here on the tray all afternoon with light sandwiches in the evening. Maisie will add and replace food as we need it."

Then she turned to the young woman and added. "Thank you, Maisie. Why don't you find a little picnic spot on the floor and join us."

"Thanks, Barbara," she said as she sat on the hearth.

Dahlia stretched and yawned. "I'd like a nap, too, but I think I'd rather take a short walk."

A trio of "No!" rang out from Stoner, Ivy and Tayton in one voice.

"There had been assassins after these people, Dahlia," Sean reminded her gently.

Stoner wasn't as kind. "Lady, what is it you don't understand?"

"The Inspector is concerned about your safety, Dahlia," Chalky tried to interpreted Stoner's unique language.

"I'm sorry," Dahlia apologized. "For a moment, I forgot." She started for the hall. "I think I'll take that nap."

"Do some push-ups while you're up there," Ivy suggested. "It'll either energize you or make you tired enough to sleep."

While Dahlia went upstairs, my grandparents settled on the couch. Jason and I sat on the wide chair in the corner. Again, we couldn't say much in private. There were too many others around.

I mulled a question over in my mind and finally asked, "Barbara, how is your mother?"

She wasn't surprised and smiled. "Thank you for asking, Christy. She so enjoyed seeing you when you were both here during your last visit. I see her every day, and she seems to have her eye on us and what's going on around town all of the time."

"I am so glad she's well," I responded and knew what Barbara meant. Her mother, Sondra Bedlum, was still in her attic apartment above our heads, watching life play-out on her many video screens from the surveillance cameras that network the city. She never left her space. Barbara and Richard visited her several times a day. Also, as they moved about their house, motion sensors activate cameras so they could talk to her openly, and they would appear on the attic screens. Sondra would be watching and listening to us even now.

• • •

The afternoon sun was lower on the horizon. The tiny sparkling lights in the garden beyond the French doors had come on.

Dahlia, having returned to the sitting room, found a seat beside Maisie on the wide fireplace hearth. "Look at that," she said as she pointed to the screen.

Grand-mère eyes were wide. She threw her hand to her chest as if she were unable to catch her breath. "Oliver, look!"

The pie-charts the talking news head was pointing to were dripping in green, the color assigned to Grand-père. "As you can see," the anchor explained, "with less than an hour left before the polls close here in the Eastern Zone, Oliver Richly has pulled substantially ahead of Nathan Alexander."

"Wonderful!" I screamed, clenching and unclenching my fists. I fanned my face with a side pillow. "Oh Jason, I don't think I can stand this."

He looked beyond the French doors to the right of our chair and his face softened. "Inspector, I would love to take Christy into the garden. It will be a while before we get information from the Midwestern Zone."

Stoner looked toward the heavy multi-paned glass doors and back at us. Then he did something I had never seen him do before. He smiled knowingly. "I'll go out and do a security run-through first, and then the garden is yours." As he passed us, he touched my shoulder gently.

"Should I accompany them?" Ivy asked.

"No," Stoner said as he rolled his eyes. "Stay in here, Trudeau."

Jason stood and, taking my hand, he pulled me up from the chair. We waited at the doors and watched Stoner walk through the garden, checking every corner of the large, five-foot high, walled-in terrace.

"Take the blanket-throw from the couch, Christy. It's November in New York. It is unusually warm, but it will be cold in the shadows," Barbara said as she offered the small light blue cashmere blanket.

"Yes, Dear," Grand-mère agreed. "And the color looks good on you."

The soft throw felt warm and comforting around my shoulders. When we walked out into the crisp eastern November air, I was glad Barbara had insisted I take it. Jason folded my hand in his as we took in the beauty of the garden.

The gardener had created a winding walk path that flowed past small ornamental potted trees, bushes and planters of mums and other fall flowers. Several artfully placed wooden benches dotted the magic garden under a canopy of city lights and distant neon that seemed to blink at us.

At first, we said nothing. We just enjoyed being together and alone. I looked back at the French doors. There wasn't a single eye focused on the garden and our precious time together.

I breathed in slowly and exhaled the same. "Jason thanks for this wonderful idea. I was feeling so anxious; I hadn't even seen the garden. You've presented it to me as a beautiful gift."

"Are you—still doubtful about us?" he asked, his voice sounded rough and gravely.

"I guess I never doubted *us,* Jason," I tried to assure him. "It had just been so long since we could experience *us* I didn't think I recognized *us* anymore. We had only started being *us* when *us* began to include the Claimed Children, the hollow ones, the entire colony of underlings and hundreds and hundreds of new friends and supporters of our campaign."

Jason said nothing for a moment. "You are absolutely right. But, Honey there is a solution."

"There is?" I questioned in amazement. I had accepted the inevitability of our situation for so long, it never occurred to me there might be a solution. "I've been so overwhelmed I could only put one foot in front of the other and soldier on."

"Our time has been spent in the public eye almost since we met," he said.

"I don't think I could have faced the public without you, Jason. You have become my rock."

"Christy," he began as he caressed my arms, "I want to hold you. I need for you to be mine. I need you alone—with me."

I smiled. "That sounds like an old romance novel."

"Just our romance," he said and pulled me to him. "Christy, we have no time alone because we don't own each other's alone time."

"Own?" I questioned in surprise.

"Okay, you know what I mean," he said as he threw his head back and laughed. "I wouldn't own you—any more than you could claim me—except as your husband."

"Husband?" My heart began to pound. "Are you asking me to marry you?"

"You know I am," he bellowed, like a fox howling at the moon after a successful hunt. "Christiana Applewait, will you marry me? We've almost talked about it before. Then my alone time would be spent with you in our alone place."

"Yes, Jason, yes!" I answered. I stepped into his arms in the closeness of the garden and felt sure I would never be alone again.

CHAPTER 37

An Unlikely Hero

How could the day change from sunshine and neon, to the blackness of night, in an instant, like the extinguishing of a candle on a night of the new moon? But, it did.

Crack, pop, pop, the repeating fire from a lethal firearm pierced the silence of the terrace. Jason and I hit the grass, he with his body partially covering mine.

"Stay down," he whispered as he crawled toward the French doors. At that moment, the doors flew open and the edge of the frame hit Jason's head.

"Get in here!" Alister Bedlum demanded. His face was red with anger as his hot 980 waved wildly in the air.

Jason and I got up and eased ourselves around the doors and past the gunman. Blood was dripping for Jason's forehead.

Ivy's body sat rigidly in the chair near the fireplace. Her eyes were fixed on Bedlum.

Barbara jumped up and whipped a cloth napkin from the refreshment table. "Jason, here, let me stop the bleeding."

As Bedlum's temper grew, the weapon in his hand began to shake. "Sit down!"

Stoner held his hands up, palms out. "Let's all just calm down."

Bedlum turned again and screeched, "I said sit down!"

Barbara stared into the emptiness that began to engulf us all. "What are you going to do, Father, shoot me, too?"

Bedlum's expression did not change. "If I have to, Missy. We come from a long line of heads of family who have had to do what was necessary to maintain power." He leveled the gun and pointed at Barbara's heart.

"We?" Barbara straightened her spine and stretched to her full height. "No. I do not come from your family at all. Not anymore."

"Barbara, sit down," Tayton warned her.

Ivy had not moved until then. She slowly inched to the edge of her seat and then, suddenly, *pow pow*. Grabbing the arms of the chair, she screamed out in pain.

"Try being the body guard with no right foot," he snickered.

My heart felt like it stopped. What could I do? Nothing. I watched Ivy's face for a sign of how badly she was hurt and was surprised. Her expression was of one in pain, and I knew she was injured. I could see by the damage to her shoe, that the bullet had nicked the side of her foot and no more. She was able to keep Bedlum from taking another shot by feigned more pain and more injury than was there.

"Toss that sidearm over here—and it had better not hit my feet," he said with an evil smile. "That way you won't have to think about it all the time."

Ivy released her weapon slowly and slid it in Bedlum's direction.

Stoner's eyes darted from Ivy to the evil one who held them all at gunpoint. "Can we talk about this?" He asked as he took one step toward the end of the gun.

With rage in his eyes, Bedlum hissed, "Are you stupid?" The end of the 980 exploded and Stoner collapsed onto the floor.

Chalky fell to his side and lifted his head to her lap. "Ward?" she gasped. Blood oozed from his side and began to soak into the carpet.

"Now—you," he growled at Chalky, "pull his service weapon from its holster and push it over here—yours, too."

Chalky did as ordered, reached in past the sticky seepage of blood and lifted Ward's revolver from its holster. She removed her own sidearm and cautiously slid the two pieces in Bedlum's direction.

"What have you done?" Silas asked as he came into the room, his hand covering his mouth.

Bedlum waved the gun around in the air and then snarled, "I did what I ordered that idiot Washington to do. They captured him with a busted up knee. So, I sought you out, furnace keeper, to do it. And—you botched it up, you sniveling mouse." Bedlim's eyes looked wild. "You only gave me half the information about their where-abouts and then you couldn't even pull the trigger on this piece of elite trash running for office."

"What?" I gasped as I jumped to my feet. The madman waved the gun at me. I flinched, expecting him to fire at any moment. Jason pulled me by the hand, and I fell onto the chair beside him.

"Who do you think has been feeding me your every move? How did I know where you'd be?" Bedlum roared—his voice shrill. "The mass-murderer of Howard Mountain told me," he yelled, pointing at Silas Drummond.

"Lady Applewait—" Silas begged.

"Silas, I am Christy, remember—and have been all these months."

"He forced me to tell him where you'd be," Silas said as his eyes flooded with tears.

"You are a weakling," Bedlum accused.

Tayton didn't move but said calmly. "What do you want? Maybe we can talk about it."

"You want a shot in the head little Blue Guard boy?"

I held my breath and waited. Out of the corner of my eye, I watched Stoner begin to stir and wondered if he would be strong enough to save us. Chalky was going through the motions of attending to him while her hand slowly doubled into a fist.

"You will lose that hand," the inheritor of all the mafia families warned through gritted teeth. "Didn't you learn anything when you saw what happened to your boss, or is he your boyfriend?

Chalky said nothing but stared at him with a steely gaze.

"Christy," Silas spoke only to me, his eyes pleading. "You must understand. He said he would hunt down and kill every one of the Claimed Children I rescued from the furnaces and smuggled into the Valley of the Keepers. Every one of them, Christy."

"I'll still do it, you lazy, weak whiner." Bedlum raised the gun and shot Silas in the shoulder.

Silas fell back onto one of the library chairs and slumped down. I watched him intently for signs of shock. When I saw him adjust himself in the chair, I was encouraged by his ability to move.

"Suffer a little, you butcher, as I work on my favorite target." He aimed at Grand-père's head. "While you marinate in your own blood—furnace-keeper—I'll finish off this arrogant wise-one." This time Bedlum was controlled as he took aim.

Stoner lunged at Bedlum's legs, waving his arms out in a wide sweep. Chalky reached toward the sociopath, but she and Stoner only succeeded in knocking Bedlum off balance. When he staggered, his 980 fired wildly in the air as falling plaster landed on the marble mantel of the fireplace.

Crack! The deep throated sound of a .30-30 shattered the house. Alister Bedlum fell with a mighty thud and rumble, like an ax had just felled a huge tree. His head struck the hearth when Maisie and Dahlia jumped out of the way.

Every eye in the room turned to follow the trajectory of the blast. Sondra Bedlum stood on the third step of the grand staircase, a Winchester carbine still poised in her hands.

"Mother!" Barbara gasped and ran into the entry to her mother's side.

I was as stunned as the rest of those in the room. Would Sondra crumble over what she had done? She had just killed her estranged husband.

Grand-père stood and hurried to her side. "Mrs. Bedlum, you have saved us all."

Immediately behind Grand-père, Tayton gently removed the rifle from Sondra's hands, secured the trigger and checked the gun for additional shells. "You are a hero," he said softly as Barbara put her arm around her mother's shoulder.

Stoner eased up on his elbow. "Ma'am, thank you for your courage. You prevented a blood bath here. I'm sure of it." To Chalky he added, "Boone, contact a removal unit. Have this body hauled out of here—and summon the investigative team who will need to interview the shooter." He looked back at Sondra. "It will be slick, Ma'am. There will be no charges. I'll make sure of that."

Grasping Mrs. Bedlum's hand in mine, I started to cry before I could get the words off my lips. "You have not only saved my grandfather, Sondra, you have played a huge part in saving our country from the prison of fear and hopelessness."

With roaring shouts and cheering from the mass media set behind us, I looked back. I needed to see if there was a second attack in another location.

"Grand-père," I gasped. "The election results are all in. You won!"

EPILOGUE

Inauguration was January 20, 2115. The sun was brilliant on the cool winter day. The crowd stretched out for blocks around the East front of the Capital building. Everyone who attended and those who watched on mass media were filled with new hope. The Length of Days Law had been over thrown and freedom had been found and returned to the people.

The ceremony that thrilled me as much as Grand-père's swearing-in was my wedding to Jason the following spring in the White House rose garden. My dress was long white satin covered in lace at the bodice. The veil was a simple cluster of white roses that fixed in my hair with a comb and draped down the left side of my head. Friends from all over the country came. Even Sondra Bedlum came out of her hiding place to attend. We celebrated life and the living of it; hope and the expectation of it; and freedom and our belief in it.

NOTES

Oliver Richly speech in chapter 27 is inspired by the cadence in Ronald Reagan's speech that includes the sentence, "You and I have a rendezvous with destiny." — Ronald Reagan, A Time for Choosing: The Speeches of Ronald Reagan, 1961-1982

Information on Billy the Kid, taken from, http://www.mesilla.com. Accessed 12/28/15

OTHER BOOKS BY DORIS GAINES RAPP

<u>Novelette:</u>

News at Eleven (Glo Magazine - Serialized Jan, Feb, March, and April 2015 Expanded to: *News at Eleven – A Novel* (Released April 2015)

<u>Novels:</u>

Length of Days – The Age of Silence
Length of Days – Beyond the Valley of the Keepers
Escape from the Belfry
Smoke from Distant Fires
Hiawassee – Child of the Meadow
News at Eleven – A Novel

<u>Collection:</u>

Christmas Feather, one of eight short stories in a wonderful collection titled, ***Christmases Past***

<u>Children's:</u>

Lincoln's Christmas Mouse

<u>Non-Fiction:</u>

Waiting for Jesus in a Can't Wait World – Advent 2014
Prayer Therapy of Jesus
Promote Yourself

Internet Presence:

www.prayertherapyrapp.blogspot.com
www.dorisgainesrapp.blogspot.com
Facebook: Doris Gaines Rapp – Author Page

About the Author

Doris Gaines Rapp, Ph.D. is a writer by birth, psychologist and teacher by education and experiences. She creates fictional characters that live in several centuries and loves the stories she tells. As a psychologist, she understands the people who appear on her computer screen; she laughs with them, cries with them, and triumphs over adversity with them. They are real and full of life. All of her works have at their heart a Christian world view.

Rapp also writes on the non-fiction topics of Self-publishing with an encouragement to promote yourself and your work; as well as Prayer Therapy, learning to pray specifically so God can answer prayers specifically.

She speaks on several topics:

Voices of Assertiveness within My Novels
Prayer Therapy
Promote Yourself
Know Your Own History

Dr. Rapp is a former counseling center director of Taylor University, Upland, IN and Bethel College, Mishawaka, IN. She currently writes and speaks full time. She and her pastor husband have survived rearing six children. They live in Indiana.